Contents

Mr. Claghorn's Daughter

Hilary Trent

Alpha Editions

This edition published in 2023

ISBN : 9789357952033

Design and Setting By
Alpha Editions
www.alphaedis.com
Email - info@alphaedis.com

PREFACE.

Some readers of this novel will charge the author with the crime of laying a sacrilegious hand upon the Ark of God; others will characterize his work as an assault upon a windmill.

I contend (and the fact, if it be a fact, is ample justification for this book) that The Westminster Confession of Faith has driven many honest souls to the gloom of unbelief, to the desperate need of a denial of God; and that to-day a very large number of the adherents of that Confession find it possible to maintain their faith in God only by secret rejection of a creed they openly profess.

Take from that Confession those Articles which give rise to the dilemma which confronts the wife and mother of this story, and nothing is left. The articles in question are the essential articles of the Confession.

He who can in honesty say of The Westminster Confession of Faith: "This is my standard: by this sign I shall conquer," he, and he only, has the right to condemn my purpose.

HILARY TRENT.

CHAPTER I.

A PHILOSOPHER AND A MARCHIONESS.

Mr. (by preference Monsieur) Beverley Claghorn, of the Rue de la Paix, Paris, was a personage of some note in that world in which he had lived for many years. His slightly aquiline nose and well-pointed moustache, his close-cropped grizzled hair, his gold-rimmed pince-nez, his hat, his boots—his attire as a whole—successfully appealed to a refined taste. The sapphire, encircled by tiny diamonds, which adorned his little finger, beautiful to the common eye, was, in the eye of the connoisseur, a rare and exquisite gem. Except as to an inch or two of stature, the outward man of Monsieur Claghorn left nothing to be desired; while as to his intellectual calibre, he to whom it was best known regarded it with respect, even with admiration; his moral deportment had never occasioned scandal; with the goods of this world he was liberally endowed. As a philosopher (for he affected that character) he should have been a contented man; being human, as philosophers must be, he was not. As against the advantages indicated, Monsieur had grievances incompatible with contentment. He was nearer sixty than forty, which was one cause of sorrow; another was that, in spite of the effort of years, he had not in fact become a Parisian. He had succeeded in approaching the type very nearly; nevertheless, though his card might proclaim him "Monsieur" and imply its owner to the Gallic manner born, the truth remained that he was not so born. His language, by dint of effort, aided by native talent, had become almost as easy and as idiomatic as the enunciations of those who formed the world in which he dwelt, yet he was poignantly aware that therein was still to be detected an echo of the twang of his youth and of his native tongue. His surname, too, as a stumbling block to his friends, was a source of vexation. Had he been born a Dobbins, a mere apostrophe would have made him a d'Obbins and content. But the uncompromising appellation of his ancestors refused to lend itself to a fraud, though venial, and even ennobling, and thus remained a source of repining; a gentle regret that his cognomen was not more fitting to his environment. But as to his name received in baptism, therewith was connected a grief so deep and a dread so great, that it was, perhaps, the most baleful of his closeted skeletons. Fortune having so far enabled Monsieur to hide the sorrow connected with his Christian name, let us also leave the matter to fortune.

To enumerate all the grievances of our philosopher would be a tedious task, but there was one of such magnitude that it may be regarded as the great grievance of his existence. This was Christianity.

That earnest conviction of the truth of orthodox Christianity should incite to propagandism is easily comprehensible. A reasonable sinner will not complain of the believer's desire to save errant souls; indeed, he may well be amazed that the believer engages in any other occupation. But why the rage for proselytizing should inspire the non-believer is less obvious. Why should the heathen rage because the zealot is deluded by hope and his eyes deceived by the cheering illusions offered by faith? If the rough road of the Christian wayfarer, its gloomy valleys and dark caverns are smoothed and illumined by the cheering light of conviction, why should the skeptic object, and beckon the fervent pilgrim from his chosen path to that broader and more alluring road selected by himself? Can it be that, like a boy who fears the coming darkness, the skeptic craves companionship, suspecting hobgoblins after sunset?

Monsieur Claghorn was indignant that the world, as he knew it, either professed a more or less orthodox belief in God, or cared nothing about the matter. Both attitudes aroused his ire.

"My dear Claghorn," urged his connexion, the Marquise de Fleury, "why not leave these matters to Père Martin, as I do? I assure you it is comforting," and the little matron shrugged her rather sharp shoulder-blades and nestled more snugly in the corner of her blue-silk sofa.

"It is degrading to the intellect."

"Ah! The intellect—I have none; I am all soul."

"You—the brightest woman in Paris!"

"Too broad, *mon ami*. Exaggeration destroys the delicate flavor of a compliment."

"Louise, you are in a bad humor. Evidently, you don't like your gown."

"The gown is ravishing, as you should have seen before this. It is you, my friend, who are angry. To what end? Angry at nothing? That is foolish. Angry at something? Considering that that Something is God——"

"There you have it,—fear. Women rule men through their passions; and priests rule women through their fears."

"*Eh bien!* Have it so. You deny God. It is daring—splendid—but what do you gain, what do you gain, *mon ami?*"

"I deny your impossible God, and in so doing, I retain my self-respect."

"A valuable possession, doubtless. Yet the fact remains that you fight windmills, or you fight the power that loosens the hurricane. Futile warfare!"

Monsieur shrugged his shoulders. A woman's argument is rarely worthy the attention of a philosopher.

"Behold," continued the little Marquise, "behold Père Martin. He is good; he is wise. What has he to gain? Only heaven. He sacrifices much on earth—pleasure, dignity, power——"

"He has more power than a king——"

"Listen, my friend, and do not interrupt. If he has power over me and such as I—which is what you mean—he uses it discreetly, kindly. I enjoy life, I hope for heaven. You enjoy life, of heaven you have no hope. Which of us is wise?"

"You believe because you think it safer."

"*Dame, mon ami!* It costs nothing."

"It is cowardly."

"Ah, well, my friend, I am a coward. Let us discuss something less gruesome. This charming Natalie! You will let her come to me, now that she is to leave the barbarians?"

"I, too, am a coward. I fear Père Martin."

"Believe me, my friend," said the Marquise, more seriously than she had yet spoken, "you do wrong. Women need religion. They must adore; they must sacrifice themselves to the object of their worship. As a rule they have a choice. They may worship God or they may worship Love. To one or the other they will devote themselves or miss their destiny. Which is less dangerous?"

"There is danger everywhere," replied the philosopher, discontentedly. "But, indeed, Louise, this matter is more serious to me, the unbeliever, than to you, the Christian. You Latins do not comprehend the reverence we of a different race assign to principle. I think it wrong, immoral, to expose my daughter to an atmosphere of falsehood."

"Monsieur, you are unjust to us Latins; and worse, you are impolite."

"I am serious. I think Christianity the curse of mankind."

"And you object to it. That is magnanimous."

"Natalie has been left in total ignorance of all religion."

"Charming—but hardly *de rigueur* for a de Fleury."

"She is a Claghorn."

"An excellent thing to be; enviable indeed, my dear,—in America. But she will be a Parisienne; we hope a de Fleury, of a house by inheritance religious. The wife of the Marquis de Fleury must uphold the family traditions. Do you not see, my friend, that it is thirty generations of nobles that insist."

Monsieur Claghorn, though in doubt as to God, believed in the generations. He had long looked forward to the time when his daughter should be united to the last scion of this ancient race. True, the title was in these days purely ornamental; but, though a philosopher, he was not of that unwise class which can see no value in adornment. He suspected that the noble Marquis, whose coronet he craved for his daughter, as well as his mama, the little lady to whom he was talking, were in truth as much interested in the material as in the spiritual attributes of the future mother of the race, but he was also aware that there were other influences to be considered.

"Perhaps Père Martin is even more insistent than the thirty generations," he suggested.

"Even so, my friend; when Père Martin insists it is my conscience that insists."

"After all, Louise, this discussion is premature. Adolphe is still at St. Cyr, Natalie at school——"

"But to-day we prepare for to-morrow. Adolphe will soon be a lieutenant, your daughter a woman. Let her come to me. Our prayers, those of Père Martin and mine, cannot harm her."

"Assuredly not, still——"

"But my good pagan, do you intend to refuse? Is it worth nothing to your daughter to be introduced by the Marquise de Fleury?"

It was worth so much that M. Claghorn had no intention of refusing. "And Adolphe?" he asked.

"Will remain at St. Cyr. Fear nothing, my friend. I shall do nothing in that matter without consulting you."

"You are always kind. It shall be as you wish." And then, after some further indifferent conversation, the Marquise was by M. Claghorn handed to her carriage for a promenade in the Bois; while the philosopher, after that act of courtesy, left her to visit La Duchesne, a fashionable seeress, who prophesied as to the course of stocks.

CHAPTER II.

TWO PAGANS DISCUSS FISH, PARIS AND THE HIGHER CRITICISM.

It was midsummer. The Marquise was in Brittany, Monsieur in Germany; or, as Madame de Fleury patriotically expressed it, among the barbarians, he having penetrated into barbaric wilds in order to reclaim his daughter, whose education, for the past two years, had been progressing under barbaric auspices.

There is, not far from Heidelberg, and in that part of the country of the barbarians known as the Odenwald, a quaint village called Forellenbach; and hard by the village, which is clustered against a steep hill-side, there dashes in cascades that foam and roar, a stream, from the dark pools whereof are drawn trout, which, by the excellent host of the Red-Ox are served hot, in a sauce compounded of white wine and butter; and these things render the place forever memorable to him who loves fish or scenery, or both.

Monsieur Claghorn and his daughter were seated in the garden of the Red-Ox. They had arrived at the inn in a carriage, being on their way to Heidelberg. From Natalie's school they had journeyed by rail to Bad Homburg; and from that resort, having despatched the girl's maid ahead by train, they had commenced a mode of travel which Natalie secretly hoped would not end as soon as had been originally anticipated; for the trip thus far had been the most delightful experience of her life.

There were reasons for this delight besides the joy derived from driving in pleasant weather, over smooth roads, through curious villages, beside winding rivers whose vineclad hills echoed the raftsman's song; beneath the trees of many a forest, passing often the ruins of some grim keep, which silently told to the girl its story of the time that, being past, was a time of romance when life was more beautiful, more innocent, less sordid than now. Not that Natalie knew much of the unpleasing features of modern life, or of any life (else had her self-made pictures of other days borne a different aspect), still the past had its attraction for her, as it has for all that love to dream; and from her Baedeker she had derived just enough information to form the basis of many a tender scene that had never taken place, in days that never were or could have been. Her dreams were not wholly of the past, but of the future as well; all impossible and as charming as innocence and imagination could paint them. School was behind her, her face toward France, a home fireside, liberty and happiness for all time to come. No vision of the days in which she had not lived could be more alluring than the visions of the days in which she was to live, nor more delusive.

Beverley Claghorn looking upon his daughter, perhaps, also saw a visionary future. He loved her, of course. He respected her, too, for had not her mother been of the ancient House of Fleury? It was no ignoble blood which lent the damask tint to cheeks upon which he gazed with complacent responsibility for their being. The precious fluid, coursing beneath the fair skin, if carefully analyzed, should exhibit corpuscles tinged with royal azure. For, was it not true that a demoiselle of her mother's line had been, in ancient days, graciously permitted to bear a son to a king of France, from which son a noble House had sprung with the proud privilege of that bar sinister which proclaimed its glory? These were facts well worthy to be the foundation of a vision in which he saw the maid before him a wife of one of the old noblesse; a mother of sons who would uphold the sacred cause of Legitimacy, as their ancestors (including himself, for he was a furious Legitimist) had done before them. It would solace the dreaded status of grandfather.

"What are you thinking of, Natalie?" he asked in French.

"Of many things; principally that I am sorry he showed them to us."

"The trout?"

"Yes, I am so hungry."

"They have sharpened your appetite. They are beautiful fish."

"I'm glad they haven't spoiled it. Why, papa, they were alive! Did you see their gills palpitate?"

"They are very dead now."

"And we shall eat them. It seems a pity."

He laughed. "Grief will not prevent your enjoyment," he said; "you will have a double luxury—of woe, and——"

"You are ashamed of my capacity for eating, papa. It is very unromantic."

Papa smiled, raising his eyelids slightly. He seemed, and in fact was, a little bored. "Haven't we had enough of this?" he asked.

"But we haven't had any yet."

"I don't mean trout—I only hope they won't be drowned in bad butter—I mean of this," and he lazily stretched his arms, indicating the Odenwald.

She sighed. Her secret hope that the journey by carriage might be extended further than planned was waning. "I was never so happy in my life," she exclaimed. "I shall never forget the pine-forests, the hills, the castles; nor the geese in the villages; nor the horrible little cobblestones——"

"Nor the sour wine——"

"That is your French taste, papa. The *vin du pays* is no better in France. The wine is good enough, if you pay enough."

"The Lützelsachser is drinkable, the Affenthaler even good," admitted Monsieur, indulgent to barbaric vintage; "but think of yesterday!"

"Think of an epicure who expected to get Affenthaler in that poor little village! They gave you the best they had."

"Which was very bad." He laughed good-naturedly. "I dread a similar experience if we continue this method of travel."

"I could travel this way forever and forever!" She sighed and extended her arms, then clasped her hands upon her breast. It was an unaffected gesture of youth and pleasure and enthusiasm.

It made him smile. "Wait until you have seen Paris," he said.

"But I have seen Paris."

"With the eyes of a child; now you are a woman."

"That is so," somewhat dreamily, as though this womanhood were no new subject of reverie. "I am eighteen—but why should Paris be especially attractive to a woman?"

"Paris is the world."

"And so is this."

"This, my dear——" the remonstrance on his lips was interrupted by the arrival of the fish.

They were very good: "*Ravissant!*" exclaimed Natalie, who displayed a very pitiless appreciation of them. "Not so bad," admitted papa.

"And so I am to stay with my cousin, the Marquise," said the girl, after the cravings of an excellent appetite had been satisfied. "Papa, even you can find no fault with this Deidesheimer," filling her glass as she spoke.

"With your cousin for a time, anyhow. It is very kind of her, and for you nothing better could be wished. She sees the best world of Paris."

"And as I remember, is personally very nice."

"A charming woman—with a fault. She is devout."

"I have known some like her," observed Natalie. "There was Fräulein Rothe, our drawing-mistress, a dear old lady, but very religious."

"I hope none of them attempted to influence you in such matters," he said, frowning slightly.

"No. It was understood that you had expressly forbidden it. I was left out of the religious classes; they called me 'The Pagan.'"

"No harm in that," commented Monsieur rather approvingly.

"Oh, no! It was all in good-nature. The Pagan was a favorite. But, of course, I have had some curiosity. I have read a little of the Bible." She made her confession shyly, as though anticipating reproach.

"There is no objection to that," he said. "At your age you should have a mind of your own. Use it and I have no fear as to the result. My view is that in leaving you uninfluenced I have done my duty much more fully than if I had early impressed upon you ideas which I think pernicious, and which only the strongest minds can cast aside in later life. What impression has your Bible reading left?"

"The Jews of the Old Testament were savages, and their book is unreadable for horrors. The Gospel narratives seem written by men of another race. The character of Jesus is very noble. He must have lived, for he could not have been invented by Jews. Of course, he was not God, but I don't wonder that his followers thought so."

"He was a Great Philosopher," answered Monsieur Claghorn with high approval. "The incarnation of pure stoicism, realizing the ideal more truly than even Seneca or Marcus. And what of the literary quality of the book?"

"The gospels are equal to the Vicar of Wakefield or Paul and Virginia. As to the rest," she shrugged her shoulders after the French fashion—"Revelation was written by a maniac."

"Or a modern poet," observed the gentleman.

Now while these latest exponents of the Higher Criticism were thus complacently settling the literary standing of Luke and John, placing them on as high a level as that attained by Goldsmith and St. Pierre, the man smoking and the girl sipping wine (for the fish had been devoured and their remains removed), two persons came into the garden. They carried knapsacks and canes, wore heavy shoes, were dusty and travel-stained. The elder of the pair had the clerical aspect; the youth was simply a very handsome fellow of twenty or thereabout, somewhat provincial in appearance.

Beverley Claghorn glanced at the pair, and with an almost imperceptible shrug of the shoulders, which, if it referred to the newcomers, was not complimentary, continued to smoke without remark. The girl was more curious.

"They are English," she said.

"Americans," he answered, with a faint shade of disapproval in his tone.

"But so are we," she remonstrated, noting the tone.

"We can't help it," he replied, resenting one of his grievances. "You can hardly be called one."

"Is it disgraceful?"

"Not at all; but I don't flaunt it."

"But, papa, surely you are not ashamed of it?"

"Certainly not. But it is a little tiresome. Our countrymen are so oppressively patriotic. They demand of you that you glory in your nativity. I don't. I am not proud of it. I shouldn't be proud of being an Englishman, or a Frenchman, or an Italian, or——"

"In fact, papa, you are not proud at all."

"Natalie," proceeded the philosopher, not noticing the interruption, "one may be well-disposed toward the country of one's birth; one may even recognize the duty of fighting, if need be, for its institutions. But the pretence of believing in one's country, of fulsome adoration for imperfect institutions, is to welcome intellectual slavery, to surrender to the base instinct of fetichism."

"Like religion," she said, recognizing the phrase.

"Like religion," he assented. "You will find when you are as old as I am that I am right."

"Yet people do believe in religion. There's Fräulein Rothe——"

"Natalie, no reasoning being can believe what is called Christianity, but many beings think that they believe."

"But why don't they discover that they don't think what they think they think?"

"There's nothing strange in that. When they were young they were told that they believed, and have grown up with that conviction. The same people would scorn to accept a new and incredible story on the evidence which is presented in favor of the Christian religion."

The girl sighed as though the paternal wisdom was somewhat unsatisfactory. Meantime the slight raising of Monsieur's voice had attracted the attention of the dusty wayfarers who, in default of other occupation, took to observing the pair.

"She is very pretty," said the youth.

The elder did not answer. He was intently scrutinizing Beverley Claghorn. After a moment of hesitation he surprised his companion by rising and approaching that person with outstretched hand.

"I cannot be mistaken," he exclaimed in a loud, hearty voice. "This is a Claghorn."

"That is my name," replied the would-be Gallic owner of the appellation in English. "I have the honor of seeing——" but even as he uttered the words he recognized the man who was now shaking a somewhat reluctant hand with gushing heartiness.

"I am Jared. You remember me, of course. I see it in your eyes. And so this is really you—Eliphalet! 'Liph, as we called you at the old Sem. 'Liph, I am as glad to see you as a mother a long-lost son."

"And I," replied the other, "am charmed." He bore it smiling, though his daughter looked on in wonder, and he felt that the secret of his baptism had been heartlessly disclosed.

"This," said Jared, "is my son, Leonard," and while the son grew red and bowed, the clergyman looked at the girl to whom his son's bow had been principally directed.

"My daughter, Natalie de Fleury-Claghorn," said her father. "My dear, this is my cousin, Professor Claghorn, whom I have not seen for many years."

"Not since we were students together at Hampton Theological Seminary," added Jared, smilingly. He habitually indulged in a broad smile that indicated satisfaction with things as he found them. It was very broad now, as he offered his hand, saying, "And so you are 'Liph's daughter, and your name is Natalidaflurry—that must be French. And your mother, my dear, I hope——"

"My wife has been dead since my daughter's birth," interrupted Monsieur, "and I," he added, "long ago discarded my baptismal name and assumed that of my mother."

"Discarded the old name!" exclaimed the Reverend Jared, surprised. "Had I been aware of that, I surely would have given it to Leonard. I regarded it, as in some sort, the property of the elder branch. Surely, you don't call yourself Susan?"

"My mother's name was Susan Beverley; I assumed her family name." The philosopher uttered the words with a suavity that did him credit. Then, apologetically, and in deference to his cousin's evident grief: "You see, Eliphalet was somewhat of a mouthful for Frenchmen."

"And so the old name has fallen into disuse," murmured Jared regretfully. "We must revive it. Leonard, upon you———"

But Leonard had taken Natalie to look at the cascades.

So, lighting fresh cigars, the two former fellow-students commenced a revival of old memories. Their discourse, especially on the part of the clergyman, contained frequent allusion to family history, which to the reader would be both uninteresting and incomprehensible. But, since some knowledge of that history is requisite to the due understanding of the tale that is to be told, the respected personage indicated is now invited to partake of that knowledge.

CHAPTER III.

A COUSIN IN THE COILS OF THE GREAT SERPENT.

Professor and the Reverend Jared Claghorn has already intimated that the name Eliphalet was an honored one in the family. An Eliphalet Claghorn had been a man of mark among the Pilgrims. His eldest son had borne his parent's name and had succeeded to the clerical vocation; an example which he had imposed upon his own first-born, and thus became established the custom of giving to a son of each Eliphalet the name of his father, in the pleasing hope that he who bore the revered appellation might be called to serve in the Lord's fold, as shepherd of the flock; which hope had generally been realized. In due course that Eliphalet who was destined to beget Beverley had been called, had answered the summons, and at the birth of his only son, had, with confident expectation of a similar call to the latter, named his name "Eliphalet."

In time the call was heard. The youth, fully assured that he, like the ancestral Eliphalets, would find his field of labor in the vineyard of God, had gone so far in acceptance of his solemn duty as to enter the well-known Theological Seminary at Hampton, there to fit himself for the only future he had ever contemplated.

Then a shock had come,—a great legacy from one of two California brothers, both long given up as dead. From the moment this fortune came into his possession, the father of Beverley Claghorn, always a stern and gloomy man, the product of a ruthless creed, knew no day of peace. He craved worldly distinction—not the pleasures which beckoned his son—with a craving which only a starved nature with powers fitting to the world can know. On the other hand, a rigid sense of duty, perhaps, too, the gloomy joy of martyrdom, urged him to reject a temptation which he persuaded himself was offered by the Prince of Darkness. He remained outwardly true to his duty, an unhappy soldier at the post assigned him, and died as his fathers had died, in the odor of sanctity; in his heart hankering to the last for the joys offered by the world to him who has wealth, and to the last sternly rejecting them.

Secretly, though with bitter self-condemnation, he had approved his son's renunciation of the theological course. Not with his lips. It was impossible for him, stubbornly believing, as he had always believed, though now with the frequent doubts and fears of the new standpoint he occupied, to openly approve the intentions displayed by the youth. Yet he acquiesced in silence, secretly hoping to see the son, who had commenced the study of the law, a power in the State. That he was never to see, and it was well that he died before the renegade Eliphalet had extinguished such hope by voluntary exile.

Beverley's history, or at least that portion of it which he chose to impart, was told in reply to the eager questioning of Jared. Perhaps he was not sorry that his old fellow-student should note his air of man of fashion and aristocrat, and he set forth the renown of the de Fleury lineage, innocently shocking his cousin by explaining the meaning and glory of that bar sinister, which he himself revered.

Jared, on his part, narrated at much greater length than his auditor sympathetically appreciated, the history of his own life. He, too, had married brilliantly—a Morley, as he informed his cousin, and one who, dying, had left him well endowed with this world's goods, and it may be that it was by reason of this fact, as well as because of superior attainments, that the speaker had developed into a teacher in that same seminary where the two had been fellow-students.

"Yes," he said in a tone of satisfaction, "I hold down the chair of Biblical Theology in Hampton. You would hardly recognize the old Sem, El— Beverley."

"I suppose not. I shall make a flying trip there some day."

"A flying trip! Surely you don't intend to abandon your country forever?"

"Not unlikely. You see, I am more of a Frenchman than anything else, and my daughter is quite French."

"She speaks English?"

"Oh, as to that, as well as anybody. She has been largely educated in England. But her relatives, I mean those that she knows, look upon her as belonging wholly to them, and——"

"I trust she is not a Romanist, Cousin."

"You mean a Catholic. Make your mind easy; she is not."

"I truly rejoice to hear it," exclaimed Jared with fervor. "But I might have known," he added apologetically, "that a Claghorn would not suffer the perversion of his child." Whereat Monsieur changed the topic.

Meanwhile, the young ones of the party had gone to investigate an echo in a glen hard by, directed thereto by the host of the Red-Ox. They were conducted by a stolid maiden, told off for that purpose, a fact which Monsieur Claghorn, from his place in the garden, noted with satisfaction.

Freed from the restraint of the presence of the philosopher, whose raiment and bearing had inspired him with awe, Leonard's engaging simplicity and frank manner added to the favorable impression of his beautiful face.

The charms of nature about them were attractive to both and it was easy to become acquainted, with so much of interest in common. The girl's enthusiasm, somewhat dampened by the philosopher, returned in the presence of a sympathetic listener, and she told the tale of their wanderings, concluding by expressing the opinion that Germany must be the most delightful of all countries.

"This part is fine," said Leonard. "But wait until you see the Black Forest."

"I hope to see it when we leave Heidelberg. Is the wine good?"

"I don't know," was the answer. "I didn't drink any wine."

"It must be very bad if you wouldn't drink it," she observed despondently. "Papa scolds about the wine of the Bergstrasse, which, for my part, I find very good. Then, at the better inns one isn't confined to the vintage of the neighborhood."

"Surely, you don't drink wine!" exclaimed Leonard.

"Not drink wine! What should I do with it?"

"It biteth like a serpent and stingeth like an adder," he quoted gravely, not at all priggishly. He was sincere in his confidence in Solomon, and his surprise and sorrow were honest.

"Wine does!" she laughed. "I never knew that before. Don't Americans drink wine?"

"Some do," he admitted. "Our best people do not drink. We think the example bad."

"*Par example!* And how do your best people manage at dinner?"

"With water."

"Decidedly, I should not like dining with your best people."

"But, Cousin Natalie—that is a very pretty name;" here he blushed engagingly—"wine makes one drunk."

"Certainly, if one gets drunk."

"Then, how can you drink wine?"

The question and the serious manner of its asking were incomprehensible to the girl, who laughed at the incongruity of the ideas suggested by drinking wine on the one hand, and getting drunk on the other. Then the subject was dropped; perhaps they recognized that it was enveloped in clouds of misunderstanding which were impenetrable.

The glen in which dwells the echo of Forellenbach is like a roofless cave, or a great well with a side entrance. Its floor being wet, Natalie remained at the entrance, trusting there to hear whatever might be worth hearing. Leonard passed into the well.

He looked back. She stood in the light, smiling upon this new-found cousin, who had such strange ideas as to wine, but withal, her eyes were kindly. If either had any premonition of the future, it must have been false or partial, or they had not faced each other smiling. He had intended to shout aloud her pretty name and thus to test the echo; but instinct warned him that this was hardly fitting. So, perhaps, with a vague desire to connect her with the trial, he compromised, and the word he shouted was "Claghorn."

It was returned to him in various modulations from all sides. The effect was startling, but even more so were the words that fell upon his ear as the echoes died away: "Who are you, and what do you want?"

The question came from above. Leonard, looking upward, saw the face of a youth who, from the top of the cliff, was peering down. Upon the head of this person, rakishly worn, was a blue cap, braided with silver and red velvet. The face had penetrating eyes, rather stern, and a mouth shaded by a dark moustache. The question was repeated, it seemed to Leonard truculently: "What do you want?"

The words were German, but easily understood. Leonard answered in English: "I don't want you."

"Then, why did you call me?" Now the words were English and the tone awakened Leonard's resentment. "Do you suppose that every one that tries the echo is calling you?" he asked.

"You called me. Why?"

Leonard labored under the disadvantage of hearing all that was said repeated many times. It was irritating; nor was the tone of the other pacific. It was even war-like. "I didn't address you," he said. "I do now: Be silent!"

The other laughed. "*Bist ein dummer Junge*, my son," he said. "I suppose you are a student. Get your card."

He disappeared, evidently with a view of intercepting Leonard who, emerging from the cave, met him almost at Natalie's side.

The newcomer was surprised to see the girl. "I beg your pardon," he said, removing his cap; then, aside to Leonard: "I will accept your card on another occasion, if you prefer. You are a student of Heidelberg, I suppose?"

"I am a student, certainly, of Hampton, in the United States. I have no card. My name is Claghorn."

The sternness of the newcomer gave place to astonishment. "I beg your pardon, and your sister's," he said, glancing at Natalie. "My name happens to be the same. Naturally, I supposed——"

"The place seems to be alive with Claghorns," exclaimed Leonard.

"And since you are from Hampton, I believe we are related," continued the newcomer. "Cousins, I suppose. You can't be Professor Claghorn?"

"I can be, and am, his son," laughed Leonard. "You are the third cousin I have found to-day."

By this time the two elders had joined the party. Monsieur Claghorn had deemed it advisable, for his daughter's sake, to follow her footsteps. The Reverend Jared, accompanying him, heard Leonard's words. "A cousin!" he exclaimed, looking inquiringly at the stranger who made the claim, and ready gushingly to welcome him.

"I think so," answered the stranger, smiling. "My father was Joseph Claghorn, of San Francisco."

"He's your first cousin, 'Liph," exclaimed the Reverend Jared, hesitating no longer, but grasping the unoffered hand of the son of Joseph. Then he added in an awestruck voice, "You must be the owner of the Great Serpent?"

"I am in its coils," replied the young man with a half sigh.

"Wonderful!" ejaculated Jared, and then glibly plunged into a genealogical disquisition for the general benefit, the result of which was that Claghorn, the son of Joseph, and in the coils of the Great Serpent, stood demonstrated as the first cousin of Beverley, the second of Natalie, the third of himself and the fourth of Leonard. The professorial fluency had the good effect of creating enough hilarity to dissipate constraint; and its cordiality embraced all present in a circle of amity, whether they would or not.

But there was no indication of reluctance to cousinly recognition. Monsieur saw sufficient comedy in the situation to amuse him, nor was he oblivious of the fascinations of the Great Serpent, which reptile was a mine, known by repute to all present, and the source of Monsieur's wealth, for that inheritance that had changed the course of his life had been thence derived. The dead brother of the now dead Eliphalet had left his share of the mine to Joseph, his partner, but had divided his savings between Eliphalet and a sister, Achsah by name. The son of Joseph, and owner of the Great Serpent, must be in the eyes of anybody the acceptable person he was in the eyes of Monsieur Claghorn, the more so as he was thoroughly presentable, being handsome, well dressed, and with rather more of the air of a man of the world than was usual in one of his years, which might be twenty-one.

"We have not learned your Christian name," said Jared, after acquaintance had been established and the youth had been duly informed of much family history. "I hope your parents named you Eliphalet," glancing, not without reproach, at the actual owner of that appellation.

"They spared me that infliction," answered the newcomer, laughing, "though they hit me pretty hard. My name is Mark"; then, perhaps noting the faint flush upon the cheek of one of the members of the group, "I beg pardon; I should have been more respectful of a respectable family name, which may be borne by some one of you."

"Nobody bears it; you are to be congratulated," observed Monsieur firmly. The Reverend Jared looked grieved, but said nothing.

Mark Claghorn informed his auditors—there was no escaping the examination of the Professor—that he was a student at Heidelberg, that his mother sojourned there with him, that she was a widow, with an adopted daughter, a distant connexion, named Paula; and having learned that the entire party was bound for that city he expressed the hope that all these wandering offshoots of the Claghorn family might there meet and become better acquainted.

CHAPTER IV.

THE DIVERSIONS OF THE CLAGHORNS.

A good-humored widow, fair, and if mature, not old, and with the allurement of the possession of boundless wealth; two lovely maids; a brace of well-disposed young men, of whom one was strikingly beautiful and guileless, the other less comely as less innocent, yet in these respects not deficient, and the heir of millions; finally, a genial theologian and a philosopher, summer and Heidelberg—given these components and it must be confessed that the impromptu reunion of the Claghorns promised present enjoyment and gratifying memories for the future. The various members of the clan acted as if they so believed and were content. There were moments, indeed, when the genial Jared was moved to bewail the absence of Miss Achsah Claghorn, as being the only notable member of the family not present. The philosopher admitted a youthful acquaintance with the lady in question, who was his aunt, and echoed the Professor's eulogy, but evinced resignation. To the others, except to Leonard, who had evidently been taught to revere Miss Achsah, she was personally unknown, hence the loss occasioned by her absence was by them unfelt.

"She is greatly exercised just now," observed Jared, "by an event which possesses interest for all of us, and which ought to especially interest you, 'Liph."

"Salvation for the heathen by means of moral pocket handkerchiefs?" drawled the philosopher, secretly annoyed by the clergyman's persistent use of his discarded Christian name.

"*She* says a sacrilegious scheme; nothing short of the desecration of your namesake's grave," retorted the Professor.

The party was grouped on the great terrace of the castle, against the balustrade of which the clergyman leaned as he addressed his audience with somewhat of the air of a lecturer, an aspect which was emphasized by his use of a letter which he had drawn from his pocket, and to which he pointed with his long forefinger.

"You are all doubtless aware," he observed, "that Miss Achsah is the sister of the late Reverend Eliphalet Claghorn, father of our cousin and friend here present" (indicating Monsieur, who bowed to the speaker), "and, as the sister of your deceased husband, Mrs. Joseph, she is your sister-in-law."

The lady smilingly assented to a proposition indisputable, and which probably contained no element of novelty to her; while Jared informed Mark and Natalie that the writer of the letter in his hand was aunt to the youth and great-aunt to the maiden. "She is also cousin to me, and in a further remove to Leonard," and having thus defined the status of Miss Claghorn, he proceeded to explain that he had reminded his hearers of the facts for the reason that the matter concerning which the lady's letter treated was of interest to all present, "except to you, my dear," he added sympathizingly to Paula, "you not being a Claghorn."

"We compassionate you, Mademoiselle," observed the philosopher to the damsel, "and I am sure," he added in a lower tone, "you are sorry for us." To which, Paula, who did not quite understand the philosopher, responded only with a smile and a blush.

"Miss Achsah's letter," continued the Professor, ignoring the by-play, and addressing Mrs. Joe, is dated two months since, and runs thus:

"'I wrote in my last of the strange events taking place in Easthampton. At that time there were only rumors; now there are facts to go upon. The tract given by our ancestor to the Lord is at this moment the property of a New York lawyer. You know that I long ago tried to buy the tomb and was refused. The trustees assure me that it will not be desecrated, that the purchaser promised of his own accord that the sacred dust should not be disturbed. I told them that they might advantageously take lessons in reverence from the lawyer, so there is a coolness between the trustees and myself.' (I am really very sorry for that," muttered the reader parenthetically)——

"As I understand," interrupted Mrs. Joe, "the land was owned by the Seminary, and the Seminary which is now in Hampton was to have been built upon it. Is that what my sister-in-law means by saying it was given to the Lord?"

"Her view is not exactly correct," replied the Professor. "I am myself one of the trustees. Possibly, Eliphalet Claghorn hoped that the Seminary would eventually be erected upon the land he gave toward its foundation. Evidently his successors, the fathers of the church, preferred Hampton to Easthampton."

"In those days Easthampton was a busy mart of trade—they *do* say the slave trade," observed the philosopher. "Hampton, as a secluded village, not liable to incursions of enslaved heathen, godless sailors or godly traders, was better fitted for pious and scholastic meditation, and——"

"Now the conditions are reversed," interrupted Jared; "Hampton is a considerable city, Easthampton a quiet suburb."

"Does Miss Achsah say what the lawyer intends to do with his purchase?" asked Mrs. Joe.

"No doubt he represents a concealed principal," suggested the philosopher, "probably a rival institution—a Jesuit College."

Jared turned pale. "You don't really suppose, 'Liph—but, no! I am sure my co-trustees could not be taken in."

Mrs. Joe cast a reproachful glance at the philosopher. "Miss Achsah would surely have detected a Jesuit plot had there been one," she observed encouragingly. "But why is she so indignant?"

"She has long wanted to purchase the ground about the tomb," replied Jared. "Naturally, she feels aggrieved that it will come into the hands of a stranger. The trustees, to my knowledge, tried to retain it, with the rest of the waste ground, and to sell only the old wharves and houses, but the lawyer insisted; in fact, paid a high price for the waste land which includes the grave."

"Mysterious, if not Jesuitical," murmured Beverley; but the clergyman affected not to hear.

"Has Miss Achsah no knowledge of the intentions of the purchaser?" asked the lady.

"This is what she says," answered the Professor, consulting the letter:

"'The trustees conceal the purpose for which the land is wanted, but I forced the information from Hacket when I informed him that, if I so desired, I could give the management of my affairs to young Burley. At this, Mr. Hacket came down from his high horse and informed me in confidence that the lawyer is to build a grand residence at the Point, and will spend an immense amount of money. All of which is not reassuring, if true. Although the place has been shamefully neglected, I was always glad to know that the Tomb was there, solitary amid the crags; only the sea-roar breaking the silence. I suppose there will be other sounds now, not so pleasant to think about.'"

"Well," observed Mrs. Joe, after a pause, "let us hope that Miss Achsah will be reconciled after the lawyer's plans are more fully developed. He seems to be willing to respect the tomb."

"What is this tomb?" asked Natalie.

"The Tomb of Eliphalet Claghorn, the first of your race in the New World," explained the Professor reverently, and not without a reproachful glance at the philosopher, who had too evidently left his daughter in ignorance of much family history.

"He came over in the Mayflower," observed Leonard in a low tone to Natalie; and then, to his surprise, found it necessary to explain his explanation, for which purpose, in company with the girl he strolled away.

They paused at a little distance, and leaning upon the stone balustrade, looked down upon the town or at the plain beyond, or across the Neckar at the hills of the Philosophenweg. Here Leonard told his foreign cousin the story of the first Eliphalet.

"A strange story," was her comment.

"A noble story," he corrected.

"All sacrifice is noble. I know a woman in extreme poverty who gave ten francs to regild a tawdry statue of the Virgin."

"Deplorable!" exclaimed Leonard severely.

"Pitiful, rather. Consider what the sum was to her! The needs she sacrificed—and for what?"

"Sacrifice wasted, and degradingly wasted."

"Wasted, doubtless; but why degradingly?"

"Granted that your poor woman was sincere"—which, however, the speaker seemed to grant but grudgingly—"the sacrifice was still degrading in that it was made to superstition."

She smiled. "What would my poor woman say of Grandfather Eliphalet?"

"It's a question, you see, of the point of view," observed Mark, who had sauntered to where they stood.

"It's a question of truth and falsehood," retorted Leonard a little stiffly, and not best pleased with the interruption of the tête-à-tête.

"Do you know the truth?"

"God is truth."

"A truly theological elucidation," said Mark.

"What do you say, Cousin Natalie?" asked Leonard wistfully.

She had been gazing across the plain at the towers of Ladenburg, gleaming in the glow of the setting sun. "Can anybody say?" she answered. "Look at the plain," she added, stretching forth her hand, "these battered walls, the city at our feet. How often have they been scorched by fire and soaked in blood; and always in the cause of that truth which so many said was false!"

"Rather, because of the schemes of ambitious men," said Leonard.

"The pretext was always religion. Priests always the instigators of the wars," said Mark.

"Priests, yes, I grant you——"

"I include those of the Reformation. The bloodiest history of this place is its history since the Reformation. The source of its horrors was religion, always religion."

"For which reason," retorted Leonard, "you would blame religion, rather than the men who made it a cloak to ambition."

"One asks: What is religion?" said Natalie. "Catholics say of Frederick, who reigned here, that he was led by ambition to his fall; Protestants, that he fell a glorious sacrifice in the cause of truth. Who shall judge?"

"False ideas of duty lead to perdition," said Leonard sententiously.

"Which would seem to demonstrate that Frederick was in the wrong," observed Mark. "That may be so, but it hardly lies in the mouth of a student of Hampton."

"Of course, I know that Frederick was the Protestant champion," said Leonard, annoyed; "but——"

"Yet he lost his cause! How can one know—how do you know the truth?" The girl looked up with an eager expression as she asked the question.

"I know because I feel it," he answered in a low tone. They were solemn words to him, and as he uttered them a longing to show truth to this fair maid arose within him.

"And if one does not know, one cannot feel," murmured Natalie sadly. "Catholics, Jews, Protestants, all feel and all know——"

"That the others are all wrong," interjected Mark.

Meanwhile, the others of the party were approaching, the Professor expatiating to Paula anent the glories of the Claghorn race; not such glories, as he pointed out, as those of which they saw the evidences in the effigies of warriors and carved armorial bearings; but higher glories, humble deeds on earth, of which the story illuminated the celestial record. The dissertation had been commenced for the general weal, but the widow and the philosopher had gradually dropped behind, leaving Paula alone to derive benefit from the lessons drawn by Cousin Jared from the Claghorn history as contrasted with that of the rulers of the Palatinate.

CHAPTER V.

HOW A PAGAN PHILOSOPHER ENTERED THE SERVICE OF THE CHURCH.

"I fear you do not sympathize with Miss Achsah," observed the widow to her companion.

"In her solicitude for the tomb of Grandfather Eliphalet? No. Reverence for my ancestor has diminished with age; my excellent aunt, as befits a lady, remains ever young and romantic."

"She ought to appreciate the lawyer's declared intention to respect the grave."

"Handsome of the lawyer, who, *du reste*, seems an anomaly."

"How so?"

"He pays an extravagant price for a dreary desert. He volunteers to keep a stranger's tomb in repair——"

"Suppose I were to tell you that I am the lawyer who is to build the handsome residence."

"I should feel honored by your confidence, and unreservedly put my trust in your motives, because they are yours."

"But you are not surprised?"

"Rather deeply interested, and no less solicitous."

"Why solicitous?"

"Because of the incongruity you present as a resident of Easthampton. That little town is not merely the sepulchre of Eliphalet Claghorn, but the grave of mirth and the social graces. Can I contemplate the possibility of your interment without sorrow?"

The gentleman's tone had lapsed into tenderness; the lady smiled. "I believe you have not seen the place for many years," she said.

"Nothing has prevented my doing so except my recollection of its attractions."

"The ground I intend for a residence," said the lady, "has great natural advantages. It faces the ocean, has noble trees——"

"And crags and boulders, a most desolate spot."

"Which a handsome house will adorn and make beautiful. We must live somewhere. If we leave California, what better place can we choose than the old home of my son's race, where his name has been honored for generations? In that region he will not be a new man."

"An old one, assuredly, if he remains there. But he will flee from the home of his ancestors. The place is sunk in somnolence; one of those country towns that the world has been glad to forget. Rotting wharves, a few tumbledown warehouses, and three or four streets, shaded by trees so big that even the white houses with their green blinds look gloomy."

"The wharves and warehouses are mine, and are to be pulled down. I like the shady streets and the white houses."

"And their inmates?" The philosopher shuddered.

"The Claghorn paragon, Miss Achsah, lives in one of them."

"Ah, Miss Achsah! You do not know Miss Achsah; she superintended my boyhood."

"The result is a tribute to her excellence."

The gentleman bowed. "She is a good woman—the personification of Roman virtue, adorned with the graces of Calvinism—but, my dear Cousin" (the lady was his aunt, if anything), "I put it to you. Is not personified virtue most admirable at a distance?"

The lady laughed. "Possibly. But I do not expect to be reduced to virtuous society only, even if I am fortunate enough to prove acceptable in the eyes of Miss Claghorn. Our Professor assures me that the Hampton circle is most agreeable; and Hampton and Easthampton are practically one."

"And what a one!" The philosopher shrugged his shoulders in true Gallic fashion. "Madame, Hampton is the home of theology—and such theology! It is filled with musty professors, their musty wives and awkward and conceited boys, in training to become awkward and conceited men. Remember, I was one of the horde and know whereof I speak. Think seriously, my dear Cousin, before you expose so beautiful a girl as Mademoiselle Paula, not to speak of yourself, to such an environment."

The lady remained unmoved, though the gentleman had pleaded eloquently. "You are prejudiced," she answered. "Confess that there is no more agreeable man than our Cousin Jared; and if his son is a fair specimen of Hampton students, they must compare favorably with any others."

"Which would not be saying much. Jared is, doubtless, a good fellow, amenable once, but now encrusted with frightfully narrow views. As to young Leonard, his extraordinary good looks and amiability render him exceptional. It is really a pity that he can't be rescued," and the speaker sighed.

A sigh born of a sincere sentiment. Monsieur was at bottom good-natured, and it affected him disagreeably to see unusual graces doomed to a pulpit or a professorial chair. It was a sad waste of advantages fitted for better things. To dedicate to Heaven charms so apt for the world, seemed to him foolish, and to the devotee unfair. He felt as may feel a generous beauty whose day is past, and who contemplates some blooming maid about to enter a nunnery. "Ah! *Si la jeunesse savait,*" he murmured.

"You will not resolve without deliberation," he pleaded, having rendered to Leonard's fate the passing tribute of a sigh. "I dare not venture to beg you to wait until after your winter in Paris, but——"

"But, Monsieur, my resolve is fixed, though known only to you. Work is already commenced. But I must request you to keep the secret from all, including my son. I wish to surprise him."

"Your success is certain. It would be presumptuous to further combat your plans; especially"—with a graceful inclination—"since you disarm me by honoring me with your confidence."

"I have a reason for that," she said frankly. "I want your aid."

"In self-immolation! Even in that I am at your service."

"My purpose can be explained in a few words," she said, indicating a chair near the balustrade, into which the philosopher gracefully sank, after bowing the lady into one beside it. "I wish to build a grand house. My son's importance in the world is an attribute of his wealth. This is not a fact to flaunt, but is to be considered, and one by which I am bound to be influenced in contemplating his future."

"A great aid, Madame, in right conduct."

"My son will find it a great responsibility."

"Inheriting, as he does, your sense of duty," suggested the philosopher.

"Precisely. Now, I have planned a career for Mark."

There was a faint movement as of a fleeting smile behind Monsieur's well-trimmed moustache. The sharp-eyed lady noticed it, but was not disconcerted.

"I recognize the possibility of my plans coming to naught," she said. "That need not prevent my attempt to realize them. I see but one career open to my son; he must become a statesman."

"In Easthampton?"

"In the United States. It is his country. Pardon me," seeing him about to interpose. "It is not on this point I ask the aid you are willing to accord. That refers to my contemplated operations in Easthampton. It happens, however, that my son's future will depend, in no small measure, upon the enterprises in question. His great need will be identification with local interests, to which end a fixed habitation is necessary. I wish to build a house which will attract attention. To put it bluntly, I intend to advertise my son by means of my house."

"You will extort the sympathetic admiration of your compatriots."

"I shall not be as frank with them as with you. You will know that mere display is not my object."

"Yours merits admiration, even while it extorts regret."

"And now you see why Easthampton is peculiarly adapted to the end in view. No man can point to Mark Claghorn and ask, 'Who is he?' His name was carved in that region two centuries since."

"But you and your son are, I believe, liberal in your religious views. The Claghorns——"

"Have always kept the faith—with one notable exception"—the philosopher bowed acceptance of the compliment—"but I object to being called liberal, as you define the term; we are Catholics, that is to say, Anglicans."

"Humph!" muttered the philosopher dubiously.

"And I intend," pursued the lady, "to proclaim my creed by an act which I know is daring, but which will have the advantage of rooting my son and his descendants in the soil of Easthampton. I intend to build, to the memory of my husband, a High-Church chapel, a work of art that shall be unequalled in the country."

"Daring, indeed! Rash——"

"Not rash; but were it so, I should still do that which I have planned. My husband longed to return to the home of his boyhood, had fully resolved on purchasing the Seminary tract. He shall sleep where his ancestor sleeps." She turned her head to conceal a tear; the philosopher turned his to conceal a smile.

"In this pious and appropriate design, my dear Cousin," he murmured——

"I shall have your sympathy; I was sure of it. I want more; I want your aid."

In view of its wealthy source the suggestion was not alarming. The gentleman promised it to the extent of his poor powers, intimating, however, that connubial fidelity might conflict with maternal ambition, a result which he deprecated as deplorable.

Mrs. Joe had, she said, fully considered that possibility. "Suppose you are right," she answered to the philosopher's argument, "even if Hampton is the home of bigotry, boldness always commands sympathy. My chapel will lend importance to a town which mourns a lost prestige. It will be talked about from one end of the State to the other; and I intend that the Seminary shall be my right hand, the Church—my church, my left——"

"And both hands full!"

She blushed. "Of course, I shall use my advantages. The Seminary is the centre of much religious effort, which, as a Christian, I shall be glad to aid. It is the centre of influence, which I hope to share. Under my roof the representatives of differing creeds shall meet in harmony and acquire mutual respect. Should it happen that my son be politically objectionable because of my chapel—why, in such a condition of affairs the liberalism that is always latent where bigotry flourishes would spring to his aid, and find in him a leader."

"Madame!" exclaimed the gentleman, "you will win."

"I hope so," she replied, pleased at the admiration she had extorted. "And now, you shall be told how you can aid me. Paris is an art centre; there are to be found the people I shall need in regard to my plans concerning the chapel. I am resolved that this shall be so noble an edifice that the voice of detraction shall never be heard. Next winter we shall meet in Paris. Will you, so far as may be, prepare the way for my access to the places and people I desire to see?"

"Assuredly. I shall enter upon the task assigned me with admiration for your plans and sincere devotion to your interests," Thus, with his hand upon his heart and with an inclination of true Parisian elegance, the philosopher entered the service of Mrs. Joe, and of the Church.

CHAPTER VI.

ART, DIPLOMACY, LOVE AND OTHER THINGS.

Thus in amity dwelt the Claghorns, employing the summer days in innocent diversion. Many were the expeditions to points of interest; to Neckarsteinach and the Robbers' Nest, to the village of Dilsberg, perched upon the peak which even the bold Tilly had found unconquerable in peasant hands; to Handschuhsheim, where sleeps the last of his race, the boy-lord slain in duel with the fierce Baron of Hirschhorn, who himself awaits the judgment in the crypt of St. Kilian, at Heilbronn, holding in his skeleton hand a scroll, telling how the Mother's Curse pursued him to where he lies; to the Black Forest, now so smiling, but which Cæsar found dark, cold and gloomy, with its later memories of ruthless knights whose monuments are the grim ruins that crown the vineclad hills, and with present lore of gnomes and brownies. In these simple pleasures youth and maiden, philosopher, theologian and worldly widow joined with the emotions befitting their years and characteristics. To Natalie it was a time of intense delight, shared sympathetically by Paula, but more serenely. Mark enjoyed keenly, yet with rare smiles and with an underlying seriousness in which an observer might have detected a trace of the trail of the Great Serpent. Leonard, seldom absent from the side of his French cousin, delighted in the novel scenes and the companionship, but at times was puzzled by Natalie's capacity to live in a past that, as he pointed out, was better dead, since in its worst aspect it had been a time of barbarism, in its best of fanaticism. He could not understand the longing and liking for a day when if knights were bold they were also boorish, when if damosels were fair they were also ignorant of books, and perchance of bathtubs. He stared in innocent wonder at Natalie's exclamation of deprecation and Mark's harsh laugh when he pointed out such undeniable facts. To him Hans von Handschuhsheim, lying dead upon the steps of the Church of the Holy Ghost, his yellow locks red with blood, and the fierce Hirschhorn wiping his blade as he turned his back upon his handiwork—to Leonard this was a drunken brawl of three centuries since, and it grieved him to see in Natalie a tendency to be interested in the "vulgar details of crime." He knew that the girl lived in the gloom of irreligion (he was not aware that she dwelt in the outer darkness of ignorance), and he sighed as he noted one result of her unhappy lack; and he never knelt at his bedside forgetful of the fact, or of his duty in relation thereto.

As to the elders of the party, they enjoyed the present after the fashion of those whose days of dreaming have passed. Cousin Jared's broad smile of satisfaction was only absent when, in the heat of disputation, the philosopher was especially sacrilegious or aggravating, and even so, it was easily recalled by the tact of the widow, much of whose time was spent in keeping the peace between the two fellow-students of bygone years. As for the philosopher, he secretly pined for the Boulevard, though he, too, found distraction, one favorite amusement being to disturb the usual serenity of Paula by cynical witticisms, totally incomprehensible to the simple maiden.

The day of separation came at length, the first to depart being the mature and the budding theologian. Adieux were interchanged at the railway station, and many hopes as to future meetings were expressed, as well as satisfaction that chance had brought about a reunion so unexpected. No doubt these expressions were sincere, yet it is possible that as to clergyman and philosopher, each recognized in secret that their real adieux had been uttered years before. Under the circumstances, and with Mrs. Joe as a new link, the old chain had served; but at heart the two were antagonists; the chain was worn out.

"Not altogether a bad sort, Jared," observed M. Claghorn, as he walked from the station and by the side of Mrs. Joe along the Anlage.

"A thoroughly good fellow."

He smiled. It was faint praise. He said to himself complacently that she would not characterize himself as "a good fellow," whereas, the politician at his side, however she might have described her companion, regarded the departed Jared as of greater value to her plans, which had not been confided to him, than could be the philosopher in whom she had confided.

The two girls and Mark, following their elders, also interchanged views concerning the travelers. The verdict as to Cousin Jared, though less irreverently expressed, was similar to that enunciated by the widow. The good-hearted theologian had won the regard of all.

"And as for Leonard," observed Paula, "he is the handsomest boy I ever saw."

"And as amiable as beautiful," averred Natalie.

"As well as a little—shall we say 'verdant'?" suggested Mark. But the girls either denied the verdancy, or, if they admitted the charge in part, maintained it was an added excellence.

Meanwhile, the travelers contemplated one another from opposite sides of their railway carriage, the consciousness of leaving a strange world and re-entering their old one already making itself felt. To the elder man the change was neither startling nor very painful, but to Leonard it was both. He did not try to analyze his feelings, but there was a dead weight at his heart, a sorrow heavier than the natural regret at parting. It was long before he spoke. "I am so glad that our cousin, Natalie, though French, is not Catholic," he said, at length.

"I fear she is worse," was the answer.

"What could be worse?"

"Total unbelief," replied his father solemnly; and the weight at Leonard's heart grew heavier.

During the short remainder of M. Claghorn's stay at Heidelberg—already prolonged far beyond the original intention—it was arranged that he should select for the widow suitable quarters for her winter establishment at Paris; and so willing was the gentleman to be of service, that, to his great satisfaction, he received *carte blanche* for the purpose, and, Natalie accompanying him, departed with the resolve that the owners of the Great Serpent should be lodged in accordance with the just demands of that magnificent reptile, having in view, among other aspirations, the dazzling of the House of Fleury by the brilliance of the House of Claghorn.

As to those other aspirations, enough to say that they were by no means compatible with the loyalty he had professed for the pious plans of Mrs. Joe. He had not forgotten that the noble arms of the Marquise de Fleury were open to receive his daughter; but under existing conditions he was willing to be coy. He remembered with satisfaction that he had not irrevocably committed himself to a matrimonial alliance which still possessed attractions: though in the presence of the dazzling possibilities now offered, it behooved him to avoid precipitation. And so reasonable was this position that he did not hesitate to disclose it to the Marquise, simultaneously exculpating himself and assuaging the lady's resentment by dangling before her the glittering possibilities presented by Paula Lynford, whom he, with politic inaccuracy, described as the actual daughter of Mrs. Claghorn, hence inferentially a co-inheritor, with Mark, of the golden product of the Great Serpent.

"*Tiens*, Adolphe!" exclaimed the lady to her son, after having listened to the entrancing tale told by the philosopher, "Heaven has heard my prayers," and she repeated the unctuous story.

"Over a million of *dot*! It is monstrous, mama."

"For these people a bagatelle. Their gold mine yields a thousand francs a minute."

"These incredible Americans!"

"There is also a son, one Marc, about your age——"

"Aha, I see! M. Claghorn destines Natalie——"

"Precisely."

The little lieutenant wagged his head. It was the tribute to a dying love. From infancy he had been taught by his mama that in Natalie he beheld the future mother of the de Fleurys. Since infancy he had seen her but rarely, and on such occasions, being admonished by his mama, had concealed his passion from its object; but thus repressed, it had bubbled forth in other channels. He had written and declaimed sonnets; he had shed tears to a captured photograph of Natalie in pantalettes. The gusts of consuming passion which, in the presence of his *amis de college*, had swept sirocco-like across his soul, had extorted the sigh of envy and the tear of sympathy; from other friends, notably from Celestine, Claire and Annette, these manifestations had extorted shrieks of laughter, which, however, had moved him, not to indignation, but to pity, for in these damsels he saw but butterflies of love, unable to comprehend a *grande passion*.

It was, then, not without a fitting and manly sigh that the Marquis de Fleury surrendered the love of his youth in obedience to his mama and the motto of his house, which was "Noblesse Oblige," and, having procured from Natalie a photograph of Paula, he did homage before it as to "*la belle Lanforre*" in person, besides altering an old sonnet which had already seen service, and finding that Lynford, or as he would have it, "Lanforre," rhymed sufficiently well with Amor.

Meanwhile, the philosopher having diplomatically engaged the services of the Marquise, the noble lady proceeded to perform with zeal the task assigned her. *La belle France*, home of romance and last citadel of chivalry, is also business-like, and its sons and daughters of whatever rank are deft manipulators of the honest penny. In negotiating for the luxurious apartment of a diplomat about to proceed to Spain for a sojourn of some months, and in dealing with furnishers of all description, from laundry to livery men, the noble lady provided herself with pocket-money for some time to come; a seasonable relief to the over-strained resources of the House of Fleury.

"*Tiens,*" exclaimed Adolphe to his mama, Mrs. Claghorn being already installed in the diplomatic quarters, "this desire of Madame Zho to inspect churches—how do you explain it?"

"She is *dévote*. Doubtless she has sinned. She wishes to erect in her own country an expiatory chapel."

Which explanation, evolved from information derived from the philosopher, aided by the speaker's fancy, elucidated the mystery contained in the patronymic "Lanforre," borne by Paula. "*Sans doute,*" mused the Marquise, "*la mère*, being American, was *divorcée*. The daughter is the child of the first husband." Which theory sufficed until the later arrival of Mark, who, as being palpably older than Paula, drove the lady to evolve another, which, fortunately, in the interest of harmony, was not confided to "Madame Zho," but which not only explained, but demanded the expiatory chapel.

Mrs. Claghorn threw herself into her pious work with a zeal which extorted the approbation of the Marquise, who, as we know, was herself a religious woman, but which to the philosopher was less admirable, since it interfered with deep-laid plans with which it was incompatible. He was somewhat consoled, however, by the fact that the lady's course facilitated an intimacy which was favorable to the realization of less secret hopes; wherefore he vied with the Marquise in forwarding the pious cause of the widow by surrounding that lady with an artistic host, whereof the members received comforting orders for plans and paintings, designs and drawings, and were refreshed by a golden shower whereof the Marquise had her quiet but legitimate share.

The philosopher contented himself with the post of chief adviser and sole confidant of the beneficent lady. For, though her intention to erect a chapel could not be concealed, the locality of the realization of her plans remained a secret, and was, in fact, privately regarded by Mark,—where the philosopher hoped it would remain,—as poesy hath it, in the air.

Meanwhile, the comparative freedom of intercourse which reigned among the younger members of the party was approved by the Marquise as an American custom sanctioned, under the circumstances, by heaven, as an aid in its answer to her prayers; but the little lieutenant, like a dog that has slipped its leash, was puzzled by an unaccustomed liberty, and found himself unable to conduct himself gracefully in a novel role. He knew that the joyous freedom befitting intercourse with Claire and Celestine was not the tone for present conditions, but for similar conditions he knew no other. If, after preliminary negotiation on the part of his elders, he had been introduced into the presence of the object of his love, himself clad *en frac*, and had found his adored robed in white and carefully disposed upon a fauteuil—with the properties thus arranged, he felt he could have borne himself worthily as one acceptable and with honorable intentions. But thus to be allowed to approach the object of a passion (which, he assured his mama, was now at a white heat), to converse familiarly, surrounding ears being inattentive and surrounding eyes uninterested; to be expected to interchange views freely pronounced by lips such as he had supposed were silent until unsealed by matrimony—these things puzzled and embarrassed him. Perhaps it was fortunate that such attempts as he made to tell his love were not understood by the object of his devotion. Paula's understanding of French, though it had achieved plaudits and prizes at school, did not suffice for the purpose, and the lieutenant was innocent of any modern language other than his own, while against his frequent efforts of an ocular character Paula's serenity was proof, though occasionally disturbed by the manifestations of that which she supposed was a severe nervous disorder of the eyes of her companion, and for which she pitied him; and, as to the sonnet which he slipped into her hand, it being beyond her construing powers, she handed it to Mrs. Joe, who read it and laughed.

But though she laughed at a production designed to draw tears, but for it, she had probably paid little heed to an occurrence which about this time attracted her attention.

She was in the Church of St. Roch, Paula at her side, and, near at hand, Mark and Natalie. St. Roch is an ancient and gloomy edifice, and the lady had found no suggestions for her chapel in its sombre interior. She turned to leave, when her attention was arrested by a tableau. Natalie's hand rested upon Mark's shoulder, and both stood as if transfixed, and gazing at something which Mrs. Joe could not see.

Had it not been for the sonnet and the reflections to which it had given rise, she would have at once admitted the palpable fact that the girl, absorbed by that upon which she gazed, was oblivious of the touch with which she had involuntarily arrested the steps of her companion. With head bent forward, her faculties were enchained by that which she saw with eyes in which wonder, compassion and wistful yearning were combined.

It was a young woman upon whom the girl's rapt gaze rested. She had been kneeling at the grating of a confessional from which the priest had just departed. A smothered cry, and the abandon with which the penitent had thrown herself upon the stone floor of the mural chapel, had attracted Natalie's attention, and unconsciously she had laid her hand on Mark's shoulder to arrest steps which might disturb that which, at first supposed to be devotion, was quickly recognized as the agony of grief.

For a moment the observers thought the woman had fainted, so still she lay after that smothered cry, and Natalie had taken a step forward to lend aid, when a convulsive shudder shook the prostrate form, and then the woman rose to her knees. Dry-eyed, her long, black hair hanging in disorder, her white face and great, dark eyes gleaming from beneath heavy brows and long silken lashes, she knelt, holding high a photograph upon which she gazed, a living statue of woe.

Mark was hardly less moved than Natalie, but more quickly remembered that he, at least, had no business with this sorrow. As he moved, the unconscious hand of his companion fell from his shoulder, and in the same moment the mourner rose and her eyes met Natalie's.

Dignified by grief, she was a majestic woman, and handsome; probably handsomer in her disorder than under the aspect of every day. Perhaps she instantly read the sympathy in the eyes, no less beautiful than her own, which were turned upon her.

"You suffer!" exclaimed Natalie involuntarily.

"And you rejoice," replied the other, indicating Mark.

"I have but this." She displayed the colored photograph she had held toward heaven. A startled exclamation broke from Mark, as he looked.

"He is dead," said the woman. "To-day was to have been our wedding day, and he is dead." The tears welled up in the listeners' eyes; the speaker was tearless, but the silent sympathy impelled her to go on.

"Three months we lived together," she continued, with Gallic frankness as to domestic details. "His father refused consent, but to-day, his birthday, he would have been free: he is dead. His mother pities me," the woman went on. "She has known love. She promised consolation in confession—as if a priest could know!"

"Yet they say that in religion," Natalie commenced timidly——

"There is but one religion—Love!" interrupted the other. "You will know. He"—her glance indicated Mark—"will be your teacher."

Mark glanced hastily at his cousin. She seemed oblivious of the woman's words. He moved further away. After awhile Natalie slowly followed; the woman left the church.

"Did you notice," asked Mark, as Natalie rejoined him, "how strikingly that portrait resembled Leonard?"

She made no answer. Other words than his were ringing in her ears: "There is but one religion—Love! He will be your teacher," and even while she sorrowed for the sorrow she had witnessed, a strange thrill passed through her—was it pain, was it joy?

The party left the church. Natalie sought the side of Mrs. Joe, leaving Mark to walk with Paula. The elderly lady asked her who was the person with whom she had talked. Natalie replied that the woman's name was Berthe Lenoir, and that she wished to be the speaker's maid, and she narrated some part of the history that had been briefly told to her.

"But, my dear," was the comment, "your father must make inquiry as to her fitness."

"That, of course," was the answer, and then she was silent. Within a week Berthe Lenoir entered her service, a woman, who by reason of her capacity, soon gained the general approval; and for other reasons, the special approval of a lover of the beautiful. "Her eyes," observed the lieutenant, "are the eyes which shape destinies."

Meanwhile, other eyes, belonging to one who believed it in her power to shape destinies, were watchful. Mrs. Joe had long since resolved that to be an American statesman, Mark needed an American wife, and since she had herself trained one for the position, she had no desire to see her labors rendered fruitless. It had needed merely the opening of her eyes to enable her to discern that there were other schemes worthy of her attention, besides that one of the philosopher, of which she herself was the object, and which, though the gentleman had supposed it hidden, had been patent to the lady, serving to amuse while it benefited her. She promptly averted the danger to her plans by confiding to the Marquise her intentions with regard to Mark and Paula. The noble lady regarded such matters as entirely controllable by parental edict, and at once resumed negotiations with the philosopher, who, in the belief that surrender of his hopes in regard to his daughter would tend to further those he cherished in respect to himself, acquiesced gracefully in the inevitable; and there being no ground for further delay, the de Fleury-Claghorn treaty was duly ratified, to remain, however, a secret for the present from all the juniors of the party, except from the lieutenant, whom it was necessary to inform of the need of a re-transference of his affections. He submitted with sorrow. The charms of Paula had, as he confided to his mama, made an impression on his heart which only active service could efface. As to resisting destiny, it never entered his thoughts. Paula was for Mark, Natalie for him. There might be consolation. "With such wealth," he suggested, "they will surely add to her dowry."

"Let us hope so," replied the Marquise. "Our Cousin Beverley will do what is possible. Meanwhile, be as charming as possible to Madame Zho and to Marc, who will have it all."

"Such luck is iniquitous! Well, since my marriage is deferred, you will consent that I go to Africa. Love is denied me; I must seek glory. *Tiens, je suis Francais!*"

Long before this, Mrs. Joe had exacted from Mark a promise to study at the University with reasonable diligence. The promise had been kept. A new semester was about to commence; he was anxious to take the doctoral degree, hence it was necessary for him to return to Heidelberg. He hardly regretted it. Of late, constraint had seemed to pervade the intercourse which had been hitherto so unrestrained, and, above all, Natalie had been unusually reserved. It was not without some regret that he departed, yet on the whole content to return to *Burschenfreiheit* and fidelity to the creed whose chief article is disdain of philistinism.

Mrs. Joe was glad to see him depart before she left for America, where the surprise intended for him was progressing. But it might take more time to build a house than make a Doctor of Civil Law; the question was how to prevent his premature home-coming.

"I will keep him," said the philosopher, in answer to her confidence as to her misgivings. "He has promised to visit me when he leaves the University. When I get him I will hold him."

The lady looked at the gentleman questioningly.

"Do not doubt my good faith," he murmured.

"And you will come with him to America," she suggested. "Perhaps you can induce the Marquise. And the little soldier—surely, he will brave the seas if your daughter does so!"

"An invasion by the Gauls. Why not? I for one shall be enchanted to see the result of your energy and taste."

"And Natalie shall see the Tomb in which she is so deeply interested, while you lay your homage at the feet of Miss Achsah and so fulfill a long-neglected duty."

"And at the feet of the chatelaine of Stormpoint. I am impatient for the day." And it was so arranged, and the lady, declining the proffered escort of Monsieur, left Paris for Havre, accompanied by Paula.

"A good fellow!" she thought, as she leaned back in the coupé, applying to the philosopher that very term which he had flattered himself she would not apply, "but too anxious to believe that I am his cousin and not his aunt."

CHAPTER VII.

A CONFERENCE OF SPINSTERS CONCERNING A RUNAWAY DAMSEL.

Five years have passed since the Claghorn reunion at Heidelberg. The Professor and philosopher have journeyed to that world concerning which one of the two claimed certain knowledge, and which the other regarded as unknowable. Thither we cannot follow them, but since men do not live for a day, but for all time, we shall doubtless come upon indications that the lives of these two, the things they said and did, are forces still. Meanwhile, we must concern ourselves with the living, and of those with whom we have to do, no one is more noteworthy than Achsah Claghorn.

Miss Claghorn was, as the representative of an ancient and very theological family, a citizen of no little note in Easthampton, the shady and quiet suburb of the city of Hampton. Her spotless white house was large; its grounds were, compared with those of her neighbors, large; the trees in the grounds were very large; the box-plants were huge of their kind. Miss Achsah herself was small, but by reason of her manner, which was positive and uncompromising, impressive. She lived as became her wealth and position, comfortably and without undue regard for conventionalities. She could afford so to live and had been able to afford it for many years; ever since she had shared with her brother, the Reverend Eliphalet, the bounty left to them by that other and younger brother who had died in California. On the receipt of that bounty she had retired from her position as schoolmistress, had bought the large, white house, and, together with Tabitha Cone, had undertaken to live as she pleased, succeeding in so doing more satisfactorily than is usual with those fortunate enough to be able to make similar resolves. Perhaps this was because her desires were more easily attainable than the desires pertaining to such conditions usually are.

The position of Tabitha Cone was nominally one of dependence, but, with a praiseworthy desire to rise superior to such a status, Tabitha persistently strove to rule her benefactress, which attempts were met with frequent rebellion. Miss Achsah was, at least intermittently, mistress of her own house; and both ladies had a lurking consciousness that she, Achsah, to wit, had reserves of strength which would enable her to become so permanently, if she were to develop a serious intention to that end. Both ladies, however, shrank from a struggle with that possible termination, much enjoying life as they lived it, and with no desire to terminate an invigorating and pleasing warfare.

For the rest, Miss Claghorn permitted no slurs to be cast upon her companion, except such as she herself chose to project. "Tabitha Cone and

I sat on the same bench at school; together we found the Lord. I knew of no difference between us in those days; I know of none now, except that I had a rich brother."

"I am sure, Miss Claghorn, I quite agree with your view," observed Paula, to whom the words were addressed.

"Which I hope is a satisfaction to you," replied the lady, her manner indicating complete indifference as to the fact. "If that is so, why do you object to my consulting Tabitha Cone about this letter?" looking over her spectacles at the pretty face.

"I hoped that my plan would meet your views, and then such consultation would perhaps be unnecessary, and—and——"

"And?" echoed Miss Achsah in an uncompromising tone, and regarding her visitor still more sharply.

"You know, Miss Claghorn, you sent for me, and were kind enough to say you desired my advice——"

"Information, not advice."

"Don't you think Tabitha Cone will derive a wrong impression if she reads that letter?" continued the persistent Paula, "Is that quite fair?"

"Tabitha Cone understands English—even Ellis Winter's—he says plainly enough that the girl is an atheist——"

"Not that, Miss——"

"A heathen, then—a damned soul" (Paula started palpably). "Splitting hairs about terms don't alter the essential fact."

"Nobody can deplore the truth more than I; but to risk its being made a subject of gossip——"

"Tabitha Cone is not given to tattle. She may gossip with Almighty God about this matter. She has known Him for many years."

Paula shuddered. To know Omnipotence in this blunt fashion grated on her nerves. "I have humbled myself many times and sought her eternal welfare in prayer," she said.

"I hope your condescension may ultimately benefit her," snapped the old lady. "I can't say I have noticed any change, certainly no change for the better."

"I referred to Natalie."

"Oh, and so that is the way to pronounce the outlandish name. My nephew Eliphalet's mother's name was Susan; my own name has been in the family two hundred years—well, and if Ellis Winter is right, your humblings seem to have done but little good. Perhaps those of the despised Tabitha Cone may have more effect, even if unaccompanied with flummery——"

"Miss Claghorn, you are not generally unjust."

"Never. But I get tired of millinery in religion. Ah! if only you would humble yourself—but there! I suppose you intone the prayer for your daily bread. Pah!"

Paula rose majestically.

"Sit down, child; I didn't mean to offend you. (The Lord has infinite patience and pity, and so for imbeciles, I suppose)" she said parenthetically and in a subdued tone, which was not heard by the visitor, who sat down, having an object in being both meek and persistent, a fact of which Miss Claghorn was aware. It was a sore temptation to let Paula have her wish, but, all the while she knew she must finally resolve to do her duty. It was that knowledge which gave acrimony to her speech.

"Paula," she said, "I ought not to have asked you to come here about this matter. I knew what you would desire and hoped you would be able to persuade me; I ought to have known myself better. I must do my duty; she must come to me."

"But, dear Miss Claghorn——"

"She is a Claghorn, and—dreadful as it is—a heathen as well, and alone in the world. I must do my duty; it is not easy, I assure you."

Paula quite believed this, and the belief did not add to her hope of success. When Miss Claghorn desired to do things which, in the eyes of others, were better left undone, she was apt to see her duty in such action. It was equally true that her duty being visible, she would do it, even if disagreeable. But the duty now before her was, for many reasons, very disagreeable, indeed, and strictly just as she was, she was but human, and the righteous indignation she felt for her own vacillation fell naturally in part upon Paula.

"At least do not let that letter prejudice you," urged Paula. "She is a sweet girl, as good as gold."

"Very likely. Gold is dross. Good girls do not deny their Maker."

This was indisputable. Paula sighed. "I am very sorry we cannot have her," was all she said.

Miss Claghorn looked at her thoughtfully and with some inward qualms at her own harshness. There was an opportunity to seasonably drop a word which for some time she had been considering as ready to be dropped, and which, if heeded, might have some consolation for the girl before her.

"You can have her—on one condition. Come now, Paula!"

"What is that?" asked the girl, hope in her eyes; some misgiving, too, for there was that in Miss Claghorn's expression which aroused it.

"Stop your shilly-shally with that little milliner-man, Arthur Cameril, and marry him. Then Natalie can pay you a good long visit."

This was more than a Christian ought to bear. Paula could do her duty, too.

"Miss Claghorn, Father Cameril has taken the vow of celibacy. The fact is well known. I am contemplating the same. I wish you good-morning," and so Paula majestically sailed away.

"Hoity-toity!" exclaimed Miss Achsah, as her visitor let herself out of the front door; and then, not disturbed, but in the belief that she had performed another disagreeable duty, she commenced the re-perusal of a letter in her hand. Which letter was as follows:

> "Dear Miss Claghorn—Your grand-niece, Natalie, has arrived in this country. She naturally at once communicated with me, and I find her situation somewhat perplexing. To speak frankly, she has run away from home. It was her father's wish that she remain in the household of the Marquise de Fleury, and she has lived with that lady since Mr. Claghorn's death. But it seems that for some time past the guardian has tried to induce the ward to marry against her inclinations.

> "I think there can be no doubt that the influences brought to bear on your grand-niece amounted to persecution, and I am disposed to regard her action as justified, having received from the Marquise (who was apprised of her destination by your niece) a letter, written in such a tone as to leave no doubt in my mind that the statements made to me by Miss Natalie are correct.

> "The plan of your grand-niece is to live independently in this country. For the present this would be most imprudent. She is very young, and though by no means inexperienced in the ways of the world, is very foreign. She is quite resolute in her determination, and is aware that her property, in my charge, aside from some French possessions, is ample for

her support. Do not gather that she is not amenable to advice, or is inclined to be obstinate. This is not the case, but she has evidently had an unpleasant experience of guardianship, and is quite resolved under no circumstances to permit any disposition of herself matrimonially. This resolve is the foundation of her intention to remain independent, an intention which no doubt will be easily combated with her advance in knowledge of our American customs in this regard.

"It would be unfair, having shown you the only shadows connected with Beverley's daughter, were I to withhold the commendation justly due her. With such acquaintance as I had formed with her on the occasion of my visit to France, I gathered a good opinion of one whom, indeed, I only knew as a child. That opinion has been strengthened by occasional correspondence and by the personal observation of the last fortnight. She seems to be a charming girl, remarkably beautiful, with a mind of her own, and, doubtless, a will of her own; nevertheless, a person that would be an acquisition in any household. Were I blessed with a domestic circle, I should be well content to have Miss Natalie enter it; but, as you know, I am not so fortunate.

"I hesitate to mention one other detail, yet feel that you ought to be fully informed; and while I can, believe me, appreciate the standpoint from which you will regard that which I have to disclose, I beg you to take a charitable view of a matter which, to one of your rooted and cherished convictions, will be of transcendent importance. It is that your grand-niece is in religion a free-thinker, and rejects the Christian faith.

"To you, as the representative of the Claghorn family, a family which for generations has upheld the standard of purest orthodoxy, this information will come as a shock. Yet when I assure you that Miss Natalie's views (such as they are) are probably held rather from a sense of filial duty and affection than from conviction, the facts will, I am sure, appeal to your compassion, as well as to that stern sense of duty and justice so admirably exhibited in your life. For many years I have been aware that the late Beverley had trained his daughter in accordance with a theory which repudiated tenets sacred in your eyes. My only reason for never imparting the fact to you was because the knowledge could only be a grief to one who held the Claghorn traditions in reverence. The interest you occasionally displayed concerning one who had chosen to be an exile was, I believe, always satisfied as far as in my power, except as to this one particular. I regret now that I withheld a knowledge which circumstances have made important. I did wrong, but I need not ask you not to connect my wrong-doing with the claims of your grand-niece.

"Kindly consider this letter carefully and let me hear from you soon. Perhaps an invitation to spend a part or all of the coming summer with you would lead to an easy solution of the difficulties presented. Your grand-niece is at present staying with my friend, Mrs. Leon, who will be pleased that she remain; but I foresee that the young lady herself will object to that.

"With regards to Miss Cone, believe me,

"Respectfully yours, ELLIS WINTER."

CHAPTER VIII.

A MAIDEN FAIR, A MODERN EARLY FATHER AND A THEOLOGIAN.

Paula emerged from the White House in an un-Christian frame of mind. The fact might to an ordinary sinner seem pardonable, and Paula herself, though by no means an ordinary sinner, thought so, too. "Impertinent bigot!" In these unusually emphatic words she mentally expressed her opinion of Achsah Claghorn.

From several points of view Paula was not an ordinary sinner. Externally, she was a very pleasing one, being in all things alluring to the eye. So nicely adjusted were her physical proportions that it could not be said that she was either tall or short, plump or meagre. A similar neutrality characterized the tints of her skin and hair. Her cheeks were never red, yet never pale; the much-used adjective "rosy" would not properly describe the dainty tinge that, without beginning or end, or line of demarcation, redeemed her face from pallor. Her nose was neither long nor short, upturned or beak-like, and while no man could say that it was crooked and remain a man of truth, yet would no truth-lover say that it was straight. In all respects a negative nose, in no respect imperfect. Her skin, ears, neck, hands, feet—all were satisfying, yet not to be described by superlatives. Her hair was neither chestnut nor yellow, nor quite smooth nor kinky, but in color and adjustment restful; her eyes were nearly violet, and their brows and lashes just sufficiently decided to excite no comment. Paula's mouth was perhaps the only feature which, apart from the charming whole, demanded notice, and he who noticed sorrowed, for it was a mouth inviting, yet not offering kisses.

It is believed that it will be admitted that outwardly Paula Lynford was not an ordinary sinner. Nor was she such as to the inner being, if she herself could be believed; for at this period of her existence she was accustomed to introspection, and that habit had disclosed to her that she was very bad, indeed, "vile," as she fondly phrased it, or in moments of extreme exaltation, "the vilest of the vile."

A serene consciousness of vileness was a recent growth in her bosom. Father Cameril (so known to a very small but devoted band of worshippers—to the world at large, the Reverend Arthur Cameril) was fond of dwelling upon human and his own vileness, and his adorers desired to be such as he. Nor did the Reverend Father deny them this delight, but rather encouraged their perception of the unworthiness indicated by the unpleasant word which had been caught from him by the dames and damsels who rejoiced in him and in their own turpitude. Father Cameril was, in a very limited circle, quite the rage in the vicinity. Since his advent spiritual titillation had been discovered in candles, attitudes, novel genuflexions and defiance of the Bishop, a wary old gentleman, who was resolved to evade making a martyr of Father Cameril, being, from long observation, assured that sporadic sputterings of ultra-ritualism were apt to flicker and die if not fanned by opposition. The good Father, meanwhile, unaware that the Bishop had resolved that no stake should be implanted for his burning, whereby he was to be an illumination to the Church, tasted in advance the beatitude of martyrdom, and reveled in mysterious grief and saint-like resignation and meekness, and while hopefully expectant, he added to his inner joys and the eccentricity of his outward man by peculiar vesture of the finest quality, beneath which the fond and imaginative eyes of his followers saw, as in a vision, a hair shirt. He was known to aspire to knee-breeches, and was hopefully suspected of considering a tonsure as a means of grace and a sign of sanctity. His little church, St. Perpetua, the new and beautiful edifice erected by Mrs. Joseph Claghorn, of Stormpoint, in memory of her husband (an offence in Miss Claghorn's Calvinistic eyes, and regarded askance by Leonard), was crowded every Sunday at Mass, a function which was also celebrated daily at an hour when most people were still abed; Paula always, the night watchman, about going off duty occasionally, and three elderly ladies, blue and shivering, in attendance. Father Cameril was Miss Claghorn's special aversion. Tabitha Cone found in him much to admire. He was a good little man, inordinately vain, somewhat limited in intellect, and unconscious of wrong-doing. He prayed that the Church might be led from the path of error in which she obstinately chose to remain, and, by canonizing Henry VIII, display works meet for repentance; in which case he would hesitate no longer, but return home, that is, to the maternal bosom of Rome, at once.

As Paula saw the good Father coming down the street, holding in his yellow-gloved hand a bright-red little book, the redness whereof set off the delicate tint of the glove, while its gilded edges gleamed in the sunlight, she was more than usually conscious of the vileness which should have been meekness, even while her anger grew hotter at the insult offered by Miss Claghorn to the natty little man approaching, "like an early Father," she murmured, though any resemblance between the Reverend Arthur in kid gloves and ætat 28, and Polycarp, for instance, was only visible to such vision as Paula's.

"You seem disturbed," he said, as the two gloved hands met in delicate pressure, and he uttered the usual sigh.

"A cherished hope," she answered, her clear violet eyes bent downward, "has been dashed."

"We must bear the cross; let us bear it worthily. I have been pained at not seeing you at confession, Paula. You neglect a means of lightening the burden of the spirit."

"My cousin objects, Father. I owe her the obedience of a daughter."

"You owe a higher obedience"—here his voice had that tone of sternness always sweet to the meek ears of his followers. "Nevertheless," he added, "do not act against her wish. I will, myself, see Mrs. Claghorn. Meanwhile, bear your burdens with resignation, always remembering the weakness, yea, the vileness of the human heart."

"I strive," said Paula, looking very miserable and unconsciously taking an illustration from a heavily-laden washerwoman passing, "not to faint by the wayside, but the load of life is heavy."

"But there are times when the heart's vileness is forgotten, the soul rises above its burdens and feels a foretaste of the life to come," interrupted Father Cameril a little confusedly as to the senses of the soul. "Try to rise to those heights."

"I do. May I ask your special intercession for a soul in darkness? One that I had hoped to gain."

"Hope on and pray. I shall not forget your request. The name is——"

"Natalie, the daughter of Mr. Beverley Claghorn. You have heard us mention them. Mr. Claghorn is dead. Until now she has lived in France, where she was born. I hope to see her soon at Easthampton."

"At Stormpoint! How pleasant for you! Paula, we shall rescue this dear child from the errors of a schismatic mother. I feel it here," and the Reverend Arthur indicated his bosom.

Paula recognized in the schismatic mother the Roman Catholic Church. She felt it sinful to leave Father Cameril in ignorance of the facts. She felt it unkind to her friend to disclose them. She could sin, if hard pushed; she could not be unkind. She concealed the unbelief.

"We knew them some years since in Europe," she said. "I mean Mr. Claghorn and Natalie. She is a sweet girl; but she will visit at Miss Claghorn's."

The Reverend Arthur's face fell. Above all earthly things he dreaded sinners of the type of Achsah Claghorn. "The situation will be difficult," he murmured. "But truth will prevail," he added, more cheerily. "Truth must prevail."

Which assurance made the girl uncomfortable, because she knew that his prayers and his labors would be directed against mere schism, whereas the case required the application of every spiritual engine at command.

So that she was not sorry that he left her, after presenting her with the little red book and urging her to read the same.

Stormpoint was not inaptly named. A huge crag jutting out into the sea, whose waves, ever darting against its granite sides, rolled off with a continuous muffled bellow of baffled rage, which, when the storm was on, rose to a roar. A cabin had once stood on the bluff, which, tradition asserted, had been the home of the first Eliphalet Claghorn, whose crumbling tomb, with its long and quaint inscription, was hard by. The Reverend Eliphalet slept quiet in death, but the howl of the storm and the roar of the waves must have kept him awake on many a night in life. Even the stately castle erected by Joseph Claghorn's widow often trembled from the shock of the blast. The region about was strewn with huge boulders, evidences of some long-past upheaval of nature, while among the crags great trees had taken root. The landscape was majestic, but the wind-swept soil was barren, and the place had remained a waste. Only a fortune, such as had been derived from the Great Serpent, could make the Point comfortable for habitation. But the task had been accomplished, and Stormpoint was the second wonder of Easthampton, the first being the wonderful chapel, St. Perpetua.

Paula gloried in Stormpoint. Not for its grandeur or the money it had cost, but because she loved the breeze and the sea and the partial isolation. Even now, as she ascended the bluff by a side path, rugged and steep, and commenced to smell the ocean and feel its damp upon her cheek, the Reverend Arthur Cameril seemed less like an early Father, and his lemon-colored kids less impressive.

On hearing her name called and looking up, she smiled more brightly and looked more beautiful than she had yet looked that day, though, from the moment she had emerged from her morning bath of salt water she had been beautiful. "Aha! Leonard, is that you?" she exclaimed.

"Where have you been?" asked Leonard, as he reached her side.

"At Miss Claghorn's. She sent for me."

Leonard's eyes opened wide. "Cousin Achsah sent for you! What for?"

"She will tell you."

"And you won't. Well, I must wait. What have you there?" taking the little red book from her hand. "'The Lives of the Hermits!' Oh, Paula; you had better read the 'Lives of the Laundresses'; these were a very dirty set."

"Leonard! How can you? A clergyman, a professor of theology!"

"Oh, I've no objection to them except that," he answered, "and I wouldn't mention their favorite vanity if they had not so reveled in it and plumed themselves upon it. Paula, Paula," he added, more seriously, "Father Cameril gave you that."

He was vexed, perhaps jealous of Father Cameril, though if so, he was unconscious, ascribing his vexation to a different source. He had a hearty contempt for the silly flummery, as he mentally described it, practised by Father Cameril, and he hated to know that Paula was enticed by it. She understood and was neither without enjoyment of his vexation nor resentment that he would not express it in words. She would have liked him to forbid the reading of the little book. It would have been a sign of steadfastness to disobey; it might have been a greater pleasure to obey.

"Well, read the book, if you can stomach it," he said. "I doubt if you will derive any benefit. I must be going. When you and Cousin Achsah take to plotting, I must investigate. Good-bye."

"Leonard, did you know that Natalie is in New York, that she has come to America to live?"

"Natalie in New York! Your news amazes me. She will come here, of course?"

"Not to Stormpoint," she answered regretfully. "To your cousin's, Miss Claghorn."

He looked his surprise. "To live there! That surely will never do."

"Oh, Leonard, I am so glad you agree with me. I tried to persuade Miss Claghorn to let her come to us. Think of it! Alone with those two old women and their quarrels. That gloomy house! It's dreadful!"

"It certainly will not do for Natalie," he observed, thoughtfully. "I wish, Paula, my cousin had consulted me rather than you."

"Why, Leonard! You don't suppose I did not urge all I could?"

"That's just it. Cousin Achsah is, of her kind, a very fine specimen, and I am her favorite and bound to respect and love her, as I do—but a nature like hers and one like yours are antagonistic."

"Then, since you respect and—and——"

"And love her, you think I don't respect and love you; but you know better, Paula."

She blushed at the snare the echo of his words had led her into. He was not so conscious. "As I remember Natalie," he said, "she was amiable and nice in all points—still she and my cousin——"

"They will be absolutely incomprehensible to each other," said Paula. "Do try and have her consent to let Natalie come to Stormpoint."

"I will do what I can. Has Mrs. Joe invited her?"

"She will be only too glad as soon as she knows. But the matter has been placed in such a light by that tiresome Mr. Winter—but there, you will find out everything from your cousin. Do what you can."

"I will. What happy days they were, those days in Heidelberg."

The violet eyes were tender with reminiscence, the pretty mouth seductive. "They were the happiest of my life," she said.

"And of mine," echoed Leonard, as he walked off, having seen neither mouth nor eyes, but a vision of the past.

CHAPTER IX.

THE ADVANTAGES OF TREADING THE BORDERLAND OF VICE.

Among the diversions indulged in at Heidelberg, during the accidental reunion of the Claghorns, there had been one particularly affected by Professor and philosopher. The early education of these two had been identical; their later training had progressed on widely diverging lines. The Reverend Jared had continued in the path in which his footsteps had been placed in childhood, while Beverley had wandered far. Yet, being by inheritance as nearly alike as may be two who, descended from a common ancestor, partake of marked ancestral traits, agreement between them in reference to a matter wherein their views clashed was impossible; which fact had sufficed to lend a charm to disputation.

A favorite theme of discussion had been discovered in the serious problems connected with the training of youth. The clergyman had a son who embodied his theories; the philosopher was the father of a daughter educated upon a plan of his own. Each was paternally satisfied with results so far, and each hoped for further development equally gratifying.

The philosopher preached from a text which may be briefly stated in the words of the proverb, which informs us that "Familiarity breeds contempt." He would apply this maxim to evil and use knowledge as the shield of youth. Whereas the Professor, relying upon the truth contained in the adage, "Ignorance is bliss," and maintaining that modified bliss in this world and perfect bliss in the world to come are the proper objects of man's endeavor, logically contended that ignorance of evil, a thing in its nature sure to breed sorrow, was to be encouraged.

"The true way to appreciate the dangers which must inevitably beset youth is to become familiar with them. Distance lends enchantment. That closer inspection of vice which may be derived from acquaintance with its borderland, wherein the feet of the novice may be taught to tread warily, will result in indifference, if not disgust. As long as there is ignorance there will be curiosity, which is more dangerous than knowledge." Thus had spoken the philosopher. To which the Professor had replied: "Yet I will not assume that you wish your daughter to tread the borderland of vice?"

"Certainly I do; limiting her steps to the borderland of the vices to which she is to be exposed. I admit that a man cannot, as readily as a woman, take cognizance of such vices. It is my misfortune and my daughter's that her mother died at her birth; but I have endeavored to make her superior to the glaring defects of her sex. She is not petty. She yearns neither for bonnets nor beatitudes. Without attempting, in the ignorance inseparable from my sex, to instruct her in detail, I have always had in view the enlargement of her mind."

"By educating her as a Frenchwoman!"

"Pardon me, no. Much as I admire the French, I do not approve their system of female education, which, by the way, resembles the course you have pursued with your son. I do not question its frequent excellent results, nor can I question its failures. My daughter's schooling has been only partially French. Travel and indiscriminate reading—I have largely relied on these."

"I am willing to admit, Cousin, that the apparent results in those matters which you deem of most importance ought to be gratifying. It is no exaggeration to say that my young cousin is a charming girl. But her life has not been lived."

"No. Therefore, we cannot fairly speculate as to the outcome. Meanwhile, as far as my system has reached, it is gratifying, as you confess."

"The same can be said of mine."

"Doubtless. But has your son's life been lived? Thus far, you have as much reason for satisfaction as I have. I hope that you will never be compelled to admit that innocence, based on ignorance, is a weak barrier to oppose to the inevitable temptations which beset young men."

"Innocence fortified by religious principle, early instilled," had been the solemn reply.

M. Claghorn understood the solemnity and braved the possible results of a confession which he was willing to make rather than be further exposed to the occasional somewhat annoying admonitory tone of his companion.

"I am a living example of the futility of that contention," he answered. "I do not wish to be understood as admitting that I have been unduly addicted to vice, which would not be true; but I have tasted of forbidden fruit. I found it unsatisfactory. I base my theory on careful observation and some personal experience."

Cousin Jared groaned inwardly, but made no answer. Exhortation was on his tongue's end, but, as the philosopher had desired, he recognized its futility.

Indulgence in wine was one of those vices which the Reverend Jared had found reprehensible, a practice which it grieved him to observe was permitted by the lax views of all those Claghorns, except himself and Leonard, who were sojourning together. It is not to be assumed that these people indulged in unseemly intoxication. Of so untoward a result the Professor had no fear. He objected to wine-drinking as offering an evil example. The fact that in so doing he discredited the first miracle of his Saviour was a difficulty easily surmounted by a nimble theologian.

"You are so fierce about wine that one would think you had a personal hatred toward liquor," Beverley had said to him laughingly.

"I have, 'Liph. Jeremiah Morley——" He said no more, remembering who Jeremiah Morley had been.

"It is fanaticism, Jared; absolutely incomprehensible. Your son, even though a clergyman, must live in the world. I don't say make him worldly, but don't let him remain in complete ignorance. He is a handsome fellow, amiable, intelligent—really too good for a parson."

"Which you intended to be; which your father, grandfather and great-grandfather were."

"Don't think I depreciate them. But your boy is hardly formed on the Claghorn pattern. He has probably more of the Morleys. His mother must have been a very beautiful woman, if he resembles her."

"As good as she was beautiful," sighed the widower. "Yes, Leonard resembles the Morleys—the best of them."

And so the discussion had terminated. It has been recorded here to indicate paternal views as to the education of youth. In the practice of the views he held, Professor Claghorn had been ably seconded by an excellent and pious wife, and had he been alive to see the result in the young man who had just left Paula Lynford, he must assuredly have observed the proved soundness of his theories and practice.

CHAPTER X.

A YOUTH OF PROMISE, A FEMALE POLITICIAN AND A YELLOW MAN.

Paula watched Leonard until he disappeared. Then she sighed. Long ago Beverley Claghorn had paid a similar tribute to the charms which extorted the sigh. In Paula's eyes the attractions which pertained to Leonard were lost in the sect to which he belonged. As a priest of the Church (it was thus that she put it) he would have been externally perfect, his physical excellence of unspeakable value to the cause of pure truth, while his conception of the priestly role would have been even nobler than that of Father Cameril. Leonard would have been no meek saint, but a saint militant, and long ere this the Bishop would have been down upon him, to the episcopal discomfiture.

If Paula grieved that Leonard labored under the disadvantage of the rigid practice of his denomination as to vesture and pulpit accessories, to those by whom such disadvantages were unrecognized his personality was no less persuasive of his fitness for noble deeds. As a rising theologian and young teacher of the divine science, he was, to those who watched his course, of excellent promise; destined to be a defender of that ancient creed which of late had been often attacked by able, if deluded, foes. To him orthodoxy looked with confidence, as to one who, when the day of battle came, would valiantly assail the enemies without, and confound the machinations of those within the household of faith. A worthy successor of his father, Professor Jared Claghorn, and to be greater, as better equipped to meet skeptical reasoning with reason clarified by faith; to demonstrate that the eye of the philosopher is but a feeble instrument for scrutiny of the works of God.

He was not ignorant of the general estimate or of the hopes of his elders, and had long been accustomed to fit himself for the position he was destined to fill, but of these aspirations he was oblivious as he walked slowly toward the town. He had never forgotten his father's words as to Natalie's unbelief. They were part of the memory of her, and now that memory was reawakened, and the words sounded again in his ears. He was deeply stirred by the knowledge that an errant soul was about to enter the inner circle of his life. He saw the hand of Providence in the fact; it was for this that she had not been turned from infidelity to error. She would not find the way to heaven by the dim rays of the obscured light of Romanism, but by the purer light of a reformed and vitalized religion, and to him was to be given the glory of being heaven's instrument. He was ambitious; his eyes had long been set on such earthly honors as come to theologians; he was prepared to welcome the theological storm of which the forecasts were already visible to those of clear perception, such as his own. In that impending struggle he knew that he would bear himself worthily, yet no glory that he could rightly anticipate therefrom seemed now so pleasing, nor awakened more fervent hope than that just born within him, the hope of rescuing a single soul. That glory would transcend all other, for though from men his work might be hidden, in the eyes of God he would be a faithful and worthy servant, and would hear from heaven the inaudible words, "Well done."

Exaltation such as this had long been rare with Leonard, whose mind of late had been fascinated rather by the mysteries of doctrine than warmed by religious fervor; and he was himself surprised that this ardent desire for a soul should enchain him; but he was gratified. To save souls was the ultimate object of his teaching; he was glad of this evidence that he had not forgotten it.

It may be that other thoughts, memories of bygone days, arose in his mind. Perhaps he recalled the beauty that had so attracted him in the garden of the Red Ox. There may have been some stirring of the blood of youth, which of late had sometimes coursed tingling through his veins; sometimes when he held Paula's hand, or noted the peachy velvet of her cheek, the clear depths of her eyes. But, if it were so, he was unconscious.

Meanwhile, Paula, who in the face of Miss Claghorn's fiat, still hoped to rescue Natalie from the impending horrors of the White House, turned toward the mansion. Her main reliance lay in anticipating the summons of Miss Achsah by an urgent invitation from the mistress of Stormpoint, to which end it was essential to seek that lady without further delay. Suddenly, as she hurried on, an exclamation of annoyance escaped her, and her steps were arrested by the sight of an ancient and mud-encrusted buggy which stood near that entrance to the house toward which her own steps were tending. She recognized the equipage of Mr. Hezekiah Hacket, and recent observation had taught her that when Mr. Hacket's carriage stopped that way, the lady of Stormpoint was not accessible to persons of minor distinction.

Aside from her general disapproval of Mr. Hacket, whose buggy, beneath its coating of mud, was yellow, and who was himself a yellow man, with teeth, hair, eyes and skin all of that unattractive hue, and unlovely in consequence of his pervading tint, Paula had no reason, so far as she knew, to resent Mr. Hacket's presence, except that it interfered with access to Mrs. Joe. Had she been aware of that which was transpiring in that apartment of the mansion which was devoted to business of state, she would have known that the visit of the gentleman was to have an important bearing upon her wish to deprive Miss Achsah of the opportunity to convert her erring grand-niece to Calvinism; which dark design Paula, since her meeting with Father Cameril, suspected.

Hezekiah Hacket, externally no more noteworthy than any very ordinary man and brother, was, in fact, an important personage in that region where Mrs. Joseph Claghorn had replanted the California branch of the family tree, intending that it should flourish and mightily expand. The shrewd lady of Stormpoint had quickly discovered that Mr. Hacket, the man of business of the Seminary, as well as of everybody that required the services of a man of business, possessed a sphere of influence eminently worthy of cultivation by political aspirants; and in all the region round about there was no such aspirant whose ambition soared as high as hers. In a realm largely dominated by a theological seminary, the existence of the political potentate called "Boss" was ignored and the word was seldom heard; but Mr. Hacket was the thing, and, all unconscious, the Seminary voted as its political guardian wished. Not the Seminary only; as the investor of the funds of others, this personage controlled the sources of power, and while deftly avoiding concentration of the secret antagonism which he knew existed against himself, by never exposing himself to the vengeance of the ballot, Mr. Hacket named the candidates for office—not infrequently those of opposing sides, so that in close elections, when a rolling wave of reform rendered the outlook uncertain, as in those not close, he remained the winner. Financially, he was strictly, though only legally, honest. Politically, he was a rogue. He was a pious man, though without a conscience and without belief. His industry was untiring. The lady of Stormpoint disliked him, at times to the point of loathing, and she courted him and smiled upon him.

"I sent for you," she said, on his appearance at Stormpoint, and offering a fair hand and an agreeable smile, both of which Mr. Hacket pretended not to see, it being his pleasant way to rule by insolence—if possible, by cringing if need were—"because in a few months my son will return home."

Mr. Hacket smoothed his yellow jaws with a freckled hand, and replied, "Just so," while the lady, who secretly desired to shake him, smiled yet more agreeably.

"Before he left home the last time," she continued, seeing that her visitor intended to remain dumb, "he had made many acquaintances. This was in accordance with your advice. What is he to do now?"

"Make more acquaintances."

"That, of course. I want him to enter the next Legislature."

Mr. Hacket had not decided that the desire expressed by the lady was his own, but he was shrewd enough to know that, crude as her ideas might be, and defective her knowledge of things political, she had the energy to attain her desire in the end, if seconded by the efforts of her candidate. He hated innovation, but he was aware that the Great Serpent held potentialities which he must not antagonize. It was not possible for him to be pleasing to Mrs. Joe, nor for her to be pleasing to him; but it was prudent to seem sympathetic. He essayed it, awkwardly enough.

"You know," he said, "your son is young and his only merit is money."

She flushed; but she knew he could not help being insolent in the presence of grace, comeliness and luxury, and all these were before him. "You mean it's the merit by which he's best known. Let it serve until others become apparent."

"It'll go far, but some it makes mad. I have an idea your son isn't over-warm in the matter."

"He didn't seem so. He wasn't aware that I am serious, and I said but little to him. Then the country was very new to him, and the people. He'd been long in Europe; his position was difficult." She had realized much more keenly than Mr. Hacket that Mark had only followed her urgency in that matter of making acquaintance because he had wished to please her. She was sure that there had been some hidden cause for indifference other than distaste for the task she had set him, and had brooded not a little over possibilities. But she was sanguine by nature; and since no love-tale had come to her ears (and she had her observers and reporters) she had concluded that, whatever the cause of his indifference, her son would become sufficiently ardent in the furtherance of her plans, when once they were more fully disclosed to him, and he had become aware that his mother had set her heart upon a political career for him. At present he probably regarded her wishes as merely a passing whim, and she knew that he was ignorant of her consultations with Mr. Hacket.

"Positions are apt to be difficult," observed the gentleman. "However, it's much too soon to discuss nominations. He'll have a year before him."

"He must have the Seminary," she said, "when the time comes."

"When the time comes," he echoed. He did not intend to commit himself, but he was becoming each moment more convinced that the lady knew her value and wished him to perceive the fact. It was equally evident that she duly appreciated his own; was, in fact, afraid of him, a pleasing assurance, which would have been yet more delightful if the gentleman, simultaneously with the recognition of this truth, had not also recognized a less agreeable fact, namely, that he was also afraid of her; sufficiently so to make it advisable that she understand he was not trifling with her. Such advice as he might give must seem reasonable, and must go beyond the suggestion of making acquaintances.

"You're working the Sem. all right," he said as graciously as he could. "Keep it up, but don't overdo it. How's Miss Achsah feel?"

"Friendly to Mark, I'm sure; not unfriendly to me, though———"

"Though your church sticks in her—is hard to swallow. I'm not surprised at that. St. Perpetual's———"

"Is there and beyond discussion."

"I always believe in looking over the whole field. St. Perpetual covers a good deal of it; so does Miss Achsah, and———"

"I had no idea that my sister-in-law is a political factor."

"Her's is, or wants to be."

"Well, let us conciliate Miss Achsah, if necessary. We're on fair terms———"

"Next time the Bishop comes here, invite her to dinner with him."

"She'll decline."

"What if she does? You always had the Professor, and she'll see that you look on her as his successor."

He rose, as if to go, but hesitated. Not because of any delicacy about volunteering the counsel that hovered on his lips, but in doubt whether it might not be well to permit her to injure her aspirations as much as she could. The certainty that she was, if she cared to be, too influential to offend him, determined him. He felt, with a sigh, that the time might come when he might be compelled to share his power; better that than risk losing it.

"I was in New York this week and saw Ellis Winter," he said. "Ellis told me that 'Liph Claghorn's daughter is in this country. He seemed to think you might invite her here."

"I intended to do so."

"Don't. She's French and, I suppose, a Romanist. Winter was close-mouthed, but I could see there was something. There's talk enough about idolatry and St. Perpetual's. I happen to know that Miss Achsah wants her, too, to convert her."

"Really, Mr. Hacket———"

"Good-bye," he said. "I've acted on the square. There's more in the matter than you think."

After his departure the lady of Stormpoint spent a few moments of indulgence in silent indignation; but when Paula came and preferred the request for that urgent invitation to Natalie, which was to circumvent the designs of Miss Claghorn, she found the lady inclined to recognize the claims of that person. Nevertheless, she promised to send the invitation, and did so that afternoon.

CHAPTER XI.

THE DEVIL WALKS TO AND FRO IN HAMPTON.

The ancient city of Hampton and its Theological Seminary are well known. To the wanderer under the elms of the quaint old town there is imparted an impression of cleanliness and a serene complacency, derived, doubtless, from the countenances of the many who, clad in sombre vesture and clean linen, pass and repass in the quiet streets. No man can be long in Hampton without feeling the theological influence; unconsciously the wayfarer adopts the prevailing manner, becomes deliberate in his walk and grave of aspect; his moral tone acquires rigidity, his taste severity; he inwardly rejoices if clad in fitting black and secretly covets gold-rimmed spectacles.

The best hotel, facing the Square, has the Hampton air, being even severely theological in aspect. Ordinary commercial travelers prefer "The United States," also a grave hostelry, though less austere in tone; but some descend at "The Hampton," reverend appearing gentlemen these, with white chokers conspicuous, and dealing in churchly wares and theological publications.

In this house Leonard had lived since his father's death had made the old home desolate, being, by reason of his personal as well as his professional attributes, a guest of note; and here there happened to him one day a new and strange experience.

He was breakfasting, later than his usual hour, when he became conscious of the scrutiny of the strangest eyes he had ever seen—eyes belonging to a woman, who, plainly clad in traveling attire, faced him from an adjacent table where she sat, with another woman, whose back was toward Leonard.

The gaze, though fixed, was not in appearance intentionally bold. The woman's eyes, dreamy, languishing, seemed to sink into his own, as though seeking what might be in the depths they tried to penetrate. It was as though, for them, the veil behind which man hides his inner self was lifted, and a sense of pleasure stole over him and willingness to surrender to this scrutiny; withal a shrinking from disclosure of that which he instinctively felt was unknown, even to himself. It required some effort to rise and leave the room.

An hour later, while waiting for the time of his morning lecture, and hardly freed as yet from the sensation resulting from his breakfast experience, while sitting in the spacious hall of the quiet house, he suddenly became aware of drapery, and looking up, encountered the eyes again; not as he had been seeing them since he had escaped them, but again bodily where they belonged, under the heavy brows of a dark-faced, large, and rather handsome woman.

"Pardon," she said in musical tones, and with a scarce perceptible smile at the ruddy flush which mantled his face. "*Est ce Monsieur Claghorn?*"

"Surely," exclaimed Leonard, "this is not——"

"The maid of Mademoiselle Claghorn," she replied, still in French. "The clerk indicated you as Monsieur——"

"Certainly. Your mistress——"

"This way, Monsieur." She led him toward the parlor, and had his ears been keen enough, he might have heard her murmur: "*Il est adorable.*"

Natalie had been, in Leonard's eyes, a very beautiful girl, and he found her now a very beautiful woman. She was tall, dark, slender and indescribably graceful, as well as with the nameless manner, born with some and never in perfection acquired, of exceeding yet not obtrusive graciousness. Had she been born a duchess, she could not have had a better manner; had she been born a washerwoman, it would have been as good, for it was born, not made. The mere beauty of her face was hardly remembered in contemplation of qualities apparent, yet not wholly comprehensible. Ordinarily serene, if not joyous in expression, there was an underlying sadness that seldom left it. Perhaps she still grieved for the father she had lost; perhaps, unconsciously, she craved the love or the religion which the Marquise had said a woman needs.

The travelers were on their way to Easthampton, having arrived in the night train from New York. On learning that less than an hour's drive would bring her to the home of Miss Claghorn, Natalie declined Leonard's escort. "I wish to see my grand-aunt alone," she explained. "She has written a most kind invitation——"

"Which I hope you will accept, Cousin."

"Which I greatly desire to accept, but——"

"If for any reason," he interrupted, "you should decide not to accept Cousin Achsah's invitation, I know that at Stormpoint——"

"I have letters from both Mrs. Joe and Paula; but my first duty, and my inclination as well, take me to my father's aunt."

Though he had at first agreed with Paula that residence with Miss Achsah would not "do" for Natalie, he saw the fitness of her decision. She recognized her own status as a Claghorn and appreciated the Claghorn claim upon her. "I am glad you feel so," he said. "You will discern Cousin Achsah's real excellence beneath an exterior which, at first sight, may seem unpromising. She is not French, as you will soon discover, but as for true kindness——"

She interrupted with a laugh. "You and Mr. Winter are both eloquent in apologizing for my grand-aunt's sort of kindness, which, it seems, differs from the French variety."

"We only mean she will seem to you undemonstrative. She is very religious."

"That does not alarm me; everybody is—except myself," and now her laugh had a cadence of sadness.

It touched him. He knew the task laid out for him by Providence, and he felt that he ought to say a fitting word. But all the time he knew that the eyes of the maid were upon him. The knowledge made him appear somewhat constrained—he who ordinarily had an ease of manner, which was not the least of his charms.

"They are well at Stormpoint, of course?" questioned Natalie. "Mrs. Joe and Paula?"

"Perfectly. You will be charmed with their home. Mrs. Claghorn has transformed a desert. The sea——"

"Paula sent me some views, and better, an appreciative description. I should think they would never wish to leave it—none of them?" She looked inquiringly at him.

"As to that," he laughed, "Mrs. Joe flits occasionally; and, of course, Paula with her. But they are becoming more and more content to remain at home. Mrs. Joe is quite a public character."

"A chatelaine—the head of the house?" Again her eyes questioned more insistently than her lips.

"Quite so," was the answer. "Mark's a rover. He's in Russia."

A sigh of relief—or regret? It was quickly checked. Leonard noticed her pallor. "You are tired," he said. "Why not rest for an hour or two here? If you will do so, I can myself drive you to Easthampton. Just now I must attend to my class at the Seminary."

But she would not wait for his escort; so he procured a conveyance, and surmising that, under the circumstances, the maid was an embarrassment, he suggested providing her with a book and the hospitality of his sitting-room, and having seen his cousin depart, he conducted Mademoiselle Berthe to his room and handed her a volume of the "Revue des Deux Mondes," which the maid accepted graciously.

"There," he said pleasantly, and in his best French, "you can look out of the window or read, as you please. I hope you will not find the time long."

She smiled in reply. Her penetrating eyes sought that other self within him, which leaped to the call and looked out of his eyes into hers. For a moment only. His gaze dropped. Wondering, he found himself trembling.

"I—I shall look in in an hour, to see if you want anything."

"Monsieur is very good," murmured Berthe. They were not far apart; her hand touched his. She looked downward.

"Good-bye," he said abruptly.

She watched him crossing the square toward the Seminary. There was a half smile upon her lips. "He is adorable," she murmured again. "Ah! I thought so," as Leonard, now some hundred yards away, looked back.

When he had disappeared she lazily inspected her surroundings, noting the various objects with faint interest. "*Son père,*" she muttered as her glance fell upon the portrait of Professor Jared Claghorn. But she examined more minutely that of his mother. "*Belle femme,*" was her comment, and though her eyes wandered from the picture, they often returned to it, verifying the close resemblance between it and the occupant of the room. "Ah-h!" she exclaimed, throwing up her arms, and then letting them fall listlessly, "*Qu'il est beau!*"

Then she tried to doze, but without much success, twitching nervously and occasionally muttering impatiently; and, at length, she rose from her chair and began to deliberately inspect the various objects lying on table or mantel. Everything that was purely ornamental she scrutinized with care, as though she would read the reason of its being where she found it. There was a peculiar expression of veiled anger in her eyes while thus engaged, and once the veil was momentarily lifted and anger was visible. Nevertheless, she laughed a moment after and replaced the object, an ivory paper cutter, where she had found it. "*T'es bête,*" she muttered.

But soon her dark eyes flashed actual rage. She had taken a prettily bound book of poems from the table, where it had been thrown, as if but recently read. She turned the pages, half carelessly, yet with a sharp eye, to see if there were any marked passages. She found one or two such, and it would have been diverting, had there been a spectator present, to note her perplexed attempts to read Mrs. Browning. But the language was beyond her powers, and she was about impatiently to replace the book when she noticed the fly-leaf, whereon in a neat, clear hand was written the inscription, "Leonard, from Paula." She stared at these innocent words with a glare that under no circumstances could have been regarded as amusing. Finally, she tore the leaf from the book and flung the book itself disdainfully from her. Then she crumpled the leaf in her hand, threw it into the waste basket, and deliberately spat upon it.

Which strange proceeding perhaps soothed her irritation, for she lay back in her chair, and after breathing hard for a little while, was soon sleeping peacefully.

Meantime, while Mademoiselle slept the sleep of one who has spent the night in travel, Leonard lectured, but less fluently than was usual. A man out of sorts is not an uncommon circumstance, and though his flushed cheeks, bright eyes, and occasional bungling speech were sufficiently remarkable in one ordinarily engrossed with his subject, nothing was said to further disturb his equanimity.

The lecture over, he walked across the square, less equable in spirit than he had been in the class-room; for there he had striven to retain his grasp of the topic in hand; now he was under no restraint and could surrender himself to contemplation—of what?

Of the stirring touch of a woman's hand, of the vision of a new world, a glimpse of which he had caught in the greedy depths of a woman's eyes. Even now he was hurrying to see these things again, while he was angry that they drew him back.

He overcame the attraction, and deliberately sat down upon a bench. He watched a little girl playing about, and might have remained watching had not the devil, who sometimes walks to and fro and up and down in Hampton, intervened.

The child was suddenly struck by a ball, batted by an urchin, who, on seeing what he had done, incontinently took to his heels. She fell, stunned, almost at Leonard's feet. The impact of the ball had seemed frightful, and for a moment Leonard thought she was killed.

The hotel was across the street. He carried her thither, intending to summon a physician, but on seeing some returning signs of animation, he took his burden to his room and laid her on the bed.

Berthe, her nap over, had witnessed the scene in the park. She heard Leonard lay the child on the bed in the chamber adjoining the room in which she sat, and was instantly by the bedside with her traveling bag, from which she produced restoratives. She gave her whole attention to the sufferer, while he looked on, pleased with these gentle ministrations.

"It may be a bad hurt," said Berthe, undoubted pity in her tone. "The brain may be injured."

"I will call the doctor,'" he said.

The doctor was at hand, his room being on the same corridor. His opinion was that no serious damage had been done. "Let her rest awhile. If she seems unusually drowsy, let me know," with which words and a glance at Mademoiselle, he returned to his room.

Berthe knelt beside the child, who was growing alarmed as her intelligence became normally acute. The Frenchwoman prattled soothingly, and Leonard stooped to add some words of encouragement. He stroked the child's hair, and his hand met the soft hand of Berthe and was enclosed within it. He trembled as she drew him downward, and a sob escaped him as his lips met hers and lingered on them in a rapturous kiss.

CHAPTER XII.

HER EYES GREW LIMPID AND HER CHEEKS FLUSHED RED.

When the carriage, which was to convey her to Easthampton, had started, Natalie commenced the re-perusal of Miss Claghorn's invitation, which ran thus:

"My Dear Grand-niece—I address you thus, for though I have never seen you, yet you are of my kindred, and all who bear your name must be dear to me. Your father was so in his youth, and if, in later years, he neglected, if he did not forget, the ties of kinship and of country, I nevertheless mourned for him, even though sensible that all things are ordered by the Lord of heaven and earth and that human regret is useless, and, if unaccompanied with resignation, sinful. Mr. Winter writes me that you are friendless. I offer that which you can justly claim from me—my friendship and a home. As far as earthly cares are concerned, I am willing to relieve you of those incident to your situation. This is plainly my duty, and for many years I have striven, with God's help, to perform with a cheerful spirit that which I have been called upon to do.

"It is this habit which impels me here to refer to your views concerning man's duty toward his Maker. I do not, because conscientiously I cannot, agree with those who profess tolerance in these matters. There should be no tolerance of sin. If we would worthily follow in the steps of Him who died that we might live, we must hate the devil and his children in the same measure that we love our Father and his children. Whose child are you?

"This is a solemn question. I urge you to seek its answer at the Throne. If you will do this, my hope will be mighty. Should you be tempted to resent my solicitude, remember that my religion is a part of my nature, the only part meriting your respect, and that it requires of me that which I have written, as well as much more not set down here, but of which I hope I shall see the fruits. Come to me as soon as possible, and be assured of a welcome. ACHSAH CLAGHORN."

The girl smiled, though sadly, as she read this letter. She did not resent the fact that it was confessedly inspired solely by a sense of duty; she rather admired the writer for the uncompromising statement; nor was she offended at the sermon contained in the epistle, or inclined to treat it lightly. It is not probable that the writer of the letter believed that her exhortation would sink deeply in the heart of an "atheist," she being probably unaware that some who know not God crave a knowledge which they find nowhere offered.

The drive was long, the horse sleepy, the driver willing that his steed should doze, while his passenger paid by the hour, for which reason he had chosen the longer road by the sea.

She looked out upon the water with a gaze of longing, as though there might arise from out the solitary deep a vision which would solve that great mystery, which for Miss Claghorn and such as she, was no mystery, but wherein most of us grope as in a fog. But, as to other yearning eyes, so to hers no vision was vouchsafed; though had her sight been strengthened by experience, she might have seen, symbolized in the waters, the life of man. For, against the shore the fretful waves were spent and lost in sand, whereof each particle was insignificant, but which in the mass absorbed the foaming billows, as the vain aspirations of youth absorb its futile energies. Beyond was the green water, still tireless and vexed, and then the smoother blue, as it neared the sky-line, undisturbed, until afar the waters lay at rest in hopeless patience, and the heavens came down and hid the secret of what lay beyond.

But, if youth looked with the eyes of age, there were no youth. She was not yet to know lessons which must be hardly learned, and it was not that one offered by the waters that she saw as she looked out upon the ocean. Far beyond the horizon, in a distant land, her eyes beheld the garden of a village inn where sat a girl, prattling with her father and commenting upon two dusty strangers, who in their turn were eyeing the maid and her companion curiously. She saw the cave, heard Leonard shout the name—and then Mark Claghorn stood before her—as he then had stood, in the jaunty cap and ribbon which proclaimed him "*Bursch*"; one of those lawless beings of whom she had heard much school-girl prattle. Even then she had contrasted the handsomer face of the simple-minded boy beside her with the harsher and more commanding features of this newcomer. And her fancy wandered on through pleasant German saunterings and Parisian scenes among the churches—to the day when Berthe Lenoir had said that Mark would be her teacher in the lore of love; and she knew that, in the moment of that saying, she had learned the great lesson, never to be forgotten.

She had cherished the secret without hope or wish that he should share it, for she knew that so sweet a thing could live in no heart but her own; and she had not been ashamed, but had been proud of this holy acquisition hidden in her heart of hearts. Her eyes grew limpid and her cheeks flushed red as she recalled how the shrine of her treasure had been profaned by the hand of one that might have known, but had disdained its worth. In the Church of St. Roch the three who had been present when love was born were again alone together. Berthe was now her maid, and Mark, his university days past, was a daily visitor at her father's house.

The scene was clear before her as he pointed to the maid, out of earshot, and gazing carelessly at the worshippers. "Has she forgotten—so soon?" he said. "Are women so?"

She had not answered. Forgotten! Who could forget?

"I have not forgotten. I often come here, Natalie."

She had had no words. What was it that had so joyously welled up within her and overflowed her eyes and closed her lips?

"I was to be your teacher, Natalie."

She looked into his eyes, and from her own went out the secret of her soul into his keeping; and she had been glad, and the gloomy church had been aglow, and as they passed out the sun shone and the heavens smiled upon a new world; for she had never seen it thus before.

That was the short chapter of the history of her love. There had been no other. He had ravished her secret that he might disdain it, and next day had said a stern good-bye, spoken as though forever.

Yet she had dared to come here, though now the impulse was strong upon her to turn and flee from a region where he might be met. It was but an impulse; for either she must come among these her relatives or return to throw herself into the arms of the vacuous hussar who loved her dowry, or failing that, into the strife and importunity from which she had escaped. Resentful pride, too, came to her aid, bidding her not flee from him who had disdained her love, though even so she knew that that which had been born within her had been so fondly cherished, had grown so mighty, that in the heart it filled there was no room for pride to grow with equal strength.

She turned again to the letter in her hand. Her unbelief had never stilled the longing to believe, and now, in the hunger of her soul, the yearning was strong. But, she asked herself, What was belief? There was much glib talk of faith, but what was faith? Could one have faith by saying that one had it? Was conviction mere assertion? The letter advised her to seek enlightenment at the Throne of God. What meaning could the words have except that she was to crave that which she had ever craved? Her soul had always cried aloud for knowledge of God. Could it be that formal words, repeated kneeling, would compel heaven to give ear? Was it thus that people experienced what they called religion? Was it so that Miss Claghorn had found it?

Such musings came to an end with her arrival at the White House. She had announced her coming by letter, wherefore Tabitha Cone, recognizing the identity of the visitor and mentally pronouncing her a "stunner," ushered her into the gloomy parlor, and informed Miss Claghorn that "'Liph's daughter" awaited her.

"I decided to call in person before accepting your kind invitation," said the visitor.

"I learn from Ellis Winter that you need a home," replied Miss Achsah, a little stiffly, but rather from awe of this blooming creature than from dislike.

"I am grateful for your offer of one; but in fairness, I thought you should know my reasons for leaving France, and essential that you should justify me."

Miss Claghorn assented not ungraciously. The frank demeanor of her visitor pleased her. "A Claghorn," was her mental comment, as Natalie told her story more in detail than Mr. Winter had done.

"You see," she added to her narrative of the matrimonial pursuit of the gallant de Fleury, "he is not a man that I could like, but my cousin——"

"You mean this French Markweeze?"

Natalie nodded. "She is a sweet woman, and undoubtedly believed herself right in the matter. Then it was, doubtless, a very serious disappointment. Lieutenant de Fleury is her son; they are comparatively poor; I am not—and so—and so——"

"You were quite right to run away," snapped Miss Achsah, with the emphasis born of indignation at this attempt to coerce a Claghorn.

"It must not be forgotten that, from her point of view, my cousin was justified in expecting me to carry out a promise made by my father. It was this that made her so persistent and induced her to attempt measures that were not justifiable. To her I must seem ungrateful for much kindness." The girl's eyes glistened with tears. In fact, this view of her conduct, which was doubtless the view of the Marquise, affected her deeply. She did not state, though aware of the fact, that her own income had, during her residence with her French guardian, been mainly used to sustain and freshen the very faded glory of the house of Fleury.

"Well, my dear," was the comment of Miss Claghorn, "I have listened to your story and justify your course; and now I repeat my invitation."

Had Tabitha Cone seen the gracious manner of the speaker she would have been as surprised as was the lady herself. But in the presence of this beautiful face, the evident honesty of the narration of the tale she had heard, the underlying sadness beneath the serene expression, it would have needed a harder nature than Miss Claghorn's to be anything but gracious. But she flushed with self-reproach when Natalie touched upon what she had for the moment completely forgotten.

"But," exclaimed Natalie, "I have not answered the question in your letter. The matter of religion, I was led to believe, would be to you most important. It is to so many; the Marquise, Père Martin, Mrs. Leon—have all been grieved—I am an infidel."

The coolness with which this statement was made shocked her auditor even more than the fact. The perplexed smile upon the girl's face; the yearning look, that seemed to recognize something wanting in her, some faculty absent which left her without a clew to the cause of the successive shocks emanating from her—these things, if only dimly appreciated by Miss Claghorn, were sufficiently apparent to make her feel as though a weight had fallen upon her heart. "Oh, my child, that is an awful thing to say!" she exclaimed.

The way the words were uttered showed that all the tenderness, long hidden, of the speaker's nature was suddenly called to life. No exhortation ever heard by Natalie had so affected her as this outburst of a hard old woman. She seized the other's hand, murmuring, "Dear Aunt!" She pitied, even while she envied, the victim of superstition, as the God-fearing woman pitied the errant soul. Neither understood the source of the other's emotion, but they met in complete sympathy. The elder woman pressed the hand that had grasped her own, and leaning toward her grand-niece, kissed her affectionately. What old and long-dried springs of feeling were awakened in the withered breast as the oldest descendant of the Puritan preacher yearned over the youngest of the line? Who shall tell? Perhaps the barren motherhood of the ancient spinster was stirred for once; perhaps the never-known craving for a mother's love moved the younger one. For a time both were silent.

"Come to me to-day, at once," whispered Miss Achsah, blushing, had she known it, and quivering strangely.

The heartiness of the invitation troubled the visitor, whose answer was less gracious than a chief characteristic required. "I will come to-day," she answered. "Let it be understood as a visit only." Then she went out, and in the lumbering carriage was driven back to Hampton.

Miss Claghorn watched her from the window. Gradually she was recovering herself and secretly feeling mightily ashamed, yet pleased, too. Tabitha came in.

"Well?" she asked.

"Well," echoed Miss Claghorn, acidly.

"What are you going to do?"

"Pray," replied the lady, as she ascended the stairs.

"Must have forgot it this morning," was Miss Cone's mental comment.

CHAPTER XIII.

WHEREAT CYNICS AND MATRONS MAY SMILE INCREDULOUS.

When Natalie returned, Leonard was occupying his old seat in the Square, a different man from the man she had met in the earlier morning. He had been shocked, grieved, even terrified, and above all ashamed; yet joy mingled with his grief, and his consciousness of new manhood was not without its glory; and, withal, his breast was filled with a flood of tremulous tenderness for the woman, and a longing for her forgiveness. His emotions were sufficiently confusing to be vexing, and he had striven to give the matter a jaunty aspect. Young men will be young men, even when students of divinity, and he had heard more than one tale of kisses. He had not much liked such tales, nor the bragging and assumption of their tellers; still, a few hours since, he would have seen no great offense in kissing a pretty woman; but a few hours since he had not known anything about the matter. He was sure now that the rakes of his college days, the boasters and conquerors, had been as ignorant as he. Otherwise they could not have told of their deeds; the thing he had done he could tell no man.

And so, though he had but kissed a woman, he felt that kissing a woman was a wonderful thing; and he failed in the attempt to look upon the matter airily, as of a little affair that would have in the future a flavor of roguishness. It was not a matter to be treated lightly; his grief and the stabs of conscience were too sharp for that—yet he had no remorse. He was not minded to repeat the act; he had fled from such repetition, and he would not repeat it; neither would he regret it. It should be a memory, a secret for hidden shame, for hidden pride, for grief, for joy.

He intercepted Natalie as she descended from the carriage, and, in a brief interview in the hotel parlor, learned of her intention to return at once to Miss Claghorn. The carriage was waiting, there was no reason for delaying her departure; there was nothing to do but to call the maid, and he dispatched a servant to do that. He volunteered to see to the immediate transmission of the luggage of the travelers to Easthampton, and made thereof an excuse for leaving before the maid reappeared; and when once without the hotel door, and on his way to the station, he breathed a sigh as of one relieved of a load.

Some days passed and Leonard had not appeared at Easthampton. One morning he received the following note from Paula:

> "Dear Leonard—I suppose you are very busy in these last
> days of the term, and we all excuse your neglect of us. I shall
> be at the Hampton station on Thursday, having promised

to see Natalie's maid (who don't speak English) on the evening train for New York. Perhaps you can meet me and return with me to dinner. Cousin Alice hopes you will."

He was careful not to find Paula until the train had gone, and he had assured himself that Berthe was among the passengers. Then he appeared.

"Why, Leonard," exclaimed Paula, "have you been ill?" The tone was full of concern. He shrank as if he had been struck.

"No," he said; "a little anxious—troubled."

"Over your freckled, gawky, thickshod theologues; what a pity you're not in the Church!"

This kind of outburst on the part of the speaker usually made Leonard laugh. To-night his laugh sounded hollow. "I suppose your Episcopalian students wear kids and use face powder," he said.

"There's no harm in kid gloves; inner vileness——"

"Is very bad, Paula; we'll not discuss it."

They walked across the Square, on the other side of which she had left the carriage. She looked up to his face to seek an explanation of the irritation discoverable in his tone; she noted that his hat was drawn down over his eyes in a way very unusual. They walked on in silence. "You will come with me?" she asked, when they had reached the carriage.

"Not to-night. You are right, I am not very well; it is nothing, I will come out this week. Has Natalie discharged her maid?"

"Not for any fault. Mrs. Leon was very glad to get Berthe, and as Natalie is situated——"

"I see. I hope she is comfortable with Cousin Achsah."

"They hit it off astonishingly well. The fact is, nobody could help loving Natalie—I am surprised that you have not been to see her."

"I know I have seemed negligent. I have a good excuse. Where, in New York, does Mrs. Leon live?"

"At the Fifth Avenue Hotel," she replied, wondering at the question.

"Well," he said, after a pause, and treating her answer as though, like his question, it was of no real interest. "I must not keep you here. You don't mind going home alone?"

"I should be glad of your company; aside from that, I don't mind."

"Then, good-bye," touching her hand for an instant. "Make my excuses to Mrs. Joe; I have been really very busy. Home, James." He closed the carriage door and walked rapidly away, leaving Paula vexed, to sink back in the soft seat and to wonder.

He walked across the Square to the region of shops and entered a large grocery store—at this time of day, deserted. "Could you give me a bill for fifty dollars?" he asked of the cashier.

"I believe I can, Professor," replied the official, drawing one from the desk, and exchanging it for the smaller bills handed him by Leonard, who thanked him and went out. That night he enclosed the single bill in an envelope, and addressed it to Mademoiselle Berthe, in care of Mrs. Leon.

As he could have told no man why he had done this, so he could not tell himself why. Cynics and matrons may smile incredulous, but the kiss he had given and received had wrought an upheaval in this man's soul. He who defers his kissing until he has reached maturity has much to learn, and if the learning comes in a sudden burst of light in still and quiet chambers, that have until now been dark, the man may well be dazzled.

He did not think her sordid. He hoped she would understand that he sent her that which he believed would be of use to her. But when, a week later, he received a little box and found within it an exquisite pin, which he, unlearned in such matters, still knew must have cost a large part of the sum he had sent her, he was pleased, and a thrill passed through him. Like him, she would remember, nor in her mind would there be any thought but one of tenderness for a day that could never come again. It would be a fair memory that would trouble him no more, but would remain forever fair, of her who had opened to him the portals of a new and beautiful world.

CHAPTER XIV.

IN THE WHITE HOUSE, A DAMSEL OR THE DEVIL— WHICH?

When Paula had said to Leonard that Natalie and Miss Claghorn "hit it off astonishingly well," she had fairly indicated the harmonious relations prevailing at the White House, as well as the general astonishment that the elder lady had so graciously received a religious outcast. It was true that Miss Achsah's innate benevolence was habitually shrouded in uncompromising orthodoxy, a tough and non-diaphanous texture, not easily penetrable by futile concern for souls preordained to eternal death; but Natalie was of her own blood, one of a long line of elect; furthermore, she had not been seduced by the blandishments of the Great Serpent, but had cast her lot, where it truly belonged, among Claghorns; and, finally, the oldest bearer of that name was doubtless influenced by the fact that the girl was motherless and friendless, and that she herself, paying the penalty of independence, was, except as to Tabitha Cone, with whom she lived in strife, alone.

Miss Cone also approved of the visitor. This had been originally an accident. Like the rest of the little world interested, Tabitha had supposed that Miss Claghorn's reception of a foreign and atheistical daughter of Beverley Claghorn would be as ungracious as was compatible with humanity; wherefore Tabitha had been prepared, for her part, to be extremely affable, foreseeing, with joy, many a battle with her benefactress wherein she would have an ally; but, taken unawares, by the time she had grasped the unexpected situation, she had become too sincere in her admiration to change her role. She chose, however, to announce an estimate of Natalie's character differing from that of Miss Claghorn. "She's a Beverley down to her shins," was Miss Cone's verdict.

"As much of a Beverley as you are a Claghorn," was Miss Achsah's tart rejoinder.

"Which, thank the Lord, I'm not. One's enough in one house. For my part, I don't admire your strong characters."

"So that your admiration of Natalie is all pretense. I'm not surprised."

"She strong! Poor dove, she's Susan Beverley to the life." Which may have been true, though dove-like Natalie was not.

Miss Claghorn made no reply except by means of a contradictory snort.

"Now," gravely continued the inwardly jubilant Tabitha, "I call Paula Lynford a strong character. There's a girl that'll get what she's after."

Something ominous in the manner of the speaker arrested the sneer on its way. "What do you mean?" asked Miss Achsah.

"What do all girls want—though, to be sure, you've had no experience," observed Tabitha (who had once contemplated marriage with a mariner, who had escaped by drowning)—"a husband."

Miss Claghorn laughed. "Very likely. But Paula's husband will need a dispensation—from the Pope, I suppose—since he calls himself a Catholic."

Tabitha echoed the laugh, less nervously and with palpable and unholy enjoyment. "You mean her cap's set for Father Cameril. She's been throwing dust in your eyes. She's after a minister, sure enough, but not that one."

"What do you mean, Tabitha Cone?" The tone of the question usually had the effect of cowing Tabitha, but the temptation was too strong to be resisted.

"I mean Leonard Claghorn."

Miss Achsah gasped. "You slanderous creature," she exclaimed, "Leonard will never marry a mock-papist—demure puss!"

"Leonard'll marry to suit himself, and not his forty-fifth cousin." And with this Tabitha escaped, leaving a rankling arrow.

As an "atheist," Natalie was a surprise to both inmates of the White House. Their ideas of atheistic peculiarities were probably vague, but each had regarded the arrival of the unbeliever with dread. Tabitha had foreboded profanity, perhaps even inebriety, depravity certainly, and she had been quite "upset," to use her own expression, by the reality. Miss Claghorn, with due respect for family traits, had never shared Tabitha's worst fears, but she had anticipated a very different kind of person from the person that Natalie actually was. She had pictured a hard, cynical, intellectual creature, critical as to the shortcomings of creation, full of "science," and pertly obtrusive with views. She had feared theological discussion, and though convinced that her armory (comprised in Dr. Hodge's "Commentary on the Confession of Faith") was amply furnished to repel atheistic assault, yet she dreaded the onset, having, perhaps, some distrust of her own capacity for handling her weapons.

But the atheist was neither scientific nor argumentative. She was so graceful, so amiable, in short, so charming, that both old women were quickly won; so gay that both were surprised to hear their own laughter. Sufficiently foreign to be of continual interest, and so pleased and entertained with her new surroundings that they would have been churlish indeed not to accept her pleasure as flattering to themselves.

At times, indeed, both had misgivings. The devil is abroad, and it was conceivable that in the form of this seductive creature he had audaciously invaded the White House for prey, such as rarely fell into his toils; but each spinster was too sure of her own call and election to fear the enemy of souls on her individual account, and Miss Claghorn doubted whether even the temerity of Satan would suffice for the hopeless attempt to capture an orthodox Claghorn; and this assurance aided the belief that Natalie, herself of the elect race, was neither the devil's emissary, nor in the direful peril that had been feared. She might think herself an infidel, but her time was not yet come, that was all.

"I am sure she has workings of the spirit," she observed to Tabitha. "She's not always as lighthearted as you think."

"I don't happen to think it. A good deal of that's put on."

"Everybody don't experience grace as early as you and I."

"Specially not in Paris," assented Miss Cone.

"She was surely guided of the Lord in leaving the influence of Romanism to——"

"'Cording to your view she hasn't escaped yet; there's St. Perpetua——"

"She's too true a Claghorn to be led into that folly."

"I don't know," observed Miss Cone meditatively, "that the Claghorns are less foolish than other people. There was 'Liph, her father; 'n there's Lettie Stanley—then your brother. St. Perpetua's his monument, you know."

"Joseph would never have approved St. Perpetua. If he'd been a Catholic, it wouldn't have been an imitation."

"His wife ought to know the kind of monument he would have liked. I've known the Claghorns long enough to know——"

"You've known some of 'em, to your eternal welfare, Tabitha Cone."

"I'm not aware that the family was consulted when my election was foreordained. You think well of 'em, and I won't deny their good qualities—but I guess the Almighty didn't have to wait until their creation to manage."

"You seem very sure of election. I hope you are not to be disappointed, but you might accept the fact with some humility."

"Your brother, Natalie's grandfather, had a license to preach—I'm not aware that you have—he taught me that the fact was to be accepted with joy and gladness."

"Joy and gladness are not inconsistent with humility."

"I'm not denyin' your right to be joyful, but your right to preach."

"Tabitha Cone, you'd try the patience of a saint!"

"*If* I had the opportunity!" And so, with whetted swords they plunged into the fray.

The newcomer was graciously welcomed at Stormpoint, though Paula bewailed her selection of abode, tending, as it did, to frustrate certain plans, which were to result in alluring Natalie to the sheltering arms of St. Perpetua. Paula was confident of the courage of Father Cameril, but even a brave man may hesitate to pluck a jewel from the den of a lion, and she knew that to such a den the good Father likened the home of Miss Claghorn.

But Mrs. Joe approved Natalie's choice. "Miss Achsah's her blood relation," she said.

"What is blood? An accident. Friendship is born of sympathy," protested Paula.

"And since that is the basis of our friendship," observed Natalie, "you will understand that when my grand-aunt offered me a home on the ground of duty, I also recognized a duty."

"A home on the ground of duty," repeated Paula, with as near an approach to a sneer as she was capable of effecting.

"Could she feel affection, who had never seen me? Remember, she stood in the place of mother to my father. I fear she had reason to believe that the fact had been forgotten."

Mrs. Joe nodded approval.

"Inclination would have led me to you," Natalie proceeded. "It may be, too, that I was influenced by the hope that I might, in some degree, brighten the life of an old woman who had outlived her near relations. I remembered how Cousin Jared, whom we all liked so well, reverenced her. And then, I approved her pride in the name. I, too, am a Claghorn."

"In short," commented Mrs. Joe, "you recognized a duty, as I believed you would, and you did right. Good will come of it," she added, "a bond between the houses."

Nevertheless, the lady's conscience was troubled. She was naturally candid and hospitable, yet in respect to Natalie, she had done violence to both attributes. In that invitation, sent in accordance with her promise to Paula, she had been careful to recognize the prior claim of Miss Claghorn, thus virtually indicating Natalie's proper course. It had been hard for her to close the gates of Stormpoint upon one whom she regarded with affection, yet Mr.

Hacket's counsel had outweighed inclination. That gentleman was, indeed, teaching some hard lessons to the lady of Stormpoint. It was almost unbearable that this wooden and yellow man, who secretly aroused all the antagonism of which she was capable, should direct her domestic affairs; yet she bore it smilingly, as was seemly in a politician, whose skin may smart, but who must grin. For, Mr. Hacket's command was wise. To add an infidel to her household of religious suspects would be a rash act which Hampton might not forgive. She had no doubt that Natalie's unbelief would become known, and if it did not, the fact that she was French would presuppose Romanism, and excite comment. Were Stormpoint to harbor a Papist, one concerning whom there could be no saving doubt, such as existed for its present inmates, all her plans might be jeopardized. In the eyes of the descendants of the Puritans, the adherents of St. Perpetua would be convicted as followers of the scarlet woman, and if the red rag of Romanism were flaunted in seeming defiance, Mark's incipient career of statesmanship might meet with a serious check.

On the other hand, there was comfort in the thought that all unpleasant possibilities would be avoided by Natalie's sojourn with Miss Achsah. Infidel or Romanist, in whatever light regarded, the dwellers in Easthampton would know with approval that the competent owner of the White House had the stray sheep in charge, and would anticipate triumphant rescue of the endangered soul, providentially sheltered where food of life would be daily offered. There would be also general satisfaction that to Miss Achsah had been given a task worthy the exercise of those energies which, in the cause of truth, she was apt to exhibit in domestic circles not her own, to the great terror of the members thereof. Mrs. Joe, herself, could find occasion to evince commendation of the expected efforts of Miss Claghorn, and, while placating that lady, could emphasize her own Protestantism. In fact, several birds might be slain with this single stone.

CHAPTER XV.

SUR LE PONT D'AVIGNON ON Y DANSE, ON Y DANSE.

It was, perhaps, because she was conscience-stricken that Mrs. Joe essayed to make atonement to Natalie by being especially confiding with her. We know, also, that she saw an opportunity of strengthening those bonds between Stormpoint and the White House, which Mr. Hacket insisted it was advisable to make as close as possible; for it became day by day more evident that Miss Achsah had taken her new inmate into her heart of hearts; other motives there may have been; certain it is that next to her yellow adviser, whom she loathed with a deeper loathing each time that she saw him anew, she opened her heart to Natalie in regard to those cherished projects which concerned Mark.

"I want to see him famous," she said. "It will be harder for him than for others, because of this wretched money."

"He has more talent than most, and, I think, sincerity," replied Natalie, pausing on the last word.

The elder lady looked sharply at the speaker. The two were alone together; occasionally they could hear the strains of Paula's organ from the distant music-room. "You saw much of him after he left the University?" she questioned.

"Yes, he was with us constantly for a time." The widow had a fine sense of hearing, which she strained to the utmost to note what might be told in the tone that remained untold by the words. She was quite aware that Mark had been for weeks a daily visitor, if not an actual inmate, of the household of Beverley Claghorn. She had herself arranged that it should be so; but she had not then feared possibilities, which had engaged her thoughts a good deal since she had heard of the rupture between the Marquise and Natalie. The tone of the girl's voice told her nothing, and the eyes that met her own were serene.

"I wished Mark to remain abroad until Stormpoint was complete. I wished to surprise him, and impress him with the fact that I am in earnest, that this place is but a means to an end."

"It is a beautiful and a fitting home for what he is and aspires to be."

"It will help. What has he said to you about Stormpoint?"

"You forget that I have not seen him since he made its acquaintance."

"Surely he was not so neglectful as not to write!"

"He wrote to my father. I don't recall what he said about Stormpoint."

The eyes bent upon the girl, who looked steadily out of the window at the sea, were keen and questioning. "Pardon me, Natalie, I hope the breach between you and the Marquise is not irreparable," said the lady softly.

Natalie looked up smiling. "Indeed, I hope not. I am not angry with her, though she is with me."

"I can hardly be sorry that you disappointed her—I never fancied her lieutenant—but I was surprised. I had supposed the matter settled with your consent."

"My dear father, it seems, did so arrange it. I quite appreciate her standpoint and know that she has much to forgive. Naturally, she approves of the customs of her country. Unfortunately, I was not trained strictly *à la mode Française.*"

"The French custom as regards betrothal is repulsive; but I supposed you were French—and——"

"I must have inherited independent views. I might have acquiesced had I not seen too much of Adolphe. You are not to think badly of him—only that he is unendurable."

"That is more damning than faint praise," laughed Mrs. Joe; "but I understand. Well, my dear, since you decline to become a 'female Markis,' as Mr. Weller has it, we must do as well for you as possible in a republic that offers no nobles."

"I am quite content with things as they are."

"That, of course, is eminently proper; but we are all slaves of destiny and there is one always possible to maidens. We shall select a permanent city home as soon as I can consult Mark; meanwhile we shall not spend our winters here; and in the winter Miss Achsah must reward our forbearance by surrendering you to us."

"I shall be glad to be with you and Paula sometimes; but, Mrs. Joe, you know I am only visiting my aunt. I intend to have a home of my own."

"That will come. Perhaps it will be with me for a time, if you can bear with another old woman. Mark and Paula will want their own establishment. Of course, they'll have Stormpoint."

She had sped her bolt. If it had been needless, it was harmless; if it had wounded, so much the more was it needed. But she felt mean—in the proper frame to meet Mr. Hacket, who was announced, to the relief of both.

The distant organ notes must have been pleasing to the ear, for, after Mrs. Joe had gone, Natalie sat long, listening and motionless; they must have been tender, for tears glistened in her eyes. When they ceased she rose and left the room and the house. In the grounds she found Paula, who said, "I came out at this moment, and saw that," pointing to the buggy; "then I knew that you would soon be here."

They strolled to a sheltered nook of the cliffside, and thence looked out upon the silver sea, peaceful under the summer sky.

"One could hardly believe that it could ever be angry," said Paula, "but you shall see it in fury; then it will be awful."

"It is awful now."

"Now!" exclaimed Paula. "Why, it is as serene as the sky above it."

"But think what it hides. Listen to the moan; see the swell of its heavy sighs."

"Natalie, I have discovered something!"

"Like Columbus," laughed Natalie.

"You are like the sea to-day. The surface wavelets laugh in the glint of the sun; but sadness is beneath. The sea hides sorrow; and you are so. You and Mark——"

And there she stopped. The other knew why. Paula was looking straight at her face, and she knew that her face had suddenly told a story.

"Does the sea remind you of Mark?" she asked in even tones, guarding her secret in her manner of utterance.

"Of both of you," answered Paula, who had quickly turned a somewhat troubled gaze upon the water. "Natalie," she added, rather hurriedly, "there is a balm for every sorrow, a sure one. *That*"—she slightly emphasized the word—"is why I thought of you in connection with Mark. Ah, if he were only religious!"

"Then he would be perfect, you think." She laughed, and Paula laughed, but the merriment seemed hollow.

"Nobody can be perfect," said Paula, after the pause which had followed the unmeaning mirth. She spoke in a low tone and timidly, but for that reason all the more engagingly; "but so far as perfection can be attained, it can only be with the aid of religion."

It was one of the words in season, which Natalie had become accustomed to hear from those about her, and which from this exhorter she always liked to hear. There was an atmosphere of calm about Paula and a serenity in her face which fascinated the unbeliever. And her admonitions, if timidly uttered, were sincere. It was as though the young preacher, though longing for a convert, feared to frighten the disciple away.

Natalie bent over and kissed the girl's cheek. "Is he unhappy? Mark, I mean."

"His life is evidence that he is not happy. He wanders aimlessly. Cousin Alice built Stormpoint for him, yet he leaves it."

"His large interests compel his wanderings."

"He has agents who make them unnecessary. Cousin Alice needs him."

"You would be glad to have him home?"

Paula looked up; her sparkling eyes answered the question. There was a pause.

"I hope he will come," said Natalie, after awhile, "and that you will have your wish."

"That he will become religious? I pray for it, so it must come."

Natalie took her hand and held it. "And you believe that religion insures happiness?" She was willing to hold on to this topic.

"I know it. The peace of God which passeth understanding. Do not turn from it, Natalie."

"I do not. I am not a scoffer. I think that I, too, could love God, only I am densely ignorant."

"But you can be enlightened. Father Cameril——"

Natalie smiled. "I hardly think he would be the teacher I would choose. I would prefer you."

"To enlighten your ignorance! I am myself ignorant. I believe—I know no more." This sounded prettily from pretty lips, and Paula was honest; but, as a matter of fact, she had some theological pretensions, a truth which she for the moment forgot.

"How is that possible?" asked the infidel. "I could believe, if I knew."

"We cannot understand everything."

"No—almost nothing, therefore——"

"We have a revelation."

"Which reveals nothing to me. I wish it did."

"Natalie, you demand too much. We are not permitted to know everything. We cannot be divine."

"And yet we can speak very positively; as if, indeed, we knew it all—some of us. But if nobody knows, nobody can be sure."

"I cannot argue; but I can tell you who tells me. God Himself. God speaks to the heart."

"Paula," cried the other, with startling earnestness, "I, too, have a heart. Teach me how to believe, and of all the wise you will be the wisest. Do I not know that life is barren? that the love of man cannot fill the heart? Ah! Paula, if that can do it, teach me the love of God!"

The tone rose almost to a cry. Paula was awed as a perception of the truth came upon her that here was a skeptic with religious longings greater than her own. "Natalie," she murmured, hiding her face on the shoulder of her companion, "we are told to ask. Pray, Natalie, to the One that knows it all."

"And will you pray for me?"

"I do."

"And do you pray for Mark?"

"Surely."

"And you know that my prayers will be answered?"

"I know it—in God's good time."

"I will pray, Paula."

They kissed one another, as though sealing a compact. No doubt Paula breathed a petition for her who, still in darkness, craved for light. Natalie prayed for the happiness of Mark Claghorn, and that she might forget him and resign him to the saint whose lips she pressed.

Then she went home. In the hall of the White House she met Tabitha. "Come!" she exclaimed, seizing that elderly damsel about the waist. "*Dansons*, Tabitha; hop, skip! *Sur le pont d'Avignon on y danse, on y danse!*" and she trilled her lay and whirled the astonished spinster around until both were breathless.

"My sakes! Have you gone crazy?" exclaimed Tabitha.

"Come to my senses!" replied Natalie, laughing merrily.

"I never saw you so French before," was Tabitha's comment.

CHAPTER XVI.

WARBLINGS IN THE WHITE HOUSE AND SNARES FOR A SOUL.

Achsah Claghorn, for many years lonely, with maternal instincts steadily suppressed, had found the first opportunity of a long life to gratify cravings of which she had been until now unconscious. Coyly, even with trembling, she sought the love of her grand-niece, being herself astonished, as much as she astonished others, by an indulgent tenderness seemingly foreign to her character. Grandmothers, though once severe as mothers, are often overfond in their last maternal role, and it may be that Miss Claghorn pleased herself by the fiction of a relationship which, though not actually existent, had some foundation in long-past conditions.

"Did your father never speak of me?" she asked.

"Often, Aunt. Especially of late years, after we had met Cousin Jared."

"But not with much affection?"

Natalie was somewhat at a loss. "He said you were his second mother," was her reply.

"Poor Susan—that was your grandmother, my dear. She was a gentle, loving creature. I think now, though perhaps I did not at the time, that 'Liph was lonely after she died. Ours was a dull house," she continued, after a pause. "Your grandfather lived more in heaven than on earth, which made it gloomy for us that didn't. Saints are not comfortable to live with, and 'Liph was often in disgrace. I hope I was never hard to a motherless boy, but—but——"

"I am sure you were not. My father never said so."

"Yet he forgot me. Perhaps it was pleasanter not to remember."

There was no reply to make. Natalie knew that her father had been so well content to forget his relatives that, until the unexpected meeting in Germany, her own knowledge of the Claghorns had been very vague.

"'Liph did write me when he married, even promised to come and see me, but he never came."

Miss Claghorn forgot the fact that in reply to her nephew's letter she had deplored his connection with Romanism and had urged instant attention to the duty of converting his wife. The philosopher may have justly enough felt that there could be but little sympathy between himself and one whose congratulations on his nuptials were in part a wail of regret, in part an admonitory sermon.

"You know, Aunt, he did intend to come."

"To see Mrs. Joe—well, no doubt he would have been glad to see me, too. I am sorry we never met after so many years."

Besides the tenderness displayed to Natalie alone, there were evidences of change in the mistress of the White House, apparent to all; and while these were properly ascribed to the new inmate, the fact that that influence could work such wonders excited surprise. The neighbors were astonished to behold the novel sight of perennially open parlor windows, and thought with misgiving upon the effect of sunshine on Miss Claghorn's furniture. At times strange sounds issued from the hitherto silent dwelling, operatic melodies, or snatches of chansons, trilled forth in a foreign tongue. "The tunes actually get into my legs," observed Tabitha to a neighbor. "The sobber de mong pare'd make an elder dance," an assertion which astonished the neighbor less than Miss Cone's familiarity with the French language. But comment was actually stricken dumb when both Miss Claghorn and Tabitha appeared in public with sprigs of color in their headgear and visible here and there upon their raiment.

"I believe you'd bewitch Old Nick himself," observed Tabitha.

"I have," replied Natalie. "He's promised me a shrub."

"I don't mean Nick that brings the garden sass," and the spinster groaned at the benighted condition of one so ignorant as to fail to recognize a familiar appellation of the enemy of souls. "You've worked your grand-aunt out of a horse."

"Your voice is that of an oracle, Tab, and I, who am stupid, do not understand."

"She's going to give you a horse."

"Then should you not rather say that I have worked a horse out of my grand-aunt? which is still oracular; wherefore expound, Tab."

"She told me herself. It's my belief she's in love with you. She'd give you her head, if you asked."

"She's given me her heart, which is better. And so have you; and you're both ashamed of it. Why is that, Tabby?"

"Well," replied Tabitha, making no denial, "you see we're not French—thank God! When we were young we were kept down, as was the fashion."

"I do not like that fashion."

"You'd like it less if you knew anything about it. It has to come out some time; that's the reason your songs get into my legs, and——"

"And?" questioningly, for Tabitha had paused.

"Well, your aunt was never in love—never had the chance, 's far's I know; but if she had, it had to be kept down—and now it comes out. Lucky it didn't strike an elder with a raft of children and no money."

"Much better that it has struck me than an elder—that will be a friar. I have no children, some money and a whole heart. But this tale of a horse?"

"Ever since you told us about ridin' in the Bawdy Bolone she's had Leonard on the lookout. He's found one over to Moffat's. She wants you to look at it before she buys."

"But——"

"I know—you've money of your own to buy horses. That's what she's afraid you'll say. You mustn't. She's set her heart on it."

The horse was accepted without demur, if with some secret misgiving as to adding a new link to the chain which was binding her to Easthampton; and it was peculiarly grateful. Ever since that day when Natalie had astonished Tabitha by improvising a waltz, her gaiety had been feverish, almost extravagant, the result of a craving for physical excitement; the desire to jump, to run, to leap, to execute for Tabitha's delectation dances which would have made Miss Claghorn stare. The horse in some degree filled the craving. She rode constantly, sometimes alone, galloping wildly in secluded lanes; sometimes sedately with Paula and an attendant; often with Leonard, an ardent equestrian, a fact not forgotten by the donor of the horse when the gift was made.

In the eyes of Miss Achsah, as in other eyes, Leonard embodied the finest type of the fine race to which he belonged, combining in his person physical graces not generally vouchsafed to these favorites of heaven, as well as those nobler attributes with which they had been so liberally endowed, and which rendered them worthy of the celestial preference. It was religious to believe that these graces of person and of manner were not given without a purpose, and aided by the same pious deduction which usually recognizes in similar charms a snare of Satan, Miss Claghorn beheld in this instance a device of Providence for winning a soul.

Besides the facilities for conversion thus utilized, Miss Achsah discerned other grounds for hope. In the frequent lapses into thoughtfulness, even sadness, on the part of the unbeliever, she recognized the beginning of that spiritual agitation which was to result in the complete submission of the erring soul to heaven; nor was she negligent in dropping those words which, dropped in season, may afford savory and sustaining food to a hungry spirit. Had Natalie displayed that mental agony and tribulation which naturally accompanies the fear of hell, and which is, therefore, a frequent preliminary terror of conversion, Miss Claghorn would have called in her pastor, as in physical ills she would have called in the doctor; but since Natalie displayed nothing more than frequent thoughtfulness and melancholy, and, as with some natures (and the lady knew it was true of the Claghorn nature) antagonism is aroused by over-solicitude, she easily persuaded herself that, for the present at least, the case was better in the competent hands of Leonard, to whom she solemnly confided it. She feared the treatment of a more experienced, yet perhaps harsher practitioner, whose first idea would be the necessity of combating Romanism. For the secret of Natalie's unbelief remained undisclosed, and Miss Claghorn dreaded such disclosure as sure to bring disgrace upon the family name. Finally, she had another reason, not the least important, for providing Leonard with the chance of winning that soul, which she hoped would become for him the most precious of the souls of men.

CHAPTER XVII.

THE SECRET OF HER HEART WAS NEVER TO BE TOLD BY HER TO HIM.

"She must be warned from Father Cameril," said Miss Claghorn.

"Do you suppose *he* could influence her?" observed Leonard scornfully. "I shall not forget my duty, Cousin Achsah. Meanwhile, remember that she is a Claghorn. That means something."

"A great deal; still, there was her father—and Lettie Stanley——"

"I think you are rather hard on her. I believe that Mrs. Stanley is a good woman."

"Will goodness alone attain heaven?"

Leonard did not answer. Mrs. Stanley's chances of heaven had no great interest for him.

If he seemed somewhat less solicitous than Miss Claghorn had expected it was because already his musings were tending in a direction not theological. "How lovely she is!" This had been his thought on his first visit to Easthampton, while Natalie's little hand still lay in his in welcome. He noted, as he watched her afterward, the fitful sadness of her eyes, and longed to share her unknown sorrow. He saw the ripe red lips and his bosom glowed, his eyes grew dreamy and his cheeks flushed pink. He had never, so Paula averred, been as handsome as on that evening.

He was now a daily visitor, equally welcome at the White House or at Stormpoint, and the relations between the two establishments were such that a hope arose within the bosom of Mrs. Joe that she might be able to report to Mr. Hacket that Miss Claghorn had actually dined with the Bishop. She ventured to confide to Miss Achsah certain aspirations in regard to Mark, and her confidence was well received and her plans applauded. Miss Claghorn thought it fitting that Mark, who was nearer to her in blood than Leonard, should assume in worldly affairs that eminence which in higher matters would be Leonard's. It was plain that when the time came such influence as she possessed would be used in Mark's behalf, barring some untoward circumstance, which Mrs. Joe was resolved should not occur. And to prevent it she warned Father Cameril that his wiles were not to be practised upon Natalie. His prayers, her own and Paula's, she informed him, must, for the present, suffice. She was aware that Miss Claghorn had personally taken charge of a matter which, to do Mrs. Joe justice, she regarded as of supreme importance. But, St. Perpetua notwithstanding, her opinions were liberal. She supposed that good people went to heaven, and she was not sternly rigid in her definition of goodness. As to where bad people went, her ideas were vague. She did not question Miss Claghorn's Christianity, though she did not admire its quality, but she knew that on the first attempt to entice Natalie by the allurements presented by St. Perpetua, the bonds of amity now existing would be strained. She even went so far as to assure her sister-in-law that Father Cameril should be "kept in his place," an assurance which was accepted with the grim rejoinder that it were well that he be so kept.

Wherefore, it would seem that those exalted aspirations which had warmed Leonard's bosom, when he had learned from Paula that his French cousin was to be a resident of Easthampton, would be reawakened, and that he would gladly attempt their realization. Alas! other, and more alluring visions, engaged his senses.

To say that he had loved the maid, Berthe, is only to say that which would be true of any man of similar temperament under similar circumstances. The kiss of those lips, over which he had so rapturously lingered, had been his first taste of passion. It may be a sorrowful, but it is not a surprising, fact, that it should affect him violently and color his dreams of a sentiment hitherto unknown. He had taken a long step in a pathway which was to lead him far, though he was as ignorant of the fact as he was of the fact that, in this respect, his education had commenced unfortunately.

He was sufficiently a man of the world to be aware that the emotion in which he had reveled could have no satisfactory result. He would no more have considered the advisability of marrying Natalie's maid than would the Marquis de Fleury; and as to any other possibility, such as perchance might have occupied the mind of the noble Marquis, it never even entered his thoughts. In his ignorance he was innocent, and had he been less so, would still have possessed in the moral lessons of his training a sufficient safeguard. Yet the kiss was to have its results. Woman's lips would, to him, bear a different aspect from that of heretofore.

And so the days passed very happily, though Leonard's conscience often pricked him. Natalie's soul was still in danger.

"Cousin," he said one day—they were sitting among the trees of Stormpoint, the girl sketching, he watching her—"Do you——?" He stopped, blushing.

She thought the blush very engaging as she looked up with a smile. Women rarely looked upon the handsome, innocent face, except smilingly. "Do I what, Leonard?" she asked.

"Do you ever think of religion? I am a clergyman, Natalie."

"I think a great deal of religion." Her eyes fell before his. He had touched a secret corner of her heart, and at first she shrank; yet the touch pleased her; not less so because of his manner which, though he was secretly ashamed of it, was in his favor. It was not easy for him to discuss the topic with her, to play the role of teacher and enlarge upon a theme which was far from his thoughts. The fact lent him the grace of embarrassment, leading her to believe that the topic was to him a sacred one. Truly, her soul was burdened. Who more apt to aid her than this young devotee, who had consecrated a life to that knowledge for which she yearned?

"You know, Natalie, as a minister——"

"It is your duty to convert me," she interrupted, looking again upward, and smiling. "That is what Tabitha says."

"Perhaps Tabitha is right. I think I ought."

"Suppose you were to try, what would you have me do?"

What would he have her do? The man within him cried: "I would have you love me, kiss me, pillow my head upon your breast and let me die there!" But the man within him was audible only to him. "I would advise you to read"—he stopped. What he had been about to say was so utterly incongruous—to advise reading the Westminster Confession, when he longed to call upon her to read the secrets of his soul!

"I have read enough," she answered. "Lately I have done better"—she hesitated; he noted the flushed cheek and downcast eyes, the tremulous tone of her voice. She was affected, he believed, religiously. He remembered the day on the terrace of Heidelberg, when he had so yearned over the wandering soul, and again with his love—for he knew it was love, and always had been—was mingled the higher aspiration to reconcile the wayward spirit with its Maker. He would have taken her hand, but he felt tremulously shy. "What have you done?" he asked gently.

Much had been told her of the sweet relief of confession to a priest. Here was a confessor, sympathetic, she knew from his tone. Yet she had no sins to confess (belief in which incongruity demonstrates her state of darkness).

"I—have prayed," she said at length, and the shy admission seemed to create a bond between them. Another shared her confidence, and the fact lightened her spirit. She told herself it was so, and had it been true the future might have been brighter; but the real secret of her heart was never to be told by her to him. She looked up, a faint sheen of tears in her eyes, a smile upon her lips.

"Indeed, you have done better," he answered, the eyes and the smile summoning that inner man with a power hard to resist. "You need no guidance from me," he said huskily. "God bless and help you, Natalie!" He placed a trembling hand upon her head, as was seemly in a priest, and, turning abruptly, walked away.

"Ah!" she sighed, as she watched him. "There must be something in religion. Fräulein Rothe was right, and my dear father was wrong."

Thus Leonard's fears concerning Natalie's salvation were quieted. If she prayed, it was plain that she was called, and though her ears might still be deaf, she would hear in the appointed time.

Had he comprehended her utter misapprehension as to orthodox tenets, he might have been awakened to a stricter sense of duty. But this was his first heathen, and he is hardly to be blamed that he did not recognize the extent of her ignorance; or, in his lack of knowledge of humanity, at all to be blamed that he failed to discern the true nature of her religious cravings, alluring to her soul because her soul was hungry; for God, perhaps—for who shall say that God has no part in human love?—but not for Leonard's God. He had never been informed of the deceased philosopher's method of training, and would, certainly, have doubted its success had he known of it. That one could attain years of discretion in a Christian country, lacking even an elementary knowledge of Christian doctrine, would have been to Leonard incredible. He could not remember the time that he had not known that in Adam's fall we all fell, and that had there been no Atonement there would be no Salvation. For so much, and similar doctrinal essentials, he accorded Natalie full credit; and, since she had escaped the taint of Romanism, he felt that no real obstacle stood in the way of her growth in grace.

Meanwhile, Natalie had no more knowledge that, unless her name had been from before creation inscribed upon the roll of the elect, she must, for the glory of God, infallibly be damned, than has a Patagonian. She felt that outside of humanity there was something on which humanity must lean, and that it was God. Priests, sisters of charity and sweet girls like Paula knew about God, and all these had told her that the way to find out what they knew was to pray; and, in her outer darkness, she prayed, her prayers the prayers of a heathen; not heard in heaven, if we are correctly informed as to heaven's willingness to hear. Yet to her they brought some solace. And in her petitions for enlightenment of her ignorance, she besought happiness for others, not for Mark Claghorn only; henceforth she included the name of Leonard.

As for him, he was no longer haunted by troublesome recollections of Berthe. He thought of her, it is true, and with tenderness, though with a smile, and accusing himself of youthfulness. He was now sure that he had never seriously loved her. It had been a *penchant*, a *petit amour*—the Gallic flavor of the words was not altogether ungrateful—and the experience would have its uses. These things happened to some men; happy they who escaped them; a humdrum life was safer. Sinning was dangerous; to weaklings, fatal; such a one would have been burned in the ordeal of fire. He had escaped, nor had he any intention of being again taken unawares. He did not attempt to palliate the grave wrong of which he had been guilty; he would have resented such palliation on the part of an apologist. In certain sins there lurks a tinge of glory, and one has a right, accepting the blame, to appropriate the glory. But his resolve that the one misstep should be the last, as it had been the first of his life, was sternly made. He was strong now, and was glad to admit that much of his strength derived its power from a sweeter passion glowing in his bosom. His heart swelled with joy that he could love, feeling only such misgivings as lovers must. It was a sin to love and long for Berthe whom he wouldn't marry. To transfer to Natalie the love he had given to Berthe, to hunger and to burn, to feed his eyes upon the outward form, unheeding the fairer creature within, to revel in visions and forbidden dreams—this was love, this the lesson his carefully guarded life had prepared him to learn from wanton lips.

Who, being in love, has not shown himself to the loved one at his best? If he was unquiet within, he was sufficiently tranquil in manner to avoid any startling manifestation of ardor. If there was art in the graceful coyness of his approach, it was unconscious art. To Natalie he appeared with more alluring gentleness, and surer fascination, than the most practised veteran of love's battles. She had seen chivalrous elegance so studied as to charm by its seeming unaffectedness; but the most successful picture is not reality, and in Leonard she noted the nature superior to art; nature softened and adorned by demeanor graced and made tender by the inward tremors of love, as a rugged landscape is beautified by the mellow tint of a gray day.

Above all, though if this was known in secret it was unconfessed, was Leonard aided by that which was to be forever hidden in the woman's heart. There were rumors of Mark's return, rumors which agitated Natalie, strive as she might to look forward to that return without emotion. How could she leave the home where love had been so generously bestowed? Mrs. Joe would no longer be ashamed that she had given her warning—and Natalie had not been sorry to believe that the lady was ashamed—for she would know that it had been needed. And Miss Claghorn—how would she understand it? How Paula? Perhaps she saw, if but dimly yet, an escape from the perplexities which inspired the questions.

CHAPTER XVIII.

A LOVER WRITES A LETTER.

If a Parisian philosopher, animated by the love of that wisdom which is deducible by philosophic methods from the study of mankind, had emerged from his abode, on a certain summer evening, in quest of the solution of that great riddle, Why is this thus? and, seeking an answer, had scanned the visages of the passers upon the Boulevard, he would, perhaps, have noticed the face and bearing of a man who strolled alone and listless; and, it being a fine evening of early summer, at an hour when, philosophers having dined, are ruminative, he might have fallen into speculation, and asking himself the meaning of this man's face, would, perhaps, have deduced discontent, becoming habitual and tending toward cynicism; and if a philosopher of the weeping, rather than the laughing variety, he would have mourned over the atom of humanity, beneath whose careworn lines and shadows of dissatisfaction there lay forgotten noble promise. And, to sum up the philosophic conclusions (for, like other philosophers, our hypothetical lover of wisdom is growing tiresome) he, being aware of the cause of much mundane misery, might have decided that the man had lost money, and would have been wrong, for the man was one whom financial loss could hardly touch. The Great Serpent might refuse to yield for weeks, aye forever, and Mark Claghorn would have been content. In truth, its annual product was a burden heavier than he thought he ought, in fairness, to be called upon to bear. He liked companionship, being naturally well disposed toward his fellows, yet, as he said to himself, the loneliness of this evening stroll in the centre of mirth and good fellowship had its reason in his wealth. A man such as he, so he told himself, is forced, in the nature of things, to purchase all the joys of life, and being purchased they had but slight attraction for him; thus ordinarily he was solitary and somewhat given to brooding, though wise enough to utter no complaint on a score wherein he certainly would have found but slight sympathy.

He strolled on, paying little heed to any, except when occasionally the clank of a sabre or the faint jingle of a spur signified a cavalryman in the vicinity; then he would glance at the cavalryman, and with a quickly satisfied curiosity, pass on, listless as before.

He entered a cafe, and calling for a "bock," lit a cigar and proceeded to seek distraction in tobacco and beer, while looking over the pages of the "*Vie Parisienne*," but apparently found no amusement in that very Gallic periodical. At last he drew a letter from his pocket. "Little Paula," he muttered, as he opened the sheet, and his tone was kindly, if not tender. "I suppose, in the end, my mother will see the fulfilment of the wish she thinks so carefully concealed," he muttered, and then, as if to find encouragement to filial duty in the letter itself, he commenced to read, and was thus engaged when he felt a hand upon his shoulder, and heard the exclamation, "Claghorn!" He looked up and, rising, accepted the outstretched hand of Adolphe de Fleury.

"I was not sure whether it was you or your ghost," said Adolphe. "When did you leave America?"

"Over a year since," replied Mark; then, unmindful of the look of surprise in the face of his companion, he added: "I hoped I might meet you. I am only here for a few hours, and the opportunity to congratulate you——"

"To congratulate! May I ask why I am to be congratulated?" interrupted the lieutenant.

"Usually a newly married man; or one about to be——"

"Claghorn, you can hardly—do you mean that you believed me married?"

"Married, or about to be. I heard from the Marquise while at St. Petersburg———"

"And I have suspected you! Know, my dear fellow, though I had rather you heard it from somebody else, that I am very far from married. I am jilted; abandoned by our fair but cruel cousin, who has fled from my mother's protection and taken refuge among the Yankees."

"Do you mean that Natalie is in America?"

"Just that, *mon cher*, and with her Berthe of the wonderful eyes."

Mark's innocence of all knowledge of the fact stated was evident in his face. He was astounded; at the same time a sense of joy swept across his soul. He looked hastily at his watch; it was too late to call upon the Marquise, unless, indeed, she had company, in which case he would not be able to see her alone. But, looking at his watch inspired him with an excuse to plead an appointment, which he did, and left his companion.

The next day he called upon Madame de Fleury, and on his return to his hotel, he wrote the following letter:

> "My Dear Cousin Natalie—Last night I arrived here direct from St. Petersburg, being merely a bird of passage, and on my way to London. I had expected to be there by this time, but after meeting Adolphe de Fleury, I deferred my departure until I could see the Marquise. Doubtless, my letters in London will convey the information which has been imparted by her. To say that I was surprised to hear that you had gone to America hardly expresses my feeling;

but surprise is cast into the shade by gratification. Now that your reasons for the step you have taken have been so freely disclosed to me by Madame de Fleury (who insisted upon reading to me passages from your letters), I hope you will not regard it as intrusive in me if I express my admiration of your independence and complete approbation of your conduct. You are in spirit a true American, and I congratulate both you and our country upon the fact. Do you remember the day I said 'good-bye' to you? Had you then any inkling of the true reason for my adieu? Your father had just informed me that since girlhood you had been the betrothed of Adolphe de Fleury. Monsieur Claghorn at the time assured me that had not this been the case I should have had his good wishes in regard to the aspirations I had just laid before him. I have never laid those aspirations before you, nor can I do so adequately in a letter; nor at this time, when so long a period has elapsed since I last saw you. What I have to say must be said in person, and so unsatisfactory is this method of addressing you on the subject that I may not send this letter.

"But, if you receive it, understand why I write it. It seems, perhaps, laughable—though it does not seem so to me— that I should be haunted by a terror which darkens the new hope that has arisen within me. You are thousands of miles away. True, it is not easily conceivable that you may become lost to me in so brief a residence in America, yet the idea is constantly with me. I blame that which I then believed the honorable reticence which I ought to maintain toward you after my interview with your father, and having heard his assurances of intentions, which I, of course, supposed were approved by you. Had I shown you the least glimpse of a sentiment which it cost me much to conceal, I might now be freed from the dread which oppresses me. I am even tempted to send you a telegraphic message; yet I picture you reading such a message and shrink from seeming ridiculous in your eyes. As to this letter, I am impelled to say as much as I have said while that which I desire to say is plainly enough indicated. I had supposed it possible to disclose and yet conceal it. But the letter is wiser than I intended it to be. My most ardent hope is that within a few days after its receipt you will listen to all that is here omitted.

"Faithfully,

"Mark Claghorn."

He sent the letter, unsatisfactory and feeble as he knew it to be. He chafed at the necessity of deferring his departure for America; but the Great Serpent was importunate, and even for love a man cannot disregard the claims of others. Engagements connected with the mine, made long since, must receive attention before he could leave Europe.

But, during the intervals of business, even pending its details, he was hourly tempted to send a dispatch and be ridiculous. But he refrained. He sailed for America four days after sending the letter. He had not been absurd; his dignity was saved. Who that is wise in a wise generation listens to intuitions?

CHAPTER XIX.

A KISS THAT MIGHT HAVE LINGERED ON HIS LIPS WHILE SEEKING ENTRANCE AT THE GATE OF HEAVEN.

At the foot of the cliff whereon Mrs. Joe had erected a monument to the Great Serpent in the form of a castle, the ocean beats in calm weather with a sullen persistence which increases with the rising wind from spiteful lashing into furious pounding against the unshaken crag, accompanied by a roar of futile rage. Stormpoint affords no nook of shelter for a distressed craft, and the rocks, submerged beneath the vexed waters, render the coast hereabout even more dangerous than does the sheer wall of stone which appals the mariner caught in the storm and driven shoreward. Once around the point, the little harbor of Easthampton offers safety, but it has happened that vessels, unable to weather Stormpoint, have been dashed against the rocks and human beings have been tossed about in the seething foam beneath the crags; or men have clung to wreckage in sight of wailing wives and mothers, and of children to be orphaned in the rush of the next black billow.

From the rocks hereabout no lifeboat can be launched at times when lifeboats are needed, therefore the coast-guard station is nearer the harbor, where there is a beach upon which the waves slide upward, spending their strength, and where even in the storm they can be ridden by resolute men; but no boat can live among the rocks in the raging waters beneath the cliff. And so, Mrs. Joe, with the approval of the authorities, had built on the ledge of the cliffside (enlarged and widened for the purpose) a house, in which were kept appliances for casting lines athwart wrecked craft. There were plenty to ridicule the benevolent lady, some on the score of the futility of preparing for an improbable disaster (less than a dozen ships had been lost there in a century; and probably not, in all that time, a hundred lives); others because while yet another ship might be driven thither, no human effort could then avert her doom. Mrs. Joe, notwithstanding these arguments, carried out her intention, and waited, hoping that she would never be justified by the event.

One day Natalie and Leonard were in the "wreck house," as the structure had come to be called; a high wind, constantly increasing, was blowing, and from their position they saw all the grandeur of the ocean, rolling in majesty toward the wall of rock, an assailing mass, seeming inspired with malevolent intelligence and boundless strength, but, caught by the sunken rocks, the onset would be broken, and, bellowing with rage, each mighty billow would recede, only to be followed by another, as angry and as awful of aspect as the last.

It was a sight before which human passion was cowed and human pride was humbled. As Leonard watched Natalie, silently contemplating the grandeur of the scene, her dark hair blowing back from the smooth white brow, beneath which eyes, as unfathomable as the ocean itself, looked yearningly out into the storm, he had a clear perception that the emotions he had harbored and nourished as to this woman were unworthy of the soul in her fathomless eyes. In the presence of nature, feebly stirred as yet, but with a promise of the mighty strength restrained, and perhaps, too, his nobler self responding unconsciously to the purity of the woman at his side, the grosser passion that had vexed him was subdued; desire for the woman was lost in desire to share the woman's heart.

The darkening heavens sinking into the gloom of the ocean, where in the distance the rolling masses of cloud and water seemed to meet, the roaring wind, the waves booming on the cliff, and the boiling cauldron of death beneath their feet—in the presence of these things words could not utter thoughts unutterable; they stood long silent.

"Who, then, is this, that He commandeth even the winds and the water, and they obey Him?" Leonard heard her murmur these words.

"Who, indeed?" he said. "How can man deny God in the face of this?"

"In the face of anything?"

"Or deny His Revelation? Natalie, it is true."

"Is it true?"

"As true as the waters or the sky—Natalie, Natalie, it is true."

His tone trembled with a tenderness deeper than the tenderness of passion. She looked and saw his eyes with a sheen of tears upon them; no gleam of earthly desire looked out of them, but the yearning for a soul. In the presence of the Majesty of God the nobler spirit had awakened and answered to the longing of the girl to know the secret of the waves, the rocks, the skies; the secret of herself and of the man beside her—the eternal truth, hidden always, yet always half revealed to questioning man.

"Religion is very dear to you, Leonard?"

"Dearer than all but God Himself. Dearer than riches, honors—dearer, Natalie, than the love I bear for you."

It was said without the usual intent of lover's vows, and so she understood it. She made no answer.

And then they saw a sight which made them forget all else—a fellow-creature, driving helplessly to destruction beneath their feet.

It was a lad, ignorant, it would seem, of the management of the frail vessel in which he was the sole passenger. Even in the hands of an experienced sailor the little boat, intended for smooth water only, would have been unsafe; now, unskilfully fitted with a mast and sail, managed by ignorant hands, and driven toward a coast that had no shelter, the storm rising each moment, the outlook was desperate for the voyager.

Leonard seized a trumpet from the appliances with which the wreck-house was furnished, and leaning far out of the window, bawled in stentorian tones, some order, which, whether heard by the boy or not, was unheeded. Indeed, the desperate situation seemed to have paralyzed him; he clung to the tiller with the proverbial clutch of the drowning man, utterly incapable of other action, if indeed other action could prevail.

Seizing a line, Leonard ran down the stairway to a platform built against the cliff and not many feet above the water. Natalie followed. The wind was rising every moment, the tide running higher with each succeeding wave, and now, as she noticed, even reaching the platform. Leonard noticed, too. "It is not safe here," he shouted to her, for the wind howled in their ears and the noise of the surge emulated the noise of the wind. At the same time he pointed to the stairway, signifying that she should return, but took no further heed of her. His one thought was to do the thing that would save the life in peril. She did not know what he was about to do, but watched him, ready to lend assistance, though without taking her eyes from the boy in the boat. Thus far it had escaped the sunken rocks, but it could not long escape the shore. The wind had blown the sail from its fastenings and it tossed upon the waves. Only the whirlpool formed by the sunken rocks and the sullenly receding waters, which had but a moment before been hurled against the cliff, stayed the wreck of the craft. It needed no experienced eye to recognize the imminence of the peril of the boy, and the sight of the solitary being, helpless and exposed to the rude mercy of the waves, was pitiful. Natalie wrung her hands and prayed in French, and while the infidel prayed the clergyman acted.

He had intended to cast the weighted end of the line across the boat and so give its passenger communication with the shore; even so, the case of the lad would have been but slightly bettered, since, though fast to the rope, to avoid being dashed against the rocks would be barely possible; but Leonard, almost in the act of throwing, saw that his intention was impracticable. He must wait until the boat had come a little nearer. Natalie, with alarm that was almost horror, saw him remove his coat and boots; she would have remonstrated, but she felt that remonstrance was useless. He stood a waiting hero, his whole being absorbed in the task before him. That task involved his plunging into the boiling surf, the very abyss of death. Who can say that some premonition of the future was not upon him, as, with uplifted head and watching eyes, he stood statue-like awaiting the supreme moment? Who knows but he was warned that better for him the whirlpool below than the woman at his side!

Keenly watching the boat, his hands had still been busy, and from the line he had fashioned a loop, which now he fitted over his head and beneath his armpits. The other end of the line he secured to a ring in the platform, and then, having said nothing to Natalie, but now taking her hand in his own, and holding it tightly, he waited.

Not long. As in a flash she saw the boat in fragments, the boy in the water, and in the same instant Leonard plunged in.

She seized the line, but let it have play. Leonard had reached the boy in one stroke, had him in his very grasp, when a huge receding wave tore them asunder, and both were lost to Natalie.

She pulled with all her strength. She knew that the boy was drowned and had no hope for Leonard; her hold of the rope aided in his rescue, as she was able to prevent his being carried away; but had it not been that the next wave swept him upon the platform, where he was instantly seized and dragged far backward by Natalie, who herself barely escaped being swept off, he must have been either drowned or dashed dead against the rocks.

For some minutes she believed him drowned. She had dragged him to a place of comparative safety and he lay quite still with his head in her lap. But after awhile he sighed and looked into her eyes, and at last sat up. "The boy?" he said.

"Gone," she sobbed.

After some moments he arose, and feebly enough, assisted her to rise, and they sat upon the stairway, and after awhile got into the wreck-house. Here Leonard knew where to find restoratives, as well as a huge blanket, in which he wrapped himself and Natalie.

And so they sat side by side, enveloped in one covering, both quite silent, until he said: "Natalie, I have been praying."

"Teach me, Leonard."

"While I live," he answered, and he turned his face and kissed her.

It was the second time that he had kissed woman, but this was a kiss that might have lingered on his lips while seeking entrance at the gate of heaven.

CHAPTER XX.

A DISHONEST VEILING OF A WOMAN'S HEART.

There was joy at Stormpoint. Before the eyes of Mrs. Joe there rose the vision of a senate spell-bound by the resonant voice of oratory, while in the same foreshadowing of the time to come Paula beheld Father Cameril triumphant over the Bishop and strong in reliance upon the stalwart arm of a soldier newly enrolled in the army of the Church Militant. Mark had returned, and it was while gazing upon his countenance that these seers saw their delectable visions and dreamed their pleasant dreams.

Upon this, the first evening of his return, the three sat together in the library of Stormpoint, Mark submitting, with that external grace which becomes the man placed upon a pedestal by worshipping woman, to the adoration of his mother and of Paula; the while secretly ungrateful and chafing because it was not possible to see Natalie before bedtime.

They had dined cosily together, and the wanderer had been treated as the prodigal of old, the substitute for fatted calf being the choicest viands procurable and the rarest vintage of the Stormpoint cellar; yet he had not enjoyed his dinner, being oppressed by vague forebodings; and it was irksome to feign a smiling interest where could be no interest until he had received an answer to his letter to Natalie. Naturally, he had inquired as to the welfare of all the Claghorns of the vicinity, and had expressed satisfaction at replies which indicated health and prosperity among his relatives.

"I would have asked them all to dinner," said Mrs. Joe, "but I knew that they would understand that we would be glad to have you to ourselves to-night. Leonard and Natalie are always considerate."

"Leonard was always a favorite of yours," observed Mark, who did not greatly relish this coupling of names, and who could hardly trust himself to discuss Natalie.

"A good young man," replied the lady. "He is almost one of us."

Mark looked quizzically at Paula, who blushed but said nothing. The blush was a relief to him. "He is a fine fellow," he said, heartily. "I have always believed in Leonard, though I don't admire his profession or his creed. But there are good men among theologians, and I'm sure he is one of them."

"But, my son," remonstrated Mrs. Joe, "that is not the way to talk of clergymen."

"Fie! mother. Would you deny that there are good men among the clergy?"

"Mark, you know I meant something very different. We only wish Leonard was in the Church."

"How can he be out of it, being a Christian?"

"There is but one Church," observed Paula gravely.

"The Holy Catholic Church," added Mrs. Joe.

"Which term you and Paula assume as belonging especially to your denomination," laughed Mark. "I doubt if even your own divines would be so arrogant. Mother, this young saint is evidently as intolerant as ever; and she is making you like herself," and he placed his hand, kindly enough, on the girl's shoulder.

Her eyes filled with tears. "Mark," she said, "you may laugh at me, but religion ought to be sacred."

"Both you and your religion ought to be, and are," he answered, and stooped and kissed her forehead; and, though she did not look up, for she dared not meet his eyes, he was forgiven.

The elder lady was surprised, but she noted Mark's action with high approval. Of all the hopes that she had woven round her son, that one which contemplated his marriage with Paula was supreme. She had trained the girl for this high destiny, though, true to her instincts, she had been as politic in this as in other objects of ambition, and neither of the two whose fortunes she intended to shape were in her confidence. She rightly divined that nothing would so surely incite to rebellion on the part of Mark as an open attempt to control him in a matter of this nature, and was wise enough to know that a disclosure of her hopes to Paula would place the girl in a false position, whereby she must inevitably lose that engaging simplicity which, aside from her beauty, was her greatest charm. The lady had, as we know, been compelled by the exigencies of policy to impart her cherished plan to more than one individual; and after she had done so to Natalie, she had been in terror until opportunity occurred to insure silence.

"You see, my dear," she had explained to Natalie, "he has not actually spoken. Paula, like any other girl so situated, knows what is coming, but of course——"

"Dear Mrs. Joe, I should not in any case have mentioned the matter."

"I ought to have been more reticent, but——"

"I am sure you did what you thought best," at which reply the lady's color had deepened and the subject was dropped.

Thus Mark's action rendered his mother happy, for, notwithstanding her sanguine disposition, she had often suffered misgivings. At times, during her son's frequent absences, her fears had risen high, and with each return home she watched him, narrowly scrutinizing his belongings, even going so far as to rummage among his letters, to discover if there existed any ground for fear. Her anxieties stilled and their object once more under the maternal eye, she was willing, since she must be, that he be deliberate in falling in love. She knew men thoroughly, so she believed, having known one a little, and was persuaded that the older he grew, the more certain was Mark to appreciate that highest womanly attribute so plainly discernible in Paula—pliancy. To man, so Mrs. Joe believed, that was the supreme excellence in woman. And there had been in Paula's reception of Mark's caress a certain coyness, becoming in itself, and which had lent an air of tenderness to the little scene. Paula had cast her eyes downward in that modest confusion proper to maidens and inviting to men; doubtless Mark would be glad to repeat a homage so engagingly received.

None of these rosy inferences were shared by Paula. During Mark's last sojourn at Stormpoint, which had been immediately after leaving France and constant intercourse with the household of Beverley Claghorn, she had made her own observations and drawn her own conclusions. Whatever the reason for Mark's action, she knew it portended nothing for her, and if she had received his fraternal kiss in some confusion, it was because she dreaded the possibility of sorrow in store for him, a sorrow connected with a secret confided to her within a few hours.

"Now that you are home again, Mark," said his mother, "I want your promise not to run away."

"You know men, mother; if I make a promise, I shall inevitably want to break it."

"But you wouldn't."

"Better not tempt the weak. Isn't that so, Paula?"

"Better not be weak."

"I am serious, Mark," said Mrs. Joe. "You must consider the future; you should plan a career."

"I have no intention of running away; certainly not to-night."

"Nor any night, I hope."

"You know," he said with some hesitation, "it is possible I may have to go to California."

"Nonsense! What is Benton paid for? I need you. We ought to select a city home, and I want your taste, your judgment."

"My dear mother, the city home will be yours. Why haven't you chosen one long since?"

"As if I would without consulting you!"

He smiled, but forebore to remind her that he had not been consulted with regard to Stormpoint. "Whatever is your taste is mine," he said. "These gilded cages are for pretty birds like you and Paula; as for me——"

"That's nonsense. I am willing to keep your nest warm, but——"

"If I were to consult my own taste, I would re-erect old Eliphalet's cabin and be a hermit."

"Mark, you actually hurt me——"

"My dear mother, you know I'm joking. About this house, then. New York, I suppose, is the place for good Californians."

"It would be pleasanter; but it might be policy to remain in the State."

He looked at her in wonder. "Why?" he asked.

"It was merely an idea," she replied, blushing, and secretly grieved that he did not understand. But it was no time to enter into those plans which were the fruit of many consultations with Mr. Hacket. "It's getting late; good-night, my dear boy. I know you'll try to please me." She kissed him, and, with Paula, left the room.

Left alone, he paced up and down the long room, nervously biting a cigar which he forgot to light. He knew he would be unable to pass in sleep the hours that must elapse before he could see Natalie. He was filled with forebodings; the vague fears which had tempted him to send an absurd telegraphic message to Natalie had troubled him since he had first recognized their presence and had grown in strength with each new day. He was unaware that presentiments and feelings "in the bones," once supposed to be the laughable delusions of old ladies and nervous younger ones, were now being regarded with respectful attention as a part of the things undreamed of in Horatio's philosophy; and, taking his attitude after the old fashion, he had reasoned with that being which man calls "himself," and, for the edification of "himself," had shown to that personage the childishness of indulging in vague and ungrounded fears. But without success. Philosophers have discovered that which old ladies always knew, that all explanations of the wherefore of these mental vagaries are unsatisfactory as long as the vagaries persist; and while they do, they vex the wise and foolish alike.

His musings were disturbed by the entrance of Paula, clad in a ravishing tea-gown, a dainty fragment of humanity. "Mark," she said, "what is the matter?" for she had been quick to notice and had been startled by the gloom of his face.

"Tired, Paula," and he smiled. Somehow Paula always made him smile.

"If I were tired, I would go to bed," she observed with a faint touch of sarcasm. "I won't advise bed to you, for I know that you do not credit me with much sense."

"Yet it is plain that you have more than I, since you have indicated the sensible course," he answered pleasantly. "That should be placing you in high esteem, since we all think well of ourselves."

"Forgive me," she said with real sorrow for her petulance, for which she perhaps could have given no reason; "but I have seen that you were troubled——"

"And like a dear little sister you overflow with sympathy. Was there ever anybody kinder or better than you? But the real fact is that I am simply tired—yet not sleepy."

"Well"—she sighed wistfully—"you will feel rested to-morrow. I came down to give you this from Natalie," handing him a note. "I would have waited until morning, but I——"

"Did right, as you always do," he answered, kissing her cheek and saying good-night, and thus dismissing her, with an evident eagerness to read the note, not lost upon Paula, and which left her no alternative but to leave him.

He opened the envelope and read:

> "Dear Mark—Your letter came this morning, and I have just learned that you will be home to-night. I cannot express to you how glad I shall be to see you again. Before we meet in the presence of others, I hope to see you alone. Your letter, dear Mark, evidently delayed by being addressed in Mr. Winter's care, has cost me some tears, both of joy and sorrow. I am impatient to see you, for it seems to me that to you, before to any other, except to Paula (who would have known by intuition), I should disclose the happiness that has come to me in my engagement to Leonard. It is but two days old, and except to Paula, is known only to ourselves. Dear Mark, it has not been easy to write these few lines. I wish I could express in them how sincerely I honor and love you, and how I wish for your happiness. I have commenced to pray, and the first time I knelt to

heaven I prayed for you; and so long as I shall continue to pray—and I think that will be always now—I shall not forget to beg that you be made happy. I hope you will wander no more, but be oftener with those that love you and who need you more than you perhaps know; and as I shall live either in Hampton or Easthampton, and as I must ever regard you as one of my earliest and my best friend, I hope we shall see each other often.

"NATALIE."

"Oh, Mark, your happiness is at Stormpoint. No one is better, more loving, or more lovable than she."

The letter stunned him. He might, had he known women as well as he (being young) believed he did—he might have read the truth in every line. He might have seen that were he to rouse his energies and plead his cause, he could win it, even yet. He might have heard the unconscious cry for rescue from an engagement contracted before his letter had reached her; he might have seen, in the pains she had taken to tell him that such was the case, his excuse and hers for asserting his rights against Leonard. These things were plain enough; perhaps the writer had intended that they should be; not consciously, indeed; but from that inner being who is part of all of us, the desperate hope of the girl's heart had not been hidden as she wrote, nor was her pen entirely uncontrolled by it.

But the postscript obscured his vision. He laughed contemptuously and thought, as men will think, "It is thus that woman estimates love. She is sorry for me, and suggests that the consolation I may need I shall find in Paula!" He did not recognize that in the postscript was the real dishonesty of the letter; that it was the salve to the conscience of the writer, believing that in the letter itself she had said too much, whereas she had said too little for the perception of a man in the haze of jealousy. Such gleams of truth as might otherwise have been visible to Mark could not penetrate that dishonest veiling of the woman's heart.

CHAPTER XXI.

A MAN ABOUT TO MEET A MAID.

One may approach the White House by way of the High Street of Easthampton, of which thoroughfare the dwelling in question is a conspicuous ornament; but for such as prefer a more secluded road, a grassy lane behind the houses affords direct access to Miss Claghorn's garden.

Mark chose the lane. Since, in obedience to Natalie's request, he must see her, he hoped to find her in the garden, where there would be less danger of interruption.

The birds twittered in the trees, joyous in the new day; the dew glimmered on the grass-blades; the scent of flowers from adjacent gardens perfumed the fresh air of a perfect summer morning. On such a morning a man about to meet a maid should have trod the earth lightly. But Mark lingered as he walked, reluctant to hear his fate pronounced by lips which he longed to kiss, but could never kiss; lips, therefore, it were better not to see. Yet, since he had been summoned, he must go on; and because of the summons there were moments when he still, if faintly, hoped. Hope dies hard; and, notwithstanding the forebodings which had vexed him ever since he had written the letter (for which writing he had since cursed his folly), there had been times when hope had risen high, and, as he even now assured himself, not without reason. If he had been self-deceived, it had not been from the complacency of the coxcomb. Surely she had loved him, or had been willing to love, had that been permitted her.

In arguing thus he was not reasoning unfairly. He had been unintentionally deceived by the philosopher, Beverley Claghorn, who had permitted the intercourse between his daughter and this young man, partly from carelessness, more because he approved of a cousinly friendship of which one of the partakers was able to gratify a noble sentiment by an addition to the dowry of the other. It had been by pointing out this ability that he had assuaged the misgivings of the Marquise; at the same time so solemnly reiterating his loyalty to the treaty with that lady, that when Mark's disclosure came it had been impossible for him to receive it otherwise than he had done—by a regretful rejection. He had been astounded by the avowal, for he had noted no sighs, no posturing, no eloquent apostrophes or melting glances from this suitor who approached him with a tale of love, having never displayed a visible sign of the tender passion. M. Claghorn's observation of lovers had long been confined to one variety. He forgot that Anglo-Saxon swains are less prone to languish in public than their brothers of Gaul. Had Adolphe de Fleury been in Paris there would have been more frequent flowers, scented billets, rapt gazes, rolling eyes and eloquential phrases; all offered for the general appreciation as much as for the lady of his love. In the absence of these familiar evidences of ardor, the philosopher was, in his own eyes, acquitted of responsibility for the surprising fact which Mark had imparted to him. For, how could he suspect a legitimate passion in a youth who had yet to sow his wild oats, and one with the capacity for acquiring an unlimited field for that delightful, if futile, and generally expensive, husbandry? No man of Mark's years could be so wise—or so foolish. That was, as the philosopher viewed human nature, not in such nature. The case was different with Adolphe de Fleury, compelled by circumstances to seize the most attractive dowry that fell in his way; and even that gallant but impecunious soldier was, doubtless, cultivating a modest crop as sedulously as circumstances permitted.

Thus had Mark been the victim of a philosophic mode of thought and had bowed to that which he had supposed would be the filial, as it had been the paternal, decision; saying good-bye, sadly, doubtless, but without betrayal of that which he believed would not be gladly heard, nor could be honorably disclosed.

The ocean lay between him and the woman that he loved before he fully realized how much must be henceforth lacking in his life, and when repentance was too late he repented that he had taken the philosopher's word for a fact of which he now sometimes doubted the existence. Many memories whispered that she, too, had loved. No word of hers had told him this; but love is not always told in words—and then he would accuse himself of the folly of permitting vain longings to control his judgment. Nevertheless, when, while still at Stormpoint, he had heard of the sudden death of Beverley Claghorn, he had resolved to do that which before he had omitted, to appeal to Natalie herself, when, most inopportunely, there came a letter from the Marquise to Mrs. Joe; a letter which informed the relatives of the deceased that the death of the father would hasten, rather than retard, the marriage of the daughter, who had already taken up her residence with the writer of the epistle, in accordance with the wish of her father. Not long after the receipt of that letter Mark had started for Russia, leaving France unvisited.

He opened the gate which led from the lane into the garden, and found— Tabitha.

Who raised her hands in astonishment, then stretched them forth in welcome: "And so you're back! For how long this time? More of a Claghorn than ever—as grim as one of the Eliphalets."

"No need to ask how you are," said Mark, his grimness softened by her heartiness. "You get younger every year. How are my aunt and———"

"And Natalie? Blooming—that's the word. You'll find things different at the White House. We haven't had a good spat in months. Soor le ponty Avinyon, on y donks, on y donks——"

"*On y danse*," repeated Mark, laughing at Tabitha's French in spite of himself.

"Yes; even my old legs. Your aunt's are too stiff. But we young things, that's Natalie and I, we cut our capers," and in the exuberance of her spirits Miss Cone essayed a caper for Mark's benefit.

"Such grace, Tabby——"

"Is worth coming from Russia to see. I'm practising; there's to be great doings here before long. What would you say to a wedding?"

"Let me salute the bride?" he said, with an attempt at gaiety which, to himself, seemed rather sickly, and suiting his action to the word.

"Well!" ejaculated Miss Cone, adjusting her cap, "many a man's had his ears boxed for that. However, I suppose it's in the air around here—but you're mistaken. I'm not the bride."

"Surely, not Aunt Achsah?"

"As if you couldn't guess! But don't say I told you. The fact is I'm so full of it I blabbed without thinking."

"Then it's a secret?"

"It won't be after to-day. Leonard told us last night. I suppose your aunt'll tell your ma to-day."

Mark promised to say nothing and went toward the house. Miss Claghorn welcomed him cordially, but made no reference to the subject of Tabitha's disclosures, though traces of her agreeable agitation were visible. "There's Natalie, now!" she exclaimed after some minutes had been spent in conversation sufficiently dreary to one of the two.

The thundering of a horse's hoofs told of a wild gallop. The old lady rushed from the house, followed by Mark, dismayed by her action and the alarm expressed in her countenance. He reached the gate in time to assist Natalie to dismount.

"My dear child!" exclaimed the elder lady reproachfully.

She was grasping Mark's hands in welcome. Her face was flushed; her dark hair, disturbed by the pace at which she had ridden, hung low upon her forehead; he had never seen her so beautiful—nor so happy. His face was pale, his hands cold in hers.

"Dear Aunt," she said, "I felt as though I must gallop; I didn't mean to in the High Street; I couldn't hold him."

"He was homeward bound," said Mark, turning to look at the horse, now being led away by Miss Achsah's "man." "He's a handsome beast."

"I have much to ask you about the Marquise," said Natalie to Mark, as they went into the house, whereupon Miss Claghorn left them.

The short-lived bloom of her face was gone; she was deadly pale. She stretched her ungloved hands toward him; it might have been a gesture of appeal. He dared not take them in his own; his longing to clasp her to his heart was too great to risk the contact. She dropped her arms.

"You wished to see me—to ask me——" He paused; his voice sounded stern in his ears, but he had no power over it.

"To—to say something. Give me a moment."

As she turned toward the window he caught a glimpse of the sheen of tears. A mighty impulse raised his arms as though to clasp her; then they fell.

"What fates impose, that man must need abide."

She turned toward him. "I thought there was much to say. There is—nothing."

"Nothing for you; for me, something. It is to wish you all happiness, to assure you of my constant—friendship."

"And that is needless. We shall always be friends, warm friends, Mark. Let it be so. And—there is something more. I should not have written as I did of Paula; I had no right. But—since I am your friend, and you are mine——"

"We shall be. Even so, give me a little time."

His words were accompanied by a sardonic smile. The words and the smile silenced her. There was a pause.

"Has the Marquise forgiven me?" she asked at length.

"She will in time. By the way, I saw Adolphe. I hope he did not persecute———"

"No, no. He left that to his mama," she answered, laughing. "To Adolphe, as a cousin, I had no objection; but——"

"You have chosen more wisely," he said gravely. "I wish you happiness, Natalie." He held out his hand; she took it, her own trembling. "God bless you, Cousin." His lips brushed her cold cheek, then he was gone.

She watched him from the window; her face was very white, her hands tightly clenched. So she stood until he had passed from view, then she went upstairs. In the hall she passed Tabitha, who exclaimed: "You scared us all—yourself, too. You look like a ghost."

"Scared?" questioned Natalie.

"Riding like that."

"Like that! I wished the horse had wings."

"You'll have 'em if you don't take care, then——"

"Then I'll fly away." The intensity of her utterance made Tabitha stare. Natalie laughed aloud, and left her still staring.

Alone in her room, she paced slowly back and forth, struggling with her pride, crushing a forbidden and rejected love. So she regarded it. With a wrung heart, Mark had respected her decision, and in the depths of her soul she blamed him, scorning the puny passion so easily beaten. "Go to Paula," she had written, while "Come to me," her heart had cried so loudly that, except he were deaf, he might have heard.

When she had written her letter to Mark she had accomplished a bitter task only after a long and desperate struggle. She loved Leonard; she had said this to herself over and over again, and it was true; and to him she had given her troth freely, fully believing that for him there would be happiness and for her content. But the lowest depths of her soul had been stirred by the letter from Mark. There were chambers there that Leonard had not entered, could never enter, and into which she herself dared not look.

Self-sacrifice is to women alluring. That which she had made had been made, at least she so believed, with honest intention, yet, since now it was irrevocable, it was too hideous to contemplate. She would call him back, and on her knees——

Shameful thought! She was betrothed to a man she loved. Had she not admitted it? Not to him only, but shyly this very morning to the fond old woman to whom she owed so much, whose last days by that very admission were brightened by a glorious sunshine never before known in a long and gloomy life. Could she now, even if in her own eyes she could fall so low— could she fall so low in the eyes of these women by whom she was surrounded? In her aunt's eyes and Tabitha's? In Paula's, to whom, in loving loyalty, she had herself confided the secret? In those of Mrs. Joe, who had so carefully warned her from this preserve? No—to that depth she could not descend, not even to bask in the cold and passionless love of Mark.

The engagement was received with universal favor. It could hardly be otherwise, since all peculiarly interested were of that sex which dearly loves to contemplate a captive man, the only male (Leonard, of course, excepted) being Mark, whose attitude, being unsuspected, was ignored. And the bridegroom was the hero of all these women: the heir of Miss Claghorn; the one of the family to whom Tabitha was willing to ascribe all the virtues; regarded with affectionate esteem by Mrs. Joe, and, as to all except his denominational qualities, worshipped by Paula. As to the question of yoking believer and unbeliever, it had certainly occurred to all the devotees of the young theologian, but, aside from the certainty that truth must find its triumph in the union, the more pressing question of clothes for the approaching wedding left but little room in pious but feminine minds for other considerations. Events had so fallen in with Leonard's wishes that an early marriage was deemed advisable in Natalie's interest. Mr. Ellis Winter had encountered difficulty with regard to certain property in France belonging to her, and her presence in Paris was essential; and it was no less desirable that while there she be under the protection of a husband. For, aside from other considerations, marriage was the easiest solution of the complications which had arisen out of the guardianship of the Marquise, which guardianship would legally terminate with Natalie's marriage. And these things opened the way for Mark's return to Stormpoint.

"Urgent business" in San Francisco had precluded his attendance at the wedding. He wrote Leonard a cordial letter, and he sent to Natalie a ruby set in small diamonds, which, Tabitha Cone confidentially imparted to Miss Claghorn, was "mean for a billionaire," and which, even in the eyes of the latter lady, with whom the donor was a favorite, looked paltry. Both would have been surprised and even indignant at the man's folly, if they had known that he had bid against a crowned head to get the gem, employing a special agent, furnished with *carte blanche* for the purpose. Natalie knew better than they, but it was not of its purity or value that she thought, as she looked at the jewel long and steadfastly, until a mist of tears suddenly obscured her vision and struck terror to her soul.

CHAPTER XXII.

MAN WALKETH IN A VAIN SHADOW.

Soon after the departure for France of the newly married pair Mark returned from San Francisco. During his absence Mrs. Joe had not failed to call Mr. Hacket in consultation, and the adviser had reiterated the old counsel that the first step in a political career was "to get around and get acquainted." In order to induce her son to continue this preliminary course it became necessary to disclose her "policy."

Mark, though somewhat languid in the matter, displayed no violent reluctance to becoming a statesman. "As to the Presidency," he observed, laughing at his mother's lofty ambition, frankly disclosed, "that is the heaven of the politician, to be attained only by the elect."

"Nothing's impossible, Mark."

"There's a constitutional provision which will prevent my going in for it for some years. Meanwhile, we can investigate and learn how Presidents start. One ended as Justice of the Peace; I might try that as a beginning."

"A Justice of the Peace!"

"Why so scornful? It's aiming high. The usual course is to begin by carrying a banner and shouting."

"Mark, I've set my heart on this."

"My dear mother, blessed is the man or woman that has the wisdom to avoid that error."

"My son," said the lady reproachfully, "you seem without interest in anything."

"I am older, hence less enthusiastic, than you," he answered, smiling, and really believing, perhaps rightly, that, notwithstanding their relation, he felt older than she; "but advise me what to do, and I will do it. I am not unwilling to be a statesman, only——"

"I have told you——"

"To get about and get acquainted. Good! I'll start at once and collar the first voter I meet and demand his friendship." So, laughing, he left her, and within an hour Mrs. Joe saw him ride forth from the gates of Stormpoint.

During his long ride he admitted the reasonableness of his mother's ambition. Aside from the obstacle of great wealth, he was as eligible as another for usefulness and such laurels as come to those who honorably pursue a political career. He might smile at his mother's lofty dreams, yet they were not impossible of attainment; whereas, his own, in so far as they offered any allurement, were both unworthy and impossible. "A man should do something better than bewail his fate," he muttered; "since I cannot love elsewhere I'll be a lover of my country."

Greatly to Mrs. Joe's satisfaction, he thenceforward diligently pursued the preliminary requisite of getting around, in so far as that could be accomplished by long, solitary rides throughout the region. He seldom appeared at dinner without a gratifying account of the acquisition of a new rustic acquaintance, while meantime, the lady of Stormpoint saw to it that he did not remain unknown to such Hampton magnates as she could induce to grace her dinner table, displaying, in the matter of hospitality, a catholicity which surprised Paula and amused Mark, who, however, was quite willing to be amused.

Philosophers who have made the passion of love a subject of investigation (and most philosophers have given some attention to this branch of learning) have noticed that the violent death of an old love is often quickly followed by the birth of a new one. A jilted man or woman is Cupid's easiest prey.

Mrs. Joe may, or may not, have been aware of the truth of the above axiom, or its fitness in the case before her; but, having been fairly successful in interesting Mark in one object of her "policy," she resolved at this time to venture further and urge upon his attention the claims of Paula to his love; and, to her great delight, she found him not inattentive to the suggestion. He told his mother, truly enough, that he had a sincere affection for Paula, and admitted that she was, as far as was compatible with humanity, faultless; for it could hardly be a fault in Paula that he could feel no throb in his pulse, or glow in his bosom, when he recalled her to memory.

"You forget," he said, "that while I might find it easy to love her" (which he did not believe), "she might not find it easy to love me."

"You need have no fear." She was about to add that Paula would love anybody that loved her, but remembered in time that this might not be regarded as a recommendation. "She is the best creature I ever knew—almost perfect."

"I believe she is," he assented with a sigh, which was a tribute to Paula's perfection. "I fear she is too good for me."

"That's a strange objection."

"I am not so sure," he replied, as he lit a cigar, preparatory to leaving the room. But when he was gone, Mrs. Joe felt that he would consider the matter, and was content.

Unconsciously to herself, and, perhaps, without the knowledge of those by whom she was surrounded, Paula was somewhat harshly treated by nature; and that, notwithstanding her beauty. She was the embodiment of purity, of affection, of all the sweeter virtues, hence, regarded as wanting in those weaknesses which are essential to the symmetry of strength; one who lacks the everyday vices of temper, of selfishness, of jealousy, is, in some degree, abhorrent to our sense of the fitness of things. It is not that we envy the possessor of all the virtues—on the contrary, total absence of vice awakens something akin to contempt—but we are impatient of a non-combative disposition. The ideal Christian, offering the unsmitten cheek, presents a spectacle which, on Sundays, we characterize as sublime; the actual Christian, making such a tender, is, on any day, an object of scorn. Even of Paula, they who knew her would have admitted that it was possible to rouse her to resentment, possibly to a deed of vengeance, just as the worm may be made to turn; but, then, humanity refuses to admire worms in any attitude.

As Mark prosecuted the study of Paula, it gradually dawned upon him that it was interesting. From wondering whether there could be "much in her," he attained the conviction that, whether much or little, what there was was beyond his ken. "Paula," he asked one day, "are you as good as you look?"

"I don't know how good I look, Mark."

"Saintlike."

"Then I am not as good as I look; only I don't think I look as you say."

"Paula, you are a mystery. That's a great thing to be, is it not?" (Somehow, he could not help talking to Paula as if she were a child.) "Explain the mystery."

"Everybody is a mystery. Explain the mystery."

"Here is an unexpected depth," he exclaimed, with some surprise. "You have dared to raise a great question. Let us seek the solution at Grandfather Eliphalet's tomb."

The tomb, renovated and neatly railed by that which Miss Claghorn secretly regarded as the sacrilegious hand of Mrs. Joe, was near the extremity of the Point. When the weary Eliphalet had been laid there to rest it had been further inland, but the ever-pounding ocean was gradually having its way, day by day encroaching upon the domain of the seemingly indestructible rocks.

"The time will come," said Mark, as the two leaned upon the railing, "when the sea will claim old Eliphalet's bones."

"And the time will come when the sea will give up its dead," said Paula.

"Perhaps," he answered gloomily; "and to what end? You will answer, in order that the dead may be judged. I still ask, to what end?"

"That is the mystery, Mark."

"Not to be answered at Eliphalet's tomb, or elsewhere. Paula, did you ever hear of Deacon Bedott?"

"You know, Mark, there are so many deacons in Hampton——"

"This one lived in Slabtown, if I remember right. He was a character of fiction, neither very wise nor very entertaining; yet when Deacon Bedott lifted up his voice and spake, he formulated one of the Great Truths that man can know."

"What did he say?" she asked after a pause.

"We are all poor critters," was the answer, with a grim laugh. "Paula, I believe it is the only truth that really does come home to a man."

"It is from the Bible," she said simply.

He looked up. "Do you mean to assert that the Deacon was merely quoting? Are you going to destroy my faith in a pet philosopher; he who said all that Plato said, or Socrates, or Seneca—or anybody?"

"For man walketh in a vain shadow, and disquieteth himself in vain," she answered in a low tone.

There was silence for a moment; at length Mark said: "It seems that the Deacon was, after all, a plagiarist."

"I think that perhaps philosophers have discovered few truths concerning man that they might not have found in the Bible, and with less labor."

"Paula, do you believe the Bible?"

"Why, Mark! It is God's word."

"And these," he said, pointing to the trees, the crags, the sea; "are these God's word?"

"They are His creation; in that sense His word."

"And you and I, and these bones, crumbling a few feet below—these are all His creation, and so His word—and we know not what they say."

She looked at him surprised. She had often sorrowed that these things did not engage his attention; she was surprised to note his earnestness.

"Paula," he said, "do you know what you were made for?"

"Made for?"

"Leonard would tell you, 'to glorify God, and enjoy Him forever,'" he said, "but he would also inform you that the chance of the purpose of your creation coming to pass is slim."

"You know I do not subscribe to Leonard's creed," she replied a little severely.

"The thirty-nine articles, though less explicit, imply that which Leonard's creed has the boldness to state. Yes, Paula, that is the great and glorious Hope offered by the Church—damnation for the great majority."

"Mark, I do not think I ought to discuss these questions."

"You mean with a scoffer," he said a little bitterly.

"I hope you are not a scoffer. I cannot judge."

"And you decline to find out. Suppose I tell you in all honesty that I want to know the reasons for the faith that is in you. That I want to know them, so that I may try honestly to adopt them, if I find it possible—I don't say easy, Paula, I say possible. Suppose I assure you of this, as I do, will you aid me to be what you think I ought to be?"

"Mark," she answered, "I am not competent. Such a one as you should not come to such as I."

"Surely you have a reason for your belief! Is it not possible to put it into words?"

"Oh, Mark!" She turned and looked upon him; her eyes were brimming with tears; she placed her hand upon his arm. "I can help you; I will help you. I can direct you to one who can solve your doubts, who can make the truth so plain that you must see——"

"And this One is?' he asked reverently.

"Father Cameril."

He burst into a loud laugh which shocked and grieved her. She left him and went toward the house; he remained gazing at the tomb.

And there, if he had really contemplated seeking Paula's love, he buried the intention with Old Eliphalet. "If your eternal welfare is to your wife a matter to be handed over to her priest, your temporal felicity will hardly be of moment to her," he thought, as he looked at the smoke of his cigar hanging blue in the summer air.

CHAPTER XXIII.

A PARSON TREADS THE PRIMROSE PATH IN PARIS.

"Bel homme!" exclaimed the Marquise de Fleury admiringly.

"*Belle femme!*" echoed the hussar sadly.

"Be everything that is charming, Adolphe, I conjure you. So much depends upon Natalie's disposition."

From which brief conversation, which took place as the speakers left the hotel where the Leonard Claghorns were established, it may be correctly inferred that a friendly reception had been accorded the newly married pair by the French relatives of the bride. The noble lady, doubtless, felt all the affection for her former ward that she had, during the visit, so eloquently expressed, so that inclination prescribed the same course that policy would have indicated. The Marquise was still the custodian of property belonging to Natalie, and settlement of accounts could be much better adjusted in a spirit of indulgent friendship than in the cold and calculating spirit of business; and though Natalie and her dowry were gone forever, in that distant land whence she had returned with a husband, there were golden maids languishing for Marquises. "These Yankees," she observed to her son, "they sell their souls for money—the men; the women sell their bodies, and such soul as goes with them, for titles. Are you not a Marquis, of the *ancien regime?* It behooves us, my child, to be gracious to this wedded priest; he may know of a *partie.*"

"I am so, mama. *Du reste*, he is *beau garçon*, and seems amiable and amusing."

"Cultivate him, my infant; a voyage to America may be your destiny. It is a rich family—fabulous. There may be maids in plenty among these Claghorns."

The two young men, except for the pacific disposition of their womankind, might have been inclined to regard one another askance. For, in the person of the possessor of Natalie and her dowry the brave hussar saw one who however innocently, was still the ravisher of his rights; while in this being, in all the glory of fur and feather, sabretache and jangling sword, boots and buttons, braid and golden stripes, with a pervading tone of red and blue, Leonard beheld a startling and, at first, unpleasing creation. But the lieutenant, admonished by his mama, and sensible of the interests at stake, and genial by nature, thawed almost immediately, and the boulevardier and the theologian were friends.

To the young Frenchman a Protestant theologian was a philosopher, rather than a priest under vows, hence a person of liberal views and probably of lax conduct. As toward a newly married man, and warned incessantly by the Marquise, he recognized that etiquette required that from him no invitation to dissipation should emanate, but that his attitude ought to be that of willingness to pilot the stranger whithersoever he might wish to go; occasionally pointing out that paths of pleasantness were open to such as might choose to wander in them. And though Leonard displayed no undue disposition to such wanderings, an intimacy resulted which was not in fact, though seemingly, incongruous.

"What is he like, this beautiful heretic?" asked the Marquise.

"Like a Greek god, as you see, mama."

"But otherwise; he is a priest, you know?"

"And, like other priests, with an eye for a pretty woman."

"But discreet, Adolphe? I hope he is discreet."

"As St. Anthony! Natalie may be easy."

"Be you equally discreet, my child. She has been most generous; and, remember, Adolphe——"

"Yes, mama. What am I to remember?"

"That when a woman marries a man for his beauty, it is not love; it is infatuation. Do not permit this Leonarr to go astray; he has proclivities."

The little hussar laughed. "You are sharp-eyed, mamma."

"Had you watched him before the painting of Eve—but enough. Do nothing to cause disquiet to Natalie."

The little man, thus admonished, promised to carefully observe her wishes; the more readily as he was aware how important the friendship of Natalie was to his mama (in view of the pending adjustment of accounts). The more he studied Leonard, the more amusing he found him. To "do" Paris (not, indeed, to the extent of the capacity of that capital) in company with a priest, was, in itself, a piquant experience. "It is like demonstrating to your director how easy it is to sin," he declared; "and *ce bon Leonarr*, he imposes no penance. *Tiens!* These others, these Protestants, they have it easy."

"He does not essay to pervert," observed the Marquise in some alarm.

"Be not uneasy. Would I be of a religion whose priests marry? Think of the wife of my confessor knowing all my peccadillos!"

"Forgive me. My anxiety was but momentary——"

"Meanwhile, let me help this *pauvre garçon*, whose eyes have, since infancy, been bandaged, to see a little bit of the world. It is delightful to note his delight."

"But with discretion, Adolphe."

"Do I not assure you he is an anchorite. You have yourself observed that he drinks no wine."

"A penance, doubtless. Père Martin is also abstemious."

"As to *ordinaire*. In the presence of a flask of Leoville, I have noted a layman's thirst in *ce bon père*."

"Do not ridicule Père Martin, my infant. *Du reste*, it is not wine that I fear in the case of this beautiful Leonarr. Continue to be his guardian angel, my son."

Under this guardianship Leonard looked at Paris, enjoying his free sojourn in a great and brilliant city with hearty, but, on the whole, innocent fervor. The sunny skies, the genial good-humor, the eating and drinking, the frequent music, the lights, the dapper men, the bright-eyed women, the universal alertness—these impart a pleasant tingle to Puritan blood; and, if the novice to these delights be young, rosy, handsome, of exuberant health, and inclined to the pleasures befitting such conditions, he finds Paris grateful to the taste. In this congenial atmosphere Leonard basked in guileless rapture. A drive in the Bois with Natalie and the Marquise, brilliant equipages dashing by, brilliant eyes flashing as they passed, was a rare delight; a stroll on the Boulevard was even more enjoyable, for here were more flashing eyes and smiling faces, less fleeting, and often coquettishly inviting an answering glance. Clothed in the results of the meditations of de Fleury's tailor, it became Leonard's frequent habit to haunt the Boulevards, indulging in a strut that would have astonished Hampton; and often was he inclined to envy the Marquis that lot which had made his abiding place among these joys. It would have been fine to be a soldier, fine to fight and win glory; to wear boots and spurs and a clanking sword, and to trail the same along the pavement as one to the manner born!

Of course, that was a day-dream, which he laughed at as easily as an older man might have done, though less scornfully. There was no great harm in day-dreams, however foolish. This whole existence had the character of a pleasant dream. Had he not felt it so, he often mentally averred, he would have accepted it more gravely.

"But it will soon be over," he said to Natalie. "It is my first holiday since I was a boy."

"Enjoy it all you can. I am glad that Adolphe has been able to make your stay pleasant."

"Really, a very amiable little fellow. French, you know, and rather lax in his views, I fear; but——"

"His views will not harm you," interrupted Natalie, smiling.

"Certainly not," he replied, a little stiffly. "It would be strange if I could not take care of myself. Meanwhile, M. de Fleury is really of great advantage to me in one respect."

"And that is?"

"I am improving wonderfully in French. That's a good thing, Natalie, a very good thing." He was quite solemn on this point.

"An excellent thing," she replied, somewhat surprised at the gravity with which he treated a matter of no great importance. "I wish, Leonard, that my affairs were concluded. I am sure you are being kept here against your wish."

"Whatever my wish, your affairs ought to come first. Let us be content that, if they do drag, I can employ the time in self-improvement."

Thus, in the praiseworthy pursuit of improvement Leonard spent much of his time. He was by no means neglectful of his wife, whose attendance, with the Marquise, was much in demand in official bureaus, and who encouraged his intimacy with the lieutenant, whom she no longer found unendurable, and whose amiable and forgiving conduct had won her heart. "They are not rich, you know," she said. "Entertain the little man all you can; the Marquise was very kind to me." An injunction which afforded another reason why it was incumbent on Leonard to procure the Marquis the distractions that he loved, in so far as purse and principle permitted, and these were found elastic.

Because, as he was forced to admit when arguing with the Marquis, a reasonable elasticity is not only proper, but essential to culture.

"*Mon bon*," observed the lieutenant, "the view you advance is narrow. The ballet, as a favorite spectacle of the people, should be studied by every student of morals. You, as a preacher——"

Leonard laughed. "I'm not a preacher; I'm an instructor in a college of divinity."

"*Eh bien!* The greater reason. How shall one teach the good, knowing not the evil? *Du reste*, are they evil, *ces belles jambes* of Coralie? They are fine creations, of pure nature; there is no padding."

"You will be my guest, if we go?"

"Since you insist; also to a *petit souper, a parti carré*, with Aimée and Louise. Coralie! *Sapristi*, no! Her maw is insatiable; the little ones are easily pleased."

And so Leonard studied unpadded nature, even going alone a second, and perhaps a third time. As to the *petit souper*, it had been decorous; and beyond the fact that Mesdemoiselles Aimée and Louise were agreeable ladies with excellent appetites, his knowledge of these damsels did not extend.

Of course, there were pursuits of a different character to engage his attention, and those which occurred under the guidance of the lieutenant were exceptional. There were the usual sights to be seen; galleries, monuments, churches, all to be wondered at, criticised and admired. Leonard approved generally, though, as to the churches, their tawdry interiors and the character of their embellishments offended his taste, as well as his religious sentiments. If, during these distractions, he was neglectful of the religious instruction which he knew his wife needed, circumstances were, to some extent, at fault. He could hardly expound doctrinal truths in a picture gallery, much less in a temple of Roman error. And, though not without qualms, he admitted to himself that he had little desire to discuss religion. There was, perhaps, no heinous sin in looking at the leg-gyrations of Mademoiselle Coralie, nor was Leonard the first wandering clergyman to embrace an offered opportunity to study ethics from the standpoint of that rigid moralist, the Marquis de Fleury; nevertheless, such studies had their effect in cooling religious fervor, and fervor is essential to him who would expound truth, with a view to compel conviction.

Finally, as bearing on this question of the doctrinal instruction of his wife, he doubted whether it was worth while. Knowledge of doctrine was no adornment in women; there was Paula, whose pretensions in this regard constituted almost her only defect. Since Natalie was probably saved, why trouble himself and her with the exposition of mysteries which she would be unable to comprehend, and concerning which the injunction was laid that they be "handled with especial care." If she had heard the call it would be effectual; if she had not been born to salvation, all the doctrine which had been taught since the days of the fathers would not—and here his self-communing stopped. Damnation, though inevitable, is not an alluring subject of contemplation when it affects one's family.

The complications attendant on Natalie's affairs prolonged the stay in Paris far beyond the period originally contemplated; but French method on one side of the Atlantic, and Mr. Winter on the other, were finally satisfied, after much passing to and fro of documents. Everybody interested was weary, and consular clerks had come to loathe the names of Natalie, Eugenie, Louise, Susan Beverley de Fleury Claghorn-Claghorn, *née* de Fleury-Claghorn. As Leonard said, to be enabled to give the Marquise a receipt in full was a harder job than to negotiate a treaty. But it was done at last; Natalie had been resolute and Mr. Winter had protested in vain; the Marquise had her discharge and, relieved of many terrors, was duly grateful. "She has been charming, truly considerate," she observed to her son. "Alas, Adolphe; it was a great loss."

"There are others," replied the Marquis philosophically.

"Heaven send it so. You must no longer delay speaking seriously to this good Leonarr, who might have influenced his wife to be the ogress desired by the abominable Winter. Urge him to look out for a *partie* as soon as he arrives in America. I will speak to Natalie. I have heard her mention two demoiselles, Achsah and Tabitha."

"*Ciel!* The appellations."

"But if the bearers are rich?"

"*Tiens!* mama. Madame Zho and *la belle* Paula are in London. I might try there; it is not so far."

"But *ce gros* Marc is with them. Paula is for him, as you know."

"He does not hurry himself, and truly I believe the little one would not be averse to me."

"Better depend upon Monsieur Leonarr."

And as a result of his mama's advice the lieutenant did, on that afternoon, broach the matter to Leonard, who, at first mystified, ended by roaring with laughter when he grasped the fact that the head of the House of de Fleury was making a provisional proposal for the hand and fortune of either Mademoiselle Tabitha, or Mademoiselle Achsah, as Leonard might advise.

"*Diable!*" exclaimed the gallant youth, when Leonard had explained the cause of his hilarity, "over seventy and rich! What a country where such opportunities are neglected! Decidedly I must make the voyage."

Leonard made no reply; the suggested picture of the noble Marquis as his guest in Hampton was not precisely alluring.

"And so there is not a single demoiselle among the Claghorns that desires a title?"

"Not one."

"Alas!" sighed the Marquis. "I was too magnanimous. You know *la belle* Paula, of course. Listen, *mon ami*, but let your lips be sealed. *Elle etait folle de moi!*"

"Paula! Crazy for you! You flatter——"

"*Parole d'honneur*. It was in her eyes, in the plaintive cadence of her tones——"

"But——"

"I know—*ce polisson de Marc, toujours Marc*. Ah, the luck of this Marc! He has a mine of gold; he will have the charming Paula. Only you, *mon bon*, have beaten him. After all, it is for Marc and me to mingle our tears."

"What do you mean by that?" asked Leonard sharply. "Why are you and Mark to mingle your tears?"

"For the reason, *mon cher*, that we love to weep," replied the hussar, with an odd glance at Leonard. "Adieu, I have an appointment," and he turned abruptly down a side street, leaving Leonard astonished at his quick retreat.

"Pshaw!" he exclaimed, after a moment. "It's absurd!" Then he pursued his way homeward.

CHAPTER XXIV.

TO HIM I WILL BE HENCEFORTH TRUE IN ALL THINGS.

Mrs. Joe and her train were in London, whither Mark had been summoned on business; and ever since Madame de Fleury had become aware of the fact she had urged the party to visit Paris. The Marquise, notwithstanding her sex, was not devoid of curiosity, and, aside from other advantages which might accrue to her from the presence of the lady of Stormpoint, she was anxious that a puzzle which had not a little mystified her be elucidated. When Mark had visited her after his chance meeting with Adolphe in the cafe, she had divined his feeling with regard to Natalie, and had at once jumped to the conclusion that it explained the flight of her ward. She recalled the intimacy which had existed between the cousins during the lifetime of the philosopher, an intimacy which she had gravely disapproved, and concerning which she had more than once remonstrated. She remembered, too, with vexation and a sense of injury, that the philosopher had soothed her solicitude for the interests of her son, by pleading the cousinly customs of Mark's country, as well as by pointing out the benefit which might accrue to her son by an increased dowry for his own daughter. Now all these hopes and rosy possibilities were extinguished; Natalie had appeared on the scene with a husband who was not Mark, and Mark and Paula were still unwed. These were all puzzling facts out of which there might be gathered some advantage for Adolphe. She had concealed from him the hopes which sometimes rose within her in contemplating the present state of affairs; but she was very anxious to know what that state portended. She had tried in vain to extract information from Natalie, and as to Leonard, the matter required delicate handling. Such inquiries as she had addressed to him had been of necessity vague, and from his answers she had derived no satisfaction. He had sometimes idly wondered what the lady was after, but until the allusion by the Marquis to a mutual mingling of tears by Mark and himself, Leonard had barely given the matter a thought. He understood now what the Marquis had implied, and saw the drift of the maternal questioning. He was annoyed, but only for a moment; he dismissed the subject as being of equal importance with the hussar's idea of Paula's infatuation for himself, concerning which he had no belief whatever.

After the lieutenant had left him, Leonard pursued his way homeward, vaguely oppressed by a sense of gloom which he attributed to the weather, which had become lowering. He was near the Church of St. Roch when a shower drove him inside its portals for shelter.

A few sightseers were wandering about the edifice; an occasional penitent occupied a chapel with lips close to the grating, on the other side of which was the ear of the absolver; in the body of the church a number knelt in prayer.

He looked at these things with curiosity, not unmingled with scorn. His attention was attracted by a plainly dressed woman standing in a side aisle; to his surprise, he recognized his wife.

She did not see him as he softly approached her. A sunbeam breaking through the clouds outside shone through a window and lit up her face, displaying to him a new expression, a look of yearning and of love which beautified it; a look he had never seen before; he recognized the fact with a vague sense of pain.

That which he saw, like that which he felt, was but momentary. She turned, looking at him at first with an abstracted gaze, then startled, as though waking from a dream. "Leonard!" she exclaimed in a low voice. It sounded like fear.

"Even so, my dear. Why are you here alone?"

"I—I—don't know. I was tired."

"Has this spectacle moved you so?" He pointed to the worshippers.

"No, not that. I wish I were as good as they; I have watched them often."

"Often?" he repeated. He was somewhat indignant at that wish, that she, his wife, were as good as these idolaters; but it was plain that she was deeply moved by something, and he was very tender. "Do you come here often?"

"I have done so, Leonard." There was humility in her tone, there was confession; had he known it, there was a cry for aid.

"Natalie," he said, with some reproach for her, and feeling not a little for himself, "I hope you are not attracted by the glitter of Romanism. Surely you can pray in your closet!"

"I do not pray in the churches," she said. "I did not know that my visits to them would annoy you."

"Not at all, my dear," he replied. "I can understand that you like to enjoy the architectural beauties and the solemn influence. But upon me the crucifixes, the holy water, the vestments—in short, the frippery—these things have a less agreeable effect. They savor of gross superstition."

It was true that she did not pray in the churches. Something restrained her; perhaps the very memories which had invited her to these wanderings in dim shadows where so many vain aspirations had been breathed. Sometimes as she would pass a chapel where knelt a penitent, confessing to a hidden priest, a strong desire would come upon her to do as the penitent was doing. Yet why? Even to herself she had not yet admitted that she had aught to confess.

They strolled slowly toward their hotel, Leonard silently reproaching himself that he had not sooner discovered and prevented this habit of haunting churches, a habit which might lead to lamentable results in one easily influenced by the external pomp and circumstance of Romanism.

However, any danger that might exist would soon be passed. Before long they would be far beyond the subtle influences of priesthood, as well as other subtle influences which he felt were not altogether healthful. He sighed, a little regretfully; after all, pleasure was sweet.

There had been some question whether they should await the possible arrival of Mrs. Joe. The discussion of this subject had been confined to himself and the Marquise, Natalie having displayed but a faint interest in the matter. Only that morning Madame de Fleury had informed him that the lady of Stormpoint had written to say that she and her party would come to Paris for a short stay and then accompany the Leonard Claghorns homeward. He was therefore surprised when Natalie suddenly exclaimed, "Leonard, let us go home!"

"Do you mean we should not wait for Mrs. Joe?" he asked.

"Why should we? She has Paula and the maids."

"And Mark. He counts for something," suggested Leonard, laughing.

"Of course; and if we wait for them, the waiting will never end. The Marquise will do all she can to keep them, and Paris is not so easily left. I foresee more difficulty in getting away gracefully, should they arrive while we are here, than if we go at once."

"We can pass through London and explain," he suggested.

"Let us go by Havre. I long to get away, and you ought to be home. I will write to Mrs. Joe. Let us decide now."

She was strangely insistent, even agitated. He noticed it and assumed that she was depressed at the thought of leaving that which was her own country, and longed to get a painful separation over. To him it was a matter of indifference by what route they traveled, so long as Mrs. Joe's susceptibilities were not wounded; and Natalie, assuring him that her written explanation would prevent that misfortune, the matter was settled.

He kissed her as they entered their apartment; for a moment she held her face close to his.

That night, being alone and prostrate upon the floor of her room, where she had sunk, humiliated and ashamed, she uttered a vow to heaven:

"To him I will be henceforth true in all things; in thought as in deed. Help me, heaven, to atone, by surrendering to him and in his service every act and every thought."

CHAPTER XXV.

MRS. JOE ON CLERICAL BUMPTIOUSNESS AND MRS. FENTON'S SHOULDERS.

The family of Stormpoint remained abroad until long after Leonard and his wife were established in the old Morley mansion in Hampton, finally returning to America without Mark, who remained in England, ostensibly on business connected with the Great Serpent. He had done nothing to advance his mother's wishes with regard to Paula, assuming that the lady had by this time recognized the futility of her hopes, and like the wise woman he knew her to be, had become reconciled to the inevitable. She was even wiser than he knew, and a part of her wisdom was to trust to the future. She would admit defeat when she found herself defeated, meanwhile acquiescing to all seeming in things as they were, placidly listening to Paula's confidences as to that celibate sisterhood which the damsel hoped some day to found, but which, as Mrs. Joe said to herself, was not founded yet.

Mark had extracted a promise both from his mother and from Paula that their letters should contain "all the news of all the Claghorns," meaning perhaps Mrs. Leonard Claghorn; and when the first letter came from his mother he opened it eagerly and read: first a great deal of political advice (at second hand from Mr. Hacket), and toward the end of the epistle, matter of greater interest.

"As to Leonard" (wrote the lady), "I fear marriage has not improved him. Natalie makes the mistake of coddling him too much. Her notion of wifely duty is extravagant. In their house a thousand things are done for Leonard's comfort, all thought of by his wife, and her eyes follow him about as though she were constantly on the watch to anticipate his wants. She is very quiet in manner and seems rather to wish to echo Leonard's opinions than to have opinions of her own; all of which has other than a pleasing effect on Leonard. I suppose, too, that he has arrived at an age (somewhat late in his case) in which the fact of his own manliness is the most important fact of existence. He has not been improved by contact with quite another world than that of Hampton, the world of Adolphe de Fleury, in which he seems to have mingled rather surprisingly. One would hardly recommend the allurements of Paris in such companionship to a young theologian. You know the angels in Paradise fell, though I do not mean to imply that Paris is paradise, or Leonard an angel, fallen or otherwise; but his engaging innocence is gone; perhaps it was inevitable. I am sorry to see in its place an undue amount of the bumptiousness often affected by members of his profession. It is quite distressing to think that he should degenerate, he who was so beautiful to look at, so gentle, yet so strong—in short, so naturally refined—a word, by the way, which I dislike, but it expresses the idea. He is not so refined as he was; he is less pleasing to the eye, there is a shadow of something in his face which I do not like—and I do *not* like the way with which he looks at Paula.

"There, Mark, I have been long in coming to it—but you are not to misunderstand me. I don't believe Leonard has a thought which could be regarded as injurious to Natalie, but I don't think he regards feminine beauty with the eyes one likes to see. I gave a little dinner a few evenings since; only the Stanleys, the Fentons, Father Cameril and the Leonard Claghorns. You remember Mrs. Fenton's style; her shoulders (very beautiful they are—I say shoulders) too much in evidence for my taste. Leonard hardly took his eyes off of them. Father Cameril, on the contrary, hardly knew what to do with his to avoid seeing them, and I don't know which of the pair made me most angry. I remember when Leonard would have been oblivious of shoulders.

"He is rather truculent, too, is Mr. Leonard, and fell foul of poor Father Cameril in a manner which roused even Paula, on the subject of the Apostolic Succession—in short, I never saw him at such a disadvantage, and I'm afraid my indignation has carried my pen away.

"Natalie is lovely. A little sad at times. She confided to me a secret which no doubt accounts for her rather noticeable pensiveness. There will be a baby in the old Morley house before the year is out."

Mark pondered over his mother's letter often, and with more misgiving than behooved a man interested in his neighbor only in ordinary neighborly fashion. He did full justice to his mother's shrewd observation, and believed that her letter was intended to convey more than appeared on the surface, and his self-communings in reference thereto were not cheerful.

CHAPTER XXVI.

INTRODUCES DR. STANLEY, SATAN AND THE PRAYER MEETING OF MATRONS.

Mrs. Leonard Claghorn had been graciously received by the matrons of Hampton. She was so interesting (they said), so foreign; and careful cross-examination of those who had penetrated into the inner sanctuaries of the Morley mansion had established the fact that there was not a crucifix in the house. On the whole, the matrons were content. Surely, the wife of a young professor, so thoroughly grounded in the faith as was Leonard—though his prominence in the Seminary, in view of his youth, might be deprecated by some—such a one could not remain heretical, even if her religious education had been defective. How awfully defective these excellent ladies did not know.

On her part, Natalie had been no less gracious. "She'll be one of them in a year," said Mrs. Joe, alluding to the matrons. "She'll be whatever Leonard says."

"I wish Father Cameril could talk with her," sighed Paula.

"He lost his chance when he contradicted Leonard at my dinner."

"She certainly is very loyal to her husband," admitted Paula.

"Altogether too subservient," observed Mrs. Joe testily. "No woman should permit her whole nature to be absorbed in that manner. No wonder he's bumptious."

"Bumptious!"

"Conceited. Pliancy, Paula, is a virtue in a wife. I was pliant myself; still the most devoted of wives ought to have an opinion of her own."

"Natalie is so sweet," urged the extenuating Paula.

"Sweet! So are you; so was I; so was Tabitha Cone to the man that gave her that monstrous watch—but sweetness may be sickening."

"Oh, Cousin Alice!"

"It irritates me, because it's not Natalie's true character. She had a mind of her own once, and a good one. Actually, she's superior to Leonard——"

"He's a very brilliant man, Cousin."

"To look at, and glib; but inferior to his wife. Men generally are. Yet she effaces herself. She overdoes her loyalty. She is playing a part!"

"Cousin Alice!" remonstrated Paula.

"I don't mean she's consciously a hypocrite, and you needn't flare. She's imbibed some absurd notions of wifely duty, and is trying to carry them out."

An impression made upon an observer as keen as Mrs. Joe must have a foundation. In her irritation the lady had expressed the truth. Natalie was playing a part.

Since the day in St. Roch when she, recalling a day long past, had lost herself in a dream of what might have been—since then she had been playing a part, the part of a penitent; the role she had assumed when later, in humiliation and conscience-stricken, she had prostrated herself before heaven, vowing the only atonement possible.

She had seen the beginning of that change in Leonard which remained a cause of irritation to Mrs. Joe; nor had she been ignorant of the influences to which it was in part to be ascribed; but her conscience had whispered that in very truth the effect of those influences was to be attributed to herself. In her marriage an essential element had been absent, and was wanting still. To complete that holy mystery and adorn it with its rarer graces, to tinge its atmosphere with consecrated incense, there must be spiritual union. If Leonard had not learned of nobler joys than the lesser gratification that engaged his thoughts, was it not because such joys had not been offered?

To those religious teachings which had been deferred she now looked forward as to the means whereby both could attain to that higher union which she craved, and which when attained would surely soothe her troubled spirit and aid in that atonement prescribed by her conscience and which she had vowed, and of which the subservience disapproved by Mrs. Joe was a minor manifestation. So, though timidly, for his reluctance (so strange to her) was apparent, she sought to bring Leonard to discussion of religious subjects.

"Was Jonathan Edwards a great man?" she asked one day, and then regretted her question, for at that passage of arms which had occurred at Mrs. Joe's table, Father Cameril had mentioned the name, a fact forgotten until it was recalled to her memory by the lowering brow of Leonard.

"A great man, indeed!" he answered; "an apostle of truth. Chattering imbeciles like Father Cameril may tell you differently."

"I was not thinking of Father Cameril. I read the title of your article, 'Jonathan Edwards, a Man Athirst for God.'"

"So he was; and one who slaked his thirst at the well of knowledge. A great and good man, Natalie, though shallow reasoners are glad to deny the merit of the greatest of metaphysicians. The truth is they're afraid of him."

"Why afraid?"

"Because his logic is inexorable, the unassailable truth he utters not lovely to all hearers. Edwards declines to abate one jot or tittle of God's message. It has become the fashion even among men of greater intellect than Mr. Cameril has been endowed with to avoid Edwards, but——"

"I should think all would crave the truth. I would like to read him."

"Not now," he said, kissing her. "Dr. Stanley advises steering clear of Edwards," he continued, laughing, "though not for the usual reasons. You must follow the fashion for awhile, Natalie."

He knew that public opinion would expect, and in time demand, his wife's union with the church. Had she been trained from childhood in orthodox tenets her preparedness for the sacrament would have been presumed, and, at some convenient season, when souls are garnered as crops are garnered, it being assumed that they ripen like the fruits of the earth, she would have been duly gathered to the fold with those other members of the congregation whose time for experiencing religion had come. But there was no presumption of early instruction in Natalie's case.

He would have been better pleased if his position had not required deference to that opinion which would demand Natalie's entrance into the doctrinal fold. If she were chosen for salvation, what difference could it make whether she was instructed as to the Confession or not? Where were the women that were so instructed? Nowhere. They had some phrases and some faint recollection of Sabbath-school lessons, but as to any real knowledge of the mysteries they professed, he knew that the laymen of his denomination were in general as ignorant as those puppets of the Romish priesthood who left such matters to their betters. And secretly he regarded this as the correct system. He was not sorry that he had a valid excuse for avoiding domestic theological discussion in the dictum of Dr. Stanley.

The doctor, who had been present on the occasion when Leonard had fallen foul of Father Cameril, and who had been amused at the husband's truculence, had also noted the anxious look of the wife. He had known Leonard almost since boyhood and liked him; he was, for reasons of his own, especially interested in Leonard's wife.

Doctor Stanley's position in Hampton was not unlike that of Satan in the world. He was endured of necessity and his services called in requisition, because in certain straits there was no getting along without him. "The parsons don't want to go to heaven," he would say, "any more than the rest of us, so when they're sick they call me in, and when they're well they smile on me; but, if I weren't a doctor, Hampton would be too hot to hold me." All of which, if true, was because Dr. Stanley was troubled with a theological itch of his own, and, though calling God the "Unknowable," claimed knowledge with as much confidence as his orthodox rivals, and with equal truculence. He was at some disadvantage in his public onslaughts on Hamptonian strongholds, since his followers were few; but at occasional lectures, the meagre proceeds whereof went to sustain a Mechanics' Library, founded by the doctor for the behoof of philosophical plumbers and carpenters, he sometimes charged upon the foe with great gallantry, if but little effect. In his private capacity he was genial, amiable and good-hearted, and, if hated as an infidel, was loved as a man. As a physician, the general faith in his skill was nearly unbounded.

His wife, who laughed at him and loved him, was that Lettie Stanley of whose ultimate salvation Miss Claghorn had grave doubt. She was, if unhappily "passed by," still of the elect race, and Miss Achsah, on the occasion of her union with the doctor, had expressed the opinion that the Reverend Josias Claghorn, father of the unfortunate, had celebrated the nuptials by turning in his grave. It was not known that she was, like her husband, an absolute unbeliever, since she sometimes appeared at public worship, and there were among the ladies of Hampton one or two who maintained that she was a pious woman. However, it was certain that she was heterodox, a grievous circumstance which gave great and just cause of offense to these descendants of the original seekers after liberty of conscience. She was active in charitable work, and though admitted to the Shakespeare Society, was not a member of any of the distinctly denominational organizations. She had been invited to the "Thursday Prayer Meeting of Matrons," and had declined, flippantly, the matrons proclaimed, and on the ground that though she was willing to be prayed for, she did not wish to be prayed at. For the rest, she was a handsome woman of middle age, with large, tender eyes and a cheery disposition, tinged with a certain melancholy, which some called cynicism.

This lady had also noted with disapproval Leonard's manner on the occasion of Mrs. Joe's dinner. "He's getting spoiled," she had observed to her husband, as they left the hospitable mansion.

"Theological manner," replied the doctor. "They can't help it. Cameril would have been as bad, if he dared. What do you think of Leonard's wife?"

"A beautiful woman, who adores her husband. I wonder why her eyes are sad?"

"Her eyes are like yours."

"Pshaw, Doctor; I'm an old woman——"

"That's nonsense. She not only resembles you as to eyes, but in disposition."

"Of course you know all about her disposition."

"It's my business to know. Mrs. Leonard's my patient, and her idiosyncrasies——"

"Are doubtless interesting, as pertaining to a handsome woman; but how do they resemble mine?"

"She's a religious enthusiast."

"Well!" ejaculated the lady; "after years of observation that is your wise conclusion. I won't say tell that to the marines, which would be undignified, but tell it to the Hampton matrons."

"The matrons of Hampton know nothing of religion; they're theologians."

The lady laughed. "If she is really like I was at her age, I am sorry for her. Had I married a man like Leonard——"

"My dear, with your excellent taste you did much better; but I thought Leonard was a favorite of yours."

"I like him, but I detest his creed."

"You don't suppose he believes it?"

"He says he does, which is of more consequence."

"How can any human being believe the Westminster Confession?"

"I don't suppose any human being does. It's a question of obstinacy, pride; a question of being caught in a trap."

The doctor laughed.

"You, my dear," continued the lady, "lack religious sentiment. You don't care. I cannot help being indignant when I see religion desecrated by religionists. It may be from the same feeling that I am sorry for a woman who adores her husband, and who must eventually find him out."

"Find him out! My dear——"

"I mean find out that he's not all that she has pictured. Leonard is a very ordinary mortal."

"But, on the whole, a very good fellow."

"Undoubtedly, but—a theologian of Hampton. I don't think you appreciate all that that may chance to mean to a woman you are pleased to call a religious enthusiast—meaning, I suppose, a woman who really craves religion."

"You must not take a word too seriously. The fact is that Mrs. Leonard has what may be termed an exalted temperament. One day I found her in tears and with traces of great agitation. She had been reading a book of ecstatic

character. I hinted to Leonard that just now that sort of thing wouldn't do—
—"

"You were quite right. I remember that I suffered——"

"I don't mean to say that the lady had been suffering; on the contrary, I think she'd been having a good time. The book, by the way, was the life of some Roman saint—but good times of that sort are not to be indulged in by a lady about to have a baby."

"What did Leonard say?"

"Oh, he was amenable—more so than I expected. Of course, I said nothing about the Catholic book. Leonard is like prospective fathers, easily scared. They are much more tractable than prospective mothers; so I scared him."

The more easily that Leonard had been willing to be scared.

CHAPTER XXVII.

THE MUSIC OF THE CHORUS OF THE ANGUISH OF THE DAMNED.

"Socrates," observed Miss Achsah, "is damned."

"If *you* say so, he must be," was the sarcastic rejoinder of Tabitha Cone.

Miss Claghorn, with a stern gaze at her companion, opened Hodge's Commentary on The Confession of Faith and read: "'The heathen in mass, with no single, definite and unquestioned example on record, are evidently strangers to God and going down to death in an unsaved condition.' That," she said, "settles Socrates."

It did not settle Tabitha, whose question touched the weak spot in Hodge's assertion. "Where'd he see the record?" she asked.

"Tabitha," remonstrated Miss Achsah with evident sincerity, "sometimes I doubt your election. The audacity of setting up *your* opinion——"

Tabitha was human and venerated print. She was a little frightened at her own temerity, and Miss Claghorn's seriousness did not tend to reassure her. "There's Brigston," she said weakly.

"Yes; and there's 'Greenland's Icy Mountains,' and 'India's Coral Strand,'" answered the lady pertinently, and closing the book and the discussion.

But, if closed at the White House, it raged furiously in the theological world. Until recently the permanent abode of Socrates had been as well known as that of Satan. No decree, whether of Roman or Protestant Pope, had been needed to establish a fact settled to the satisfaction of all (except, perhaps, to that of the Athenian sage) by the Eternal Decree of Omnipotence. It was reserved for a deluded doctor of the rival Seminary of Brigston to promulgate doubts of a self-evident truth. Such an affront to Westminster and the immutable justice of God was not to be borne in silence by Hampton.

A storm of unexampled fury burst from theological clouds, and Leonard, sniffing the odor of battle, joyously saw that his day had dawned. Into the fray he plunged, a gallant knight armed with the sword of orthodoxy, battling in the name of God and by the lurid light of hell, in order that the music of the chorus of the anguish of the damned might still arise, a dulcet melody, to heaven.

And while the din of the holy war filled the air, Natalie welcomed a little babe, the light of whose clear blue eyes melted her soul in tenderness. To look into their celestial purity was to see heaven's glory reflected in the azure depths. The deeper springs of tenderness, closed to the rude touch of

Leonard's passion, were opened, and love undefiled gushed forth in a stream of unspeakable gladness. Her health remained delicate, and she was long confined to the house, but, aside from a pleasant languor, being physically at ease, she found in the care of the infant sufficient occupation. She was glad that she could be much alone with the boy, and held many and sweet communings with that soul she had discovered in his eyes. She never wearied of reading the mystery of those clear depths and, always connecting the child with heaven, in her simple belief, imagining the newcomer as lately from that blissful region, she built upon her fancies a system of theology which would have startled and confounded the Hampton Matrons. And, as before, in sight of the grandeur of God upon the waters, Leonard's lower self had been humbled, so now, the beauty of a pure soul, all its glory set forth in motherhood, chastened his earthly nature, and he bowed with the reverence of simple souls to saints.

Leonard's creed was, as is the case with creeds, a matter apart from his life; wherefore there was nothing strange in the fact that he could leave the presence of the two pure creatures, and retiring to his study, damn countless souls to hell in essays of exceeding force and brilliancy. Young as he was, all Hampton gloried in these labors whereby Brigston was smitten and abashed. There were champions more learned, being older; but, being older, their pens were encumbered with caution and hampered by the knowledge that pitfalls and traps lurk in the dark thickets of theological controversy. But Leonard had the daring of youth. Logic was logic, and truth not for a day, but eternal. Truth led to the Westminster Confession, which damns the great majority, Socrates included. To quibble with the plain meaning of plain words would be to follow the heretical Brigstonian, to deny the inspiration of Scripture, to be a traitor to his party and his creed. If the same decree which damned Socrates consigned the great majority of his own friends and acquaintances to the same everlasting misery, it couldn't be helped. And, in fact, there was no reason why Leonard should shrink from that which thousands of men and women profess to believe, yet marry and bring forth children doomed, the while eating dinner in content.

Echoes of the merry war reached Natalie, but her curiosity was but faintly stirred. She saw that Leonard avoided the topic when alone with her, and was now content to learn nothing from her husband; seeing in her child her best teacher in heavenly lore. Her exhibition of maternal love extorted some disapproving comment; Mrs. Joe called it "uncanny," Tabitha said she was a queer mother, Miss Claghorn disapprovingly likened her adoration to Romanism—"Idolatry," she said to Tabitha.

"Yet," replied Tabitha, "she hardly ever hugs or kisses him. She just looks at him, and if you catch her at it she passes it off."

"Just as you or I might if the cook were to come in while we were saying our prayers."

"Something 'ill happen to the child," said Tabitha ominously.

Miss Claghorn did not dispute it; the two were so perfectly in accord as to their sentiment in this matter that there was no chance for dispute.

Thus, in a strange, secret relation, mother and child lived more than a year together, and then Tabitha Cone's oracular prophecy was fulfilled. Something happened to the child, which something was death; and Natalie was stricken as by a thunderbolt.

The most alarming phase of her illness was of short duration; she had been long unconscious, and during that period they who watched her had noticed, with something akin to awe, the heavenly peacefulness and sweet smile of her face. From her mutterings they gathered that she roamed in celestial regions with her boy. Dr. Stanley was evidently not favorably impressed with these supposed visions, and as soon as it was feasible ordered her removal to Stormpoint, where the sun shone brighter than in the old house, and where there would be fewer reminders of her loss.

Leonard, who had been severely stricken by the death of the child and worn with anxiety on his wife's account, acquiesced. The complete change of scene which the physician desired involved his absence from her side. "Of course you'll visit her daily, if you choose," said the doctor, "but if you are constantly together she will inevitably talk of the child and of heaven, and we must keep her away from heaven." Natalie remonstrated, but rather feebly. Since the birth of the child Mrs. Joe had seen less cause to complain of undue absorption in the husband by the wife. Thus, to keep Natalie from contemplation of heaven, Leonard returned to contemplation of hell; for the war still raged, though with some slackness. Leonard girded up his loins and prepared to inject the spirit which had somewhat diminished during his own absence from the lines of battle.

The mistress of Stormpoint watched her new inmate keenly. "It's natural that she should love her child, even though he's dead," she said to Paula, "but she talks with him. I heard her."

"Her faith is perfect," exclaimed Paula with solemn enthusiasm. "She knows he lives forever."

"That's all very well; but he don't live at Stormpoint."

"She feels his presence, though she cannot see him."

"She says she does. Of course, it's fiddlesticks; but the doctor ought to know."

And the doctor, being informed, agreed with Mrs. Joe that conversation with angels was not to be encouraged. "A very little roast beef and a great deal of fresh air," was his prescription, "A trip somewhere when she is stronger. Meanwhile, keep bores away—Father Cameril and Leonard."

"I can't lock Leonard out."

"I wish you could; he has a grievance and may be tempted to unburden his soul to his wife."

"I have heard of no grievance."

"You will; the reaction has come. Yesterday they crowned him with laurels; to-day they are damning him—of course, in parliamentary phrase—from the president of the Seminary down to the janitor."

"Impossible! Why, Doctor, only a few days since Dr. Burley spoke of him in the highest terms."

"A few days since! Ask him now. Leonard has played the frog to Burley's ox. It was right to confute Brigston with Greek texts; they produced a good deal of fog and little illumination. But Leonard must shove himself in as interpreter between the heavyweights and the populace. Of course his action was abhorrent; it is to me. There ought to be an *esprit de corps* in all professions. I shouldn't approve if some young medical spark were to give away *our* secrets."

The physician, if flippantly, spoke the truth. Leonard had been rash, as youth is wont to be. Wise and venerable heads had from the beginning wagged in disapproval of his excess of zeal. To bury the Brigstonian deep beneath the fragments of his own exploded logic was well, but it was also well to be wary, to lay no hasty hand upon and drag forth mysteries which could not bear the light of day. Leonard was brilliant; but brilliancy was not caution. Theological argumentation, to be convincing, must be obscure; mystification, rather than conviction, is the prop of faith.

"I'm sorry he's in trouble," observed the lady.

The doctor shrugged his shoulders. "Inevitable!" he exclaimed. "He's obstinate and conceited. His last pamphlet, 'Dr. Burley's True Meaning,' is monstrous. What right had he to give Burley away in that manner? If Burley had wanted to state his meaning, wouldn't he have done it? Leonard swallows the whole Westminster Confession at a gulp, and points out that Hampton and Burley do the same thing. What maladroit presumption! He ought to know that Hampton only bolts the morsel because it must. Its contortions during the process of deglutition ought to be charitably concealed. Who is Leonard that he should tear away the veil which hides a harrowing spectacle?"

Which burst of eloquence was not wholly intelligible to the lady, who, however, saw the need of dragging the doctor down from his hobby. "Well, he must not discuss these matters with his wife," she said, "if you disapprove."

"No. For ladies in the condition of our patient the Westminster Confession is too lurid. Needless to say to a matron of your experience that in the case of a bereaved young mother the brain should not be excited, the affections over-stimulated, the fancy be allowed to rove at will, either amid the joys of heaven or the horrors of hell."

Wherefore Paula was instructed to avoid conversation concerning themes celestial or infernal, and was thus deprived of a pleasure; for there had been much loving talk between her and Natalie concerning the child, now abiding in heavenly regions. Perhaps Natalie sorrowed a little, noting that Paula no longer lingered over the favorite topic; if so, she made no comment; her thoughts were her own.

"What is true marriage?" she asked one day.

"I—I don't know," replied Paula, taken unawares, and not sure whether this new topic were celestial or infernal. "Celibacy, as the ideal state——"

"A wife vows obedience," interrupted Natalie—she had heard Paula before on celibacy—"that's a small matter. Who wouldn't be obedient?"

"But, suppose a husband were to require something wrong," suggested Paula, disturbed by the fleeting vision of a wife of St. Perpetua deprived of fish on Fridays by a wicked spouse.

"He wouldn't be a true husband. My ideal of marriage is unity in all things—tastes, hopes, beliefs——"

"Belief, of course. And to the realization of that ideal a churchwoman would lead her husband."

"Or, if the husband were the better Christian, he would lead his wife."

After due consideration, Paula repeated the monosyllable "if?"

"And, if he showed no disposition to lead his wife, which might be the case for some good reason, she ought to try and attain his standpoint. Then she would evince that perfect sympathy which all the while the husband may be longing for."

"I—I suppose so," replied Paula, always dreading an approach toward forbidden ground.

"If a wife had wronged her husband, even without intention," Natalie went on, after a considerable pause, "that fact would stand in the way of complete sympathy."

"There could be no wrong without intention—that is, no fault."

"But still a wrong; one that the doer might find it harder to forgive than the sufferer. If you were my wife. Paula——"

"Say husband," said Paula, laughing, "and since you find obedience so easy, I order you to prepare to let me drive you to the White House in the pony-phaeton."

CHAPTER XXVIII.

CURSING AND BEATING HER BREAST, SHE FELL UPON THE GRAVE.

Mrs. Joe sought, and very easily obtained, Leonard's confidence in regard to the grievance to which Dr. Stanley had alluded. Hampton had been only too glad, so he averred, to accept his aid in overcoming Brigston; and if that was in the way of accomplishment (and who could deny it?) the fact was more attributable to him (Leonard) than to any other man. "I simply popularized Dr. Burley's learned, but certainly obscurely-written article, giving its author full credit; and now he says I misrepresented him, and his complaint is echoed by every toady in Hampton. The papers, even the secular papers, are actually making sport of me."

"But Dr. Burley can't deny what he wrote."

Even Leonard smiled at her simplicity. "He can deny what I wrote, although, in other words, it is exactly what he wrote. And that is morally just as bad."

The lady was full of sympathy; the more so as his "bumptiousness" was gone. He had been plainly deeply wounded, yet out of consideration for his wife, he had borne his grief in silence. In Mrs. Joe's eyes this abnegation deserved recognition. There was a way by which he could humiliate his enemies, and yet be of so much importance that they would not venture to show resentment. She had, as we know, already "worked the Seminary" in behoof of her "policy." She could work it a little more, and help both Leonard and herself. Her donations to the library had not heretofore been of large amounts, for she shrank from ostentation, but she had always intended to be magnificent on some convenient occasion. By being so through Leonard, she could avoid display and yet possess its advantages, for the Seminary authorities would, of course, know the source of a donation from a modestly anonymous lady, coming through the hands of Leonard.

So this matter was easily arranged. "And," suggested the lady, "after you have given notice of the donation and have heaped coals on Dr. Burley's head, go away for awhile. It will do you good, and they can think their conduct over."

The idea appealed to Leonard, who saw the situation dramatically; but when Mrs. Joe proposed that he accompany herself, Paula and Natalie on a visit to Mrs. Leon at Newport, he declined with some perturbation. "I'll go to New York," he said. And, on the whole, Mrs. Joe thought this was best, though she was surprised.

She was glad when he had departed, believing that his absence would have the effect of rousing Natalie from a condition incompatible with the life of every day, in that it would result in wholesome longing for her husband. And the politic lady soon saw her hope justified. Leonard had been gone but a day when Natalie announced a desire to return to her own house; not to remain, but to order some domestic arrangements, more especially with the view of making Leonard's study more attractive than it had been, even in those days of "coddling" which Mrs. Joe had once found objectionable, but whose returning symptoms she now hailed with approval.

At Natalie's request she was driven past the cemetery, where she alighted, and, bidding the coachman wait, she sought her child's grave. Some tears came to her eyes as she laid flowers on the still fresh earth and stood for many minutes leaning on the headstone. Her thoughts were far away. In a room in Paris she saw a woman humbled by a consciousness of wrong; and here, at the most sacred spot on earth, she renewed her vow of atonement.

She returned slowly to the carriage and was driven to the Morley mansion, where she was welcomed with effusion by the maids. From them she for the first time learned that her husband had often worked far into the night, and while listening to their comments, she reproached herself that she had left him alone. The house, with its closed shutters, was gloomy even on this bright day; what had it been in the long nights?

She instructed the servants to prepare a light luncheon for her at noon and leave it on the dining table, paying no further heed to her. She intended, she said, to arrange her husband's books.

But first she went upstairs. There beside her bed was the child's crib, cheerless without its sheets and embroidery. The empty room, from which daylight was nearly excluded chilled her. The rugs were removed and her heels clicked sharply on the bare floor, making hollow echoes as she walked. She overcame the oppressive sense of desolation and went about her tasks.

She put the child's trinkets away; the spoon which had been useless, the cup from which he had never drunk, the gold chain given by Mrs. Joe, and which, partaking of the nature of the Great Serpent, had been found too heavy for agreeable wear; these were laid among her treasures. His clothes, except the little gown he had worn when dying, were put aside to be sent to poor women, already mothers or about to become such. Leonard had once suggested kindly that they were too fine. "The mothers won't think so," she had replied.

This work finished, she closed the door of the room and walked down the broad, old-fashioned stairway, every foot-fall echoing through the ancient house of which she seemed to be the only occupant; and though she knew the maids were at their tasks and within reach, the impression affected her unpleasantly. She glanced more than once over her shoulder as she descended the staircase and walked through the echoing hall.

She entered the library—a large room, dedicated, at least nominally, even in the days of Jeremiah Morley, to its present purpose, and later, by Cousin Jared and her husband, lined from floor to ceiling with books, a cheerful room when lighted, but now, with bare floor and closed shutters, a gloomy vault in whose distant corners, where the shadows were dark, the spirits of former occupants might lurk and peer at this invader. The uncanny impressions that had been with her were deepened by the sombre fancies awakened by the aspect of the room, in which the confusion attendant on Leonard's labors was everywhere apparent. Books were everywhere—on chairs, on tables, on the floor, face downward in the shelves.

She took up a small volume. Its evident antiquity attracted her and she read the title-page: "Delay Not; or, A Call to the Careless," by the Reverend Eliphalet Claghorn. Numerous names on the fly-leaves disclosed that the book had been handed down through many Claghorns. The last name was her husband's; preceding that his father's, to whom it had been given, as testified by the inscription, by "E. Beverley Claghorn." E. Beverley Claghorn, she knew, had been her own father. Turning the pages, her attention was arrested.

She read for hours. Sunk in a heap on the floor, forgotten by the servants, her eyes gloated on the page written by her ancestor. No romance had ever enchained her attention as did all this "Call to the Careless." If the writer had so charmed the reader of his own generation, the dead hand that had composed the pages which held this reader spell-bound must have been guided by a brain cunning in the author's craft. Whatever was the story, the woman lived in its terrors; she cowered and moaned, her eyes stood out, and her face was a face distorted by the horror of a soul in fear. But she could not leave the story. Enthralled until the last page had been turned, she only then looked up, and her eyes, which that morning had been bright with the light of hope, born of the resolve to resume her duties as a wife, were now dull with the shadow of an awful dread.

She glanced fearfully around and tried to rise, but crouched again upon the floor, one hand still clutching book and dust-cloth, the other held as though to shield her from a blow. She uttered no word, but a strange, hoarse rattle came from her throat, as though she would have prayed, had her voice been at her command. At last she rose, half staggering, retreating backward toward the door, as though she feared some presence, and, not daring to turn, must face it. Thus she passed out of the room and from the house.

She walked, at first, with uncertain steps, then more firmly, and with ever swifter stride. The by-streets through which she passed were quiet, almost deserted; she was hardly noticed, though in one or two observers a faint curiosity was aroused by the figure of the well-dressed, hatless woman, beaproned and clasping to her breast a dust-cloth and a book. As for her, she noticed nothing as she hastened on.

Without pause, with ever-increasing pace, which had now become a run, she entered the gates of the cemetery, threading its alleys, seeing nothing with her bodily eyes; for their horror and despair were no reflection of the mournful yet peaceful scene in which she passed. She came to the grave of her child. Again she crouched as she had done in the library of her home; her despairing eyes were turned upward and her hands raised in appeal to the serene and pitiless sky.

Words came to her in the language of her childhood. "My God," she cried, "Fiend that dwellest beyond the sky, have mercy. Pitiless Father, who didst condemn thy Son for sport, whose nostrils love the scent of burning men, whose ears find music in their agony, whose eyes gloat upon their writhings, take me to thy hell of torment and release my child."

And so, with frantic blasphemy, cursing God and beating her breast, she fell forward upon the baby's grave.

CHAPTER XXIX.

DR. STANLEY DISCOURSES CONCERNING THE DIVERSIONS OF THE SAINTS.

At the hour agreed upon, Mrs. Joe left Stormpoint to fetch Natalie. As the latter had done in the morning, and in order to inspect the newly-erected headstone, she alighted from her carriage at the cemetery and passed through various alleys, when, as she approached her destination, she suddenly halted.

A woman was stretched upon the grave, who, on hearing the ejaculation of Mrs. Joe, partly raised her head, disclosing an earth-bedaubed face, and emitting sounds not human, but rather the moans of a tortured animal.

Mrs. Joe ran and seized her shoulder, and at the touch Natalie half arose. Her gleaming eyes, her face distorted and soiled with earth—these presented an appalling spectacle.

The lady of Stormpoint could hardly have told how the task was accomplished, but she succeeded in inducing the frantic woman to enter the carriage, and, thus separated from the grave, she became quieter, though never ceasing to mutter phrases which caused the listener to shudder. Mrs. Joe was a woman of varied experience. She had heard the oaths of mining camps when pistols and knives were out and frenzied ruffians were athirst for blood; she would have thought no form of profanity strange to her ears; yet she had heard no blasphemy equal to that uttered by her companion, repeated as a weary child asleep may repeat some hard-learned sentence impressed upon a tired brain.

Arrived home, and Natalie in her bed, and withal lying quiet, and the carriage dispatched at full speed for Dr. Stanley, there was time to consider the next step.

"Send for Father Cameril," urged Paula.

"What is Leonard's address?" asked the lady, ignoring the suggestion.

"Dear," said Paula, caressingly, and taking Natalie's hand, "where is Leonard?"

"In hell," was the answer. "I am overjoyed in hearing the howlings of hell. My joy is increased as I gaze upon Leonard in the midst of that sea of suffering."

"Good Lord deliver us!" ejaculated Mrs. Joe. Paula fell upon her knees. "Father in heaven!" she commenced.

Natalie looked at her with languid interest "The sight of hell-torments exalts the happiness of the saints," she said.

At this delectable quotation from Jonathan Edwards Mrs. Joe wrung her hands; Paula uttered a half scream and burst into tears; in the same moment Dr. Stanley was ushered into the room.

"A frightful shock!" was his verdict. "Absolute quiet! No tears; no exorcisms," with a warning finger upheld for Paula. "I'll send a nurse at once and return soon."

By night he was again in the house, having received bulletins from the nurse in the meanwhile. The patient was asleep; had been so for nearly three hours. "Excellent!" he said to Mrs. Joe, finding that lady awaiting his report in the library. "It's a fine brain, Mrs. Claghorn. Let us hope it may prove a strong one. Can you explain further than you could this afternoon?"

"The keeper of the cemetery knows nothing. Her maids are here. I sent James for them, and have kept them to be questioned by you."

The maids only knew that Mrs. Leonard had visited the house, and had spent the day in the library; that one of them, noting that her mistress had neglected the luncheon that had been laid out for her, had ventured to look into the room. "She was crouched on the floor, reading; I could not well see her face. When I spoke she waved her hand, as though I was not to interrupt. That was about two o'clock. I went back to the kitchen, just putting the tea on the range so's to heat it. Then neither Martha nor I thought anything more about her, until about five Martha thought she heard the front door slam. We looked in the library; she was gone. She hadn't touched the lunch." Such, relieved of some circumlocution, was the report of the maid most glib of speech. They were dismissed by the doctor.

"She has done," was his comment, "that which creed-adherents usually omit. She has read, and as a consequence is crazed."

"Crazed as a consequence of reading!" exclaimed Mrs. Joe.

"Mrs. Leonard has sustained a shock; there must be a cause. No external injury is discoverable. The cause is to be found in her moral, or, if you please, her spiritual constitution—I don't care what you call it—among other things in strong maternal yearnings—subjective causes these, and not sufficient to explain the seizure; there must have been an agent. The maid found her deeply absorbed; people that read crouched on the floor are so; therefore a book——"

"I took this from her," exclaimed the lady, producing the Reverend Eliphalet's "Call to the Careless."

"Aha!" exclaimed the doctor, pouncing upon the volume and glancing at the title-page, "here we have it; here's enough to convert a lying-in hospital into Bedlam."

Mrs. Joe gazed upon the fat little volume in the hand of the speaker, with the same expression with which a novice might contemplate an overgrown spider impaled upon the card of a collector.

"This unctuous treatise," proceeded the doctor, who, finding his hobby saddled, was impatient to mount, "was written by a shining light of that family to which you and I have been graciously permitted to ally ourselves. In this volume are recorded the ecstatic transports of one of the most blessed of the blessed Claghorns. Our patient may have derived her tendency to exaltation from this very rhapsodist. Here, with the Reverend Eliphalet, we may revel in angelic joys; with him, we may, god-like, gloat over sinners damned, and, enraptured, contemplate Flames, Torment and Despair; here our ears may be charmed with the Roars of Age, the Howls of Youth, the Screams of Childhood and the Wails of Infancy; all in linked sweetness long drawn out; all in capital letters, and all extorted by the Flames that Lick the Suffering Damned!"

"Doctor!" exclaimed the lady, scandalized at that which she supposed was a burst of profanity.

"Shocked? Well, shocking it is—in me, who refuse to believe it, but edifying in Eliphalet. Ah! madam, the evil that men do lives after them. Was truth ever better exemplified? Listen to this: The writer pictures himself in heaven and looking down into hell. 'What joy to behold Truth vindicated from all the horrid aspersions of hellish monsters!' (that's me) 'I am overjoyed at hearing the everlasting Howlings of the Haters of the Almighty! Oh! Sweet, sweet. My heart is satisfied!'"

The lady attempted to interrupt, but the doctor continued to read: "The saints in glory will see and better understand (than we do) how terrible the sufferings of the damned are! When they have this sight it will excite them to joyful praises,' that's a choice bit from Jonathan Edwards. What do you think of the diversions of 'the saints in glory?'"

"It's blasphemy!"

"Blasphemy! Tell it not in Hampton! But listen to Jonathan again. Here is his picture of a sinner just condemned. His parents are witnesses of his terror and agony, and thus they righteously gloat: 'When they shall see what manifestations of amazement will be in you at the hearing of this dreadful sentence; when they shall behold you with a frightened and amazed countenance, trembling and astonished, and shall hear you groan and gnash your teeth, these things will not move them at all to pity you, but you will see them with a holy joy in their countenances and with songs in their mouths. When they shall see you turned away and beginning to enter into the great furnace, and shall see how you shrink at it, and hear how you shriek and cry out, yet they will not be at all grieved for you; but at the same time you will hear from them renewed praises and hallelujahs for this true and righteous judgment of God in so dealing with you!'"

"If," interjected the listener, "that is written there, the devil wrote it."

"The devil may have had a hand in the matter, but it was written by no less a person than Jonathan Edwards, regarded, and justly, by the Reverend Eliphalet and others, as a great man. He is also quoted here as saying to his hearers, 'If you perish hereafter, it will be an occasion of joy to all the godly'; one is hardly surprised that he didn't get on with his congregation. Imagine Father Cameril making that announcement with you and Miss Paula in the front pew."

"Doctor, if you are not inventing——"

"I could not. My imagination is not warmed by the flames of hell or by celestial visions. This book is filled with similar elegant extracts."

"I have heard enough, Doctor. Really——"

"Permit me one or two more. We have hardly heard the author himself as yet."

"But to what end?"

"You were incredulous when I asserted that a day's reading in Leonard's library would account for the present condition of his wife. It's only fair to allow me to justify my assertion."

"You have read enough to drive *me* crazy, if for one moment I believed it."

"Hardly. *You* are not a recently bereaved mother; *you* are not just emerging from a condition consequent upon disturbance of the physical economy which has reacted upon the mental; *you* are not inclined to mysticism, to see visions, to find pictures in goblets of water or in grate fires; in short, while you have your own idiosyncrasies, they are not of a character to render you liable to this sort of transport. But there are organizations which, though seduced by mystic lore, can hardly contemplate such matters without injury. The compiler of this book, the men he quotes, the ecstatics in general— revivalists, hermits, nuns and monks in all ages—do you believe that as a class they were well balanced? Peering into heaven is a dangerous business."

"The men you have quoted seem to have peered into hell."

"That is the Puritan mode of ecstatic enjoyment. Our Catholic—I beg your pardon, our Roman Catholic—enthusiasts, being more artistic, and lovers of the beautiful, prefer contemplation of heaven. Unlike the smug Puritan, they do not spare their bodies. They fast and flog, wear hair shirts, roll in ashes and wash seldom, but their eyes are turned upward; they urge the spirit to rejoice. Your fat and well-fed Calvinist prefers a gloom irradiated by the flames of hell, in which he can behold the writhing victims of God's vanity——"

"Doctor, you are as bitter as all your brethren; you unbeliever———"

"I don't know that I'm more of an unbeliever than you are. I'm sure if the Reverend Eliphalet has not by this time modified his opinions, he has no expectation of meeting you in heaven. Hear him as he warns humanity against the devices of Satan: 'Of which,' he says, 'the traces are visible even in the church. In these days there hath arisen a delusive hope as to infants. Some hold, and a few dare to assert, though with bated breath, that all infants die in the grace of God. Who saith this? Not God, who, by His Eternal Decree, hath declared that none but His Elect are saved. Not our Confession of Faith, formulated at Westminster in earnest prayer and reverence for the Word. Not the framers of that Confession, of whom I may mention Twisse, as having specially wrote against this new-born folly, extorted by the cunning of the Enemy of Souls by means of the bleatings of foolish mothers—search the Scripture, reader! Nowhere shalt thou find any saved but His Elect.'"

"Abominable!" ejaculated the lady.

"Poetical. 'Bleatings of foolish mothers' is quite so. And now our good man actually drops into the poetry of the Reverend Michael Wigglesworth, whose 'Day of Doom' he quotes at length. I will not inflict the whole fifteen stanzas upon you; but listen to a morsel or two. This is the Argument: The Still-born appear at the Seat of Mercy, and put in a plea for grace that might have weight in Senegambia, but which has none in the heaven of Eliphalet and of Hampton:

'Then to the bar they all drew near who died in Infancy,
And never had, or good or bad, effected personally,
But from the womb unto the tomb were straightway carried
(Or at the least, ere they transgressed), who thus began to plead.'

"Their plea is that since Adam, the actual delinquent, has been 'set free, and saved from his trespass,' they are on better grounds entitled to consideration. To the finite intelligence there would seem to be some force in the infantile argument. What says Omnipotence?

'I may deny you once to try, or grace to you to tender,
Though he finds Grace before my face who was the chief offender.
You sinners are, and such a share as sinners may expect,
Such you shall have, for I do save none but mine own elect;

Yet to compare your sin with their who sinned a longer time,
I do confess yours is much less, though every sin's a crime;
A crime it is, therefore in bliss you may not hope to dwell,
But unto you I shall allow THE EASIEST ROOM IN HELL.'"

The doctor closed the book. "I submit that I have proved my contention," he said. "Do you doubt now that Mrs. Leonard was affected by her browsings among Leonard's books? The men who wrote the matter of which this volume is made up were largely the founders of Hampton, men whose names she has heard venerated as almost inspired of God."

"Even so, how could she believe such absurdities?"

"I do not assert that she believed. Belief in the impossible is impossible. But have you never been deeply impressed by fiction; never been scared by a ghost story? Have you shed tears over the sorrows of Colonel Newcome? The few quotations you have heard cause you to shrink, though you are well aware they are but foolish words. But if you could *see* the scenes herein depicted, I do not think you could bear the prospect. I am sure *I* should howl as lustily as any hellish monster here referred to. Well, Mrs. Leonard being so constituted, has actually *seen* these horrors, and, in the central figure, has contemplated the writhings of her child."

"Oh, Doctor!" she spoke in a subdued tone, her eyes expressing more than her words.

"Even you, here in this well-lighted and cheerful room, with me, a very material and matter-of-fact person, beside you, even you can feel a faint reflection of the terrors in which this woman spent the day. Alone, without food, a deserted room, a gloomy house, but lately cheerful with the prattle of a childish voice, forever silent, but of which the echoes still linger in the mother's ears—here's enough and more than enough to disturb an exalted temperament, a morbid imagination. Add this"—the doctor shook the book in his hand—"and what need of belief, if by belief you mean the result of a reasoning process? The ideas suggested *here took possession of her!* Belief! Pshaw! nobody believes in this stuff; but Hampton says it believes."

"But that's monstrous!"

"Nothing more common than loud assertions of belief where is no belief. That's politics, partisanship."

"But this is religion——"

"So-called."

"But——"

"The Westminster Confession is a written document. The men who composed it knew what they wished to say, and said it so clearly that nobody can misapprehend their meaning. Your own creed of compromises—pardon me, compromise is always the resort of politicians who understand their business—was wiser, or luckier; its Articles are all loopholes in regard to this doctrine of Election———"

"Doctor, your ignorance of my church is so palpable that I decline to take your word concerning Hampton and the Confession of Faith. I've never read it———"

"Even its adherents are not so rash. It becomes a serious matter as to one's self-respect to maintain a monstrous absurdity, after one knows it. Nevertheless, the Westminster Confession teaches as truth all that the Reverend Eliphalet says, or that Michael Wigglesworth grotesquely sings. Moreover, it is annually published under the title of 'The Constitution and Standards of the Presbyterian Church in the United States of America'—a solemn declaration that God, before the creation of man, damned the great majority to everlasting agony so excruciating as to be beyond conception, and all for His own glory and pleasure."

"Yet I know, and you ought to know, that Christianity offers salvation to every soul through the medium of its Founder."

"Denied *in toto* by Westminster. According to the Confession, not even Jesus Christ could diminish the number of the damned, fixed before the creation of a single soul. If Mrs. Leonard's baby was born to be damned, damned he is."

"Now I know you are asserting what is not so. I have heard infant damnation denied by Hampton professors."

"And may again. I do not claim that a single human being believes the Westminster Confession; but I do maintain that he who acknowledges that Confession as his standard, and retains membership in that church, which annually promulgates the same as truth, either believes an outrageous absurdity, or says he believes it. If he is not willing to do this, he has no right in the organization; why, only the other day Dr. Willis was requested to get out because he declined to say he believed that which he does not believe."

"Doctor, I am sorry to say it, but your statements are not credible———"

"Don't apologize. Of course they are not; but they are true. I certainly don't blame you for doubting my word. But you shall ask Hodge; I'll lend you his commentary. Hodge hopes as to infants, but is honest enough to admit that in the Confession there is no ground for hope. He damns all heathen incontinently, which includes all the babies I ever knew, though he may have known babies that were not heathen. And, after all, why this solicitude for babies? Why is it less monstrous to condemn to eternal torture a being six feet long than one of three? Why, on the last occasion I was in a church I heard these words: 'The sentiment which sorrows over what God reveals as His will is simply maudlin. When the Christian finds out who are in the regions of despair he will neither be affected by their number nor by the duration of their punishment.' That's not much better than 'bleating mothers.' And in the meanwhile"—he concluded a tirade so rapidly uttered that his auditor had had no opportunity to interrupt—"they are quarreling about Socrates and tobacco, crusading against my bottle of claret, and sending missionaries to Japan." Who "they" were he had no opportunity to designate, for at this moment a messenger from the nurse announced that the patient was awake.

When the doctor and the lady entered the room, Natalie looked at them, but betrayed no surprise. Mrs. Joe was startled by the expression of her face, which was peaceful, even happy. "Heaven is beautiful," she said, without other preface. "Birds and flowers and little children. Oh! the happy little children and Lenny among them; all so happy, so rosy! Ah, I am glad!" And even as she sighed her gladness she sank into slumber. The doctor watched her anxiously for many minutes; then he signed to Mrs. Joe to follow, and they softly left the room.

"Is it death?" asked the lady, who had been frightened by his anxious face.

"Such visions often mean death; there's nothing certain yet, but every hope. Go to bed, Mrs. Claghorn; I shall remain here."

But though the lady declined to go to bed, the discussion was not resumed.

About four in the morning he went alone to the room, and soon returned with a smiling face. "She is sleeping naturally," he said. "A few hours since I feared for her reason; now I have great hope. I shall return at eight o'clock. Let nobody go near her. Burn that thing; she must never see it again." He pointed to the "Call to the Careless," and left the house.

CHAPTER XXX.

STARTLING EFFECT OF "DR. BURLEY'S TRUE MEANING."

Leonard remained in New York, ignorant of the events which had transpired at Stormpoint, concerning which, however, he was soon informed by a letter written by Mrs. Joe, a letter which conveyed the intelligence that his wife had fainted in the cemetery "as a consequence of over-exertion," that Dr. Stanley wished the intended visit to Newport to be made as soon as possible, that there was no need of his presence in Easthampton, and that if he were to come there he would probably find his wife already departed. All of which, though dictated by the physician, had been written with misgiving, as conveying an insufficient statement of the facts. But the doctor had been peremptory. "Keep them apart," he had said. "The only subject on which Leonard can expatiate just now is damnation, and of that the wife has had more than enough."

Leonard evinced no desire to follow the Newport party. Misled by the communication from the lady of Stormpoint, and yet more influenced by reluctance to enter the household of Mrs. Leon, of which household he assumed Berthe Lenoir to be still an inmate, he was willing to enjoy a holiday which he thought he had fairly earned. Mrs. Joe, though surprised by his acquiescence, was relieved. She was still more surprised when her keen vision detected that Natalie was equally relieved. "It seemed," she observed to the doctor, "to lighten her heart."

"Instinct," he replied, and made no further comment; but though ordinarily very discreet as to professional matters, he mentioned the circumstance to his wife, at the same time advancing a theory which startled that lady.

Freed from anxiety concerning Natalie, whose letters, though very short, reported continuing improvement in the matter of health, Leonard resolved, for the present at least, to forget the ingratitude of Hampton, and to enjoy to the fullest his bachelor outing. He recalled his strolls on Parisian Boulevards, and in fancy lived in past delights, promenading Broadway with the old Parisian strut, though modified, and not oblivious of the fact that here, as in Paris, were handsome eyes, not unwilling to return the glance of one who had been likened to a Greek god.

Sometimes, indeed often, he lamented that his lot had not been cast in the great world. His instincts truthfully told him that, as a man of action, he would have presented no mean figure; there were even moments when he wished, though he knew the futility of such a wish, that he might never see Hampton or hear of theology again. This he knew well enough was but the natural reaction from the strain of his recent labors, but he toyed with the thought, half playfully, half regretfully, as indicating one of the things that might have been. If there were any conscience-pricks they were too feeble to be felt; he had ceased to be a boy (so he said to himself); the boy, for instance, he had been when, on the Heidelberg terrace, he had yearned over the erring soul of his cousin. The religious sentiment which once had glowed so ardently in his bosom was burned out, consumed in the heat of partisan theology; but though he knew this, he did not know the meaning of the fact. To him it meant that his salvation was assured, and with that conviction the great concern of life had passed into the peace which passeth understanding.

Just now, however, he was not giving much attention to his personal religious attitude, as he moved among the city's throngs well-clad, rosy and with the form and grace of an athlete and the eager eyes of innocence and unconscious desire. In the delight of the holiday, a delight which sometimes rose to a surprising fervor, he thought of certain Parisian peccadillos, and more than once half resolved to renew his acquaintance with the ballet and *belles jambes*, like unto those of Mademoiselle Coralie, which gamboled ravishingly in the haze of memory; but he rejected the imprudent suggestion; he might be recognized, and Brigston would rejoice in unholy glee, if its most potent adversary—he wondered if this fact were known to the passers-by— were discovered in a temple of dubious recreation. Such recollections brought Paris very vividly before his eyes, and for some reason also the memory of Berthe and of that rapturous kiss; and perhaps at such times the handsome face assumed the look of which Mrs. Joe had disapproved.

The remembrance of Berthe recalled Natalie, who, as he believed, was in the house with her former maid, and Natalie's beauty, and he was filled with tenderness, and his soul yearned with a great longing, and had it not been that Berthe was there he would have fled to Newport. He recognized now a fact of which he had, in a vague way, been long conscious, the fact that ever since the birth of the boy he and his wife had grown somewhat apart. She had been engrossed with the child, and he with his theological war. He regretted it, and resolved that it must not be so in the future. Loving one another as they did, it would be easy to grow together again. He would tell her how grievously he had been treated by Hampton, in its envy; and on the beautiful bosom that he loved and that was his own, would pour out his griefs and find sweetest solace. If she would only curtail her visit!

One day there came a letter from his wife which he opened in the eager hope that it would announce the termination of her stay in Newport. He was disappointed in this, and was further rendered uneasy by the tone of constraint in which it was written, or which he imagined; for if there were constraint, it was hard to point out just where it lay; yet he felt, if he could not see, that the pen of the writer had been heavy in her hand. But he was more than uneasy; he felt resentment rising within him as he read the postscript, which was as follows: "Do you believe that there is an eternal hell and that many are condemned? Will you answer this as briefly as possible?"

He studied the written words with growing annoyance. The curtness of the question seemed to indicate that to the questioner the matter was of minor import—trivial, in fact; if she really thought thus, then all his recent labors had been labor in vain. Nothing had so angered him as suggestions of this character, frequently made by a godless secular press. One journal had, with pretended gravity, argued that since all heathen and their progeny must be damned, extermination was more merciful than the hopeless attempt at conversion, and at least as practicable; another had flippantly suggested that Professor Claghorn be required to demonstrate the utility of theological seminaries, since no product of those institutions could, by any possibility, be instrumental in saving a single soul—and so on. All of which he had borne with a fair show of equanimity, but he had smarted; and now Natalie's question seemed, at first sight, an echo of the unworthy journalistic jibes. There might be various opinions concerning hell; it was conceivable that the great majority preferred an attitude of incredulity as to its inevitable destination; but, at least, it was a serious subject.

But later readings of the letter seemed to indicate that it had been written with a heavy heart. There was affection in it, but a tone of gloom as well, which, though Natalie admitted that her health was completely restored, was too apparent to permit the supposition of a trifling postscript. The inference, then, must be that she had arrived at a not uncommon stage of religious agitation, often preliminary to conversion, a stage which he knew to be frequently of intense suffering to the neophyte, though satisfactory to pious observers, who were inclined to see in the lowest depths of misery the sure precursor of the highest joy. He had, himself, at an unusually early age, passed through a similar experience, and though that period of anguish was so far behind him that he could not recall its terrors, he knew that they had been very dreadful, and that his parents, to whom he had been as the apple of their eye, had been correspondingly complacent. There was, in these days, less of the agonized form of religious experience, but he could easily understand that it might happen to Natalie, who, in religion, was still but a babe.

The only way to deal with the matter was the way in which it had been treated in his own case. There must be no slurring of the truth. He would disdain that course in private as much as he had disdained it in public. Hampton might shrink from disclosure of eternal verity; he would not.

Wherefore, he sent to Natalie his pamphlet, entitled, "Dr. Burley's True Meaning," not sorry that she should see how clearly and uncompromisingly he could state matters which others had been willing to obscure. The true meaning of the Confession, and, therefore, of the Bible, and, therefore, of the learned biblical scholar whose text Leonard illuminated, was that the majority of mankind was on the way to a hell, eternal, and of torture inconceivable.

The pamphlet was relentless, as was proper; but in his accompanying letter to his wife Leonard was very tender. He showed her that there was but one course to pursue in the face of indisputable truth, and that was resignation to the will of heaven. Weak humanity might grieve over God's will; such sorrow was certainly pardonable by man, but was nevertheless rebellion; and, before complete reconciliation to God could be assumed, must be dismissed from the heart. Leaving religion, he proceeded to tell his wife that his longing for her was growing absolutely insupportable, and he was much more fervid in his petition that she hasten her return home than he had been in his doctrinal expositions. He dispatched his letter, and returned to his former avocations, but with little spirit; he longed for Natalie, and had no room for other than the thoughts that accompanied his longing. In a few days he was able to start for home, Natalie having, in a very short letter, in which she made no comment on the one he had last written, announced her arrival in Hampton by a train due there a few minutes later than the one from New York by which he traveled, and when he finally alighted at the station, he was tremulous with anticipation, and his disappointment was proportionate when the Newport train arrived with none of the expected travelers.

There was nothing to do but to bear a revulsion of feeling, which was actually painful. He walked across the Square to his home, and found the maids with everything prepared for his arrival, and with a letter from Natalie which informed him that she would be in Hampton on the following morning.

He went early to bed, discontented and fretful. He slept badly, and in the night got up and wandered restlessly about, and in his wanderings made a discovery which might have remained unnoticed had the fancies which vexed his repose been of a different character.

After the birth of her child, Natalie had occupied a room separate from her husband's, in order that the latter, whose literary labors were exacting, should not be disturbed. In his prowling Leonard discovered evidences that this arrangement was to be continued, and as he stood in the gaslight considering the tokens whereby he inferred that one room was reserved for masculine, the other for feminine occupancy, he mentally pronounced the arrangement unsatisfactory, and experienced a feeling of vexation amounting to resentment.

But resentment gave way when, next morning, having seen Mrs. Joe and Paula drive away to Stormpoint, and having followed Natalie to the room which he had inspected the night before with dissatisfaction, he once more held her in his arms. The light that gleamed from her eyes, the roseate hue upon her feverish cheeks, the rich red lips upon which he pressed his own hungrily—the beautiful reality, fairer than the fairest vision of his hours of longing, banished every thought but one.

He held her long in a close embrace. He was very happy, and when she had withdrawn from his arms he sat upon the edge of the bed telling her of his disappointment of the day before, and of his nocturnal prowlings, and laughingly advancing his objections to the sleeping arrangements she had ordered. Meanwhile, she said but little, being engaged in searching for something in her trunk. At length she found whatever she had been seeking. "Leonard," she said, "go down to the library. I must speak to you, but not here."

The manner and the tone puzzled him—then he remembered. He sighed involuntarily. It was an inopportune moment to discuss conversion—but since she was in its throes——He went downstairs; his face betrayed vexation.

Soon she entered the room where he awaited her, seated in a big chair. She knelt before him, taking his hand in hers. "Leonard," she said, "I am sorry you don't like the arrangement of the bedrooms."

Her solemnity had led him to expect something of greater importance than this, which was, however, decidedly a more welcome topic. "You know, dearest," he said, with a quizzical look, "as husband and wife——"

"Leonard! Leonard! We dare not be husband and wife."

He stared at her in amazement. "What do you mean?" he said.

"I mean this," she answered, producing "Dr. Burley's True Meaning." "Oh, Leonard! How could the same man write that book and be a father?"

CHAPTER XXXI.

HE CLASPED HER LITHE BODY WITH A CLUTCH OF FURY.

Mrs. Joe had not obeyed Dr. Stanley's injunction, to burn the "Call to the Careless," but had studied that delectable composition sufficiently to compel her to exonerate the doctor from her suspicion, that he had invented much of the matter, which he had, in fact, read from the text before him.

Her researches had not been without an object. It is, perhaps, unnecessary to point out that this lady's conscience was sufficiently elastic for ordinary purposes, even for ordinary political purposes, and it might have with stood the assaults made upon it by her investigation, had she been of the usual sex of politicians. She could go far in the interests of her son, but long ago she had borne another child, whose smile as it faded in death had ever been, at odd moments, before her, and constantly before her during her wanderings in fields theological, and she had but recently seen a woman crazed by contemplation of her baby in hell. When she had learned, by means of her studies, that a great ecclesiastical body still dooms the vast majority of those born of woman to everlasting woe, it came upon her like a blow in the face that, in order to see her son in the legislature, she had aided in promulgating the diabolical creed which, in the face of nineteen centuries of Christianity, is still waved aloft as the Standard of a Christian Church.

Upon the first shock of this knowledge she followed the inevitable course of the conscience-stricken, and proceeded to argue with the inward monitor. "Nobody believes that now," she insisted; "the actual belief has been modified to accord with common sense. No Christian can admit that God is a demon, and no Christian can teach impossible falsehood." In answer to which, Conscience pointed to the title-page, which proclaimed the Confession to be the "Standard of the Presbyterian Church in the United States of America.'" She resolved to seek enlightenment at the acknowledged head of human wisdom in Hampton, and called for the purpose on the great Dr. Burley himself. Him she encountered as he was emerging from his front door. "Does Hampton actually uphold the Westminster Confession?" she asked.

"Certainly, my dear madam, so does Brigston."

"I'm not interested in Brigston. I am in Hampton."

"And we are all glad that it is so. But, I see—I've always been afraid of it; you are going to try and get us all over to St. Perpetua, ha! ha!"

"And does Hampton really believe——?"

"Only what is true. I must be off to my lecture now; we must have it out some other time. How's the Bishop? Fine fellow; wish we had him. Good-bye; Mrs. Burley will be *delighted to* see you," and the doctor waved the lady into the house and made his escape.

Having no desire to call upon Mrs. Burley, the lady of Stormpoint remained in the vestibule only long enough for the gentleman to get away; she then descended the steps and was about to enter her carriage, when she was accosted by Dr. Stanley, who, after the usual salutations, asked her if she had seen Leonard recently.

"I am about to call on him now—on unpleasant business."

"That's a pity. You'll wish you had stayed at home. I have just left him; he's as cross as three sticks, which I suppose are crosser than the proverbial two."

"I suppose because the newspapers are still nagging him."

"Perhaps; yet if you could manage a confidential talk with Mrs. Leonard, it might be a good thing."

"Ah! You've noticed that there's domestic trouble? I have suspected it. Why was he willing to stay away from Newport? Why was his wife reluctant to come home?"

"Perhaps you can find out. Doctors can't ask indiscreet questions more than other people."

"And you think I can, or will?" In answer to which the physician merely shrugged his shoulders.

The lady drove away, her distaste for the task before her not diminished by the encounter. She was quite sure that the physician would not have made the allusions, which had fallen from him, unless he believed that the domestic status in the Morley mansion was of grave significance. Which, in fact, it was; a dark shadow loomed, ever larger, in the old house.

Leonard was very unhappy. Natalie's ignorance, in respect to his longings, her utter absence of sympathy; these formed the side of the shadow visible to him. He was irritable, at times harsh; but more deadly in its possible results was a sullen resentment, so deep that its ferocity and strength were unsuspected by himself. He was gazing moodily out of the library window when Mrs. Joe's equipage stopped at the door, and in another moment the lady was ushered in.

"What is it?" he asked shortly. His manner was divested of its usual graces. He looked moodily at the floor.

"Only a matter of business. Leonard, have you informed the Hampton people of the gift of which I spoke to you?"

"It has been mentioned."

"Leonard, I ought not to give it."

"You don't mean you have met with serious losses?" he exclaimed, impressed by her manner.

"No, no! But my views have changed; that is, I have made discoveries. Will it annoy you, personally, if the gift is not made?"

"I shall regret it; but nobody will blame me, if that's what you mean."

She was relieved. Still, it was painful to withhold a promised gift, especially painful to deprive him just now of the credit of being her almoner. "I wish you to take this," she said, handing him a cheque. "Let it go to the poor of the town, the hospital, the blind asylum——"

He took the slip of paper she held out to him. He was startled by the amount. "Mrs. Joe——" he commenced.

"We can arrange as to details," she interrupted. "Oblige me by taking it now."

He saw that she was somewhat agitated, and knew that she feared that the withdrawal of the gift to the Seminary might have wounded him. This was her way of curing such wounds. It would be ungracious to refuse the cheque, yet even as he looked at it, a strange foreboding was upon him.

He sat down saying he would prefer to give her a receipt as trustee. "As you say, we must arrange as to details. Meanwhile, I suggest a portion of the sum for the Missionary Fund——"

"Not one penny of it," she answered with energy.

"Do you object to the conversion of the heathen?" he asked surprised.

"I do," was her emphatic answer. "Leave them alone. I suppose there are among them some that look with hope beyond the grave. I will not be an instrument to destroy that hope."

He jumped at once to the conclusion that she had been reading some of the frothy and ill-considered articles of the secular press in regard to the Hampton-Brigston controversy, and again the suspicion arose in his mind that Natalie was influenced by the wretched diatribes of the newspapers.

"I should fail in my duty as a Christian, Mrs. Joe," he said coldly, "if I made no effort to disabuse your mind of prejudice. Your capacity to aid a noble cause is so great——"

"God knows," she interrupted earnestly, "I desire to use that capacity for good. I have done grievous harm hitherto."

"I do not understand."

"Leonard, look at this. It is a fair statement. I know it because I have tested every line of it in the Seminary Library. Can I give money to bring tidings of their eternal damnation to the heathen? They are happier without such knowledge."

He took from her hand a cutting from a newspaper. It was an attack on his theology: "As a mitigation of the misery which flows from the Westminster Confession," wrote the journalist, "probation after death has been suggested by weaklings. We know how that suggestion has been received. In June, 1893, the General Assembly of the Church convicted Dr. Briggs, its author, of heresy, and stigmatized sanctification after death as 'in direct conflict with the plain teachings of the Divine Word, and the utterances of the Standards of our Church'; a deliverance which consigns to hell myriads of Jews, Mohammedans and honest doubters of Christendom—all to be added to the number of heathen in hell. Concerning these last, various computations have been made by theologians of a mathematical turn; the American Board estimates that five hundred millions go to hell every thirty years, or as Dr. Skinner has it, thirty-seven thousand millions since the Christian era. Dr. Hodge states that none escape. The last-named learned commentator on the Confession of Faith is even hopeless as to Christian infants, concerning whom he says, 'It is certainly revealed that none, either adult or infant, are saved, except by special election,' and that it is not 'positively revealed that all infants are elect.'"

The article proceeded to argue that, if all this were true (which the writer denied), to impart the knowledge to the heathen would be cruel, and that if it were not true, so much the less should lives and money be spent in the dissemination of false views of God's mercy and justice.

"Beyond the fact that the writer is thoroughly illogical, slipshod and evidently malicious, there is no fault to be found with his statements," observed Leonard, as he returned the cutting to the lady.

"Leonard, my conscience will not permit me to disseminate a faith which knows no mercy."

He respected Mrs. Joe; he could even sympathize with her views, though, regarding her as a child in doctrine, he did not think it worth while to attempt to explain to her the enlightening and consolatory effect of the "high mysteries," which are to be handled "with especial care." "Let the matter rest awhile," he said. "I will arrange as to the hospital and for a donation to the blind asylum. We can agree as to the distribution of the rest of the fund later.

You will not always be so hard on Hampton. Theology is not learned in a day, Mrs. Joe, and, you will excuse me for saying it, you have not given as much thought to the matter as some others."

"I am not foolish enough to pretend to a knowledge of theology. That would be as absurd as the exhibition presented by men who pass years in striving to reconcile eternal damnation and common justice." Having fired this shot, the lady took her departure.

The door had scarce closed upon her when Leonard called Natalie. An impression, revived by his visitor and her newspaper cutting, that his wife's attitude had its inspiration in the empty criticisms of the press, had aroused his anger. He resolved that the present mode of living should terminate. He had rights, God-given, as well as by the laws of men; he would enforce them if he must.

In their intercourse recently, Leonard had refrained from harshness, but he had been unable to conceal a resentment, hourly growing in strength; his manner had been hard and sullen. Without exhibiting actual discourtesy he had shown plainly enough that he preferred to be alone, and, except when it was inevitable, husband and wife had hardly met or spoken together for days.

Hence, when Natalie heard him call, a flush, born partly of apprehension, partly of hope, suffused her cheek. She came toward him, smiling and rosy, a vision of radiant loveliness. The pleading tenderness of her eyes was answered by the wolfish gleam of a gaze that arrested her steps. He seized her in his arms, clasping the lithe body in a clutch of fury, kissing her red lips and clinging to their sweetness with a ferocity that terrified her. In this shameful embrace they wrestled a moment until the man's violence enfeebled himself. She broke from him, standing before him an image of outraged modesty, panting, indignant and bewildered.

"Leonard!"

He sank into a chair and covered his face with his hands. His own self-respect was shocked. He was humiliated, and his shame increased his resentment.

"What is it?" she asked, placing a trembling hand on his shoulder, and noting that he shuddered at the touch.

"What is it?" he repeated. For a moment a fury to strike her possessed him. By an effort he calmed himself.

"Natalie," he said, in a slow, measured tone, "do you regard me as your husband?"

"You know I do, Leonard."

He sighed despairingly. How was he to bring a knowledge of facts to this woman incapable of comprehending them, or what they signified for him?

"Natalie," he said, and now he took her hand in his, noting its cool freshness again his own hot palm. "We cannot live thus; we are married. We must be husband and wife."

"You dare not create victims of hell," she whispered.

"Natalie, you would impiously abrogate God's holy ordinance. Marriage is enjoined by Scripture. Sin of the most heinous character is born of neglect of this ordinance of God."

"Leonard, Leonard," she cried, "you can have no assurance that your children will be saved. Only the elect."

"All, dying in infancy are elect," he answered impatiently. "That is the universal belief of to-day."

She grew very white as she looked at him; her eyes were big with horror. "Do you mean," she asked hoarsely, "that we should murder our babies?"

"Murder!" he exclaimed, amazed.

"Since only infants are certainly saved——"

He burst into a discordant laugh. "Natalie," he said, "as a reasoner you would do credit to Brigston."

"I can see no other way," she said after a pause. "My reasoning may be defective, but you do not show me its defects. Surely you believe the Confession and the catechisms?"

"Every line of either," he answered defiantly and in anger. Had he not labored night and day for a year past to demonstrate the truth of the "Standards"?

"Then," she answered sadly, "you have no right to become a father. Fathers and mothers are instruments of the devil. According to your belief, no sin can compare with the sin of bringing forth a creature so offensive to God that it must suffer eternal punishment. You may believe that you and I are both to dwell together in hell. If that be our fate we must submit. But our children, Leonard! Shall we earn their hatred in life, and watch their torments in unquenchable fires?"

"Do you compare yourself and me, and children born of us, to the depraved mass of humanity? Have you no assurance of God's gracious mercy?"

"God's gracious mercy!" she repeated. "God's gracious mercy!"

"Natalie," he said, making a great effort to speak calmly. "You who but a short time since had no religion, surely you will concede that I know something of that which has been the study of my life. I tell you that your reasoning is frantic nonsense; it would be blasphemous if it were not for your ignorance."

"You believe the Confession true—every line. I have studied it; I have studied your book. Prior to that I had spent a whole day, in this very room, reading——"

He laughed, but as before there was no mirth in the laugh. "A whole day," he said, "and this profound research enables you to contend with me in a science that I have studied all my life."

"On that day," she answered, shuddering, "the fires of hell blazed before my eyes and I heard the wails of damned souls. In a day much may be learned. If what I then saw be true—I do not know—you say it is; you say hell is——"

"And say it again," he interrupted. "If I had never known it before, I would know it now."

"Then, Leonard, you must justify me. Since God cannot save the innocent——"

"He punishes the guilty only."

"Having himself decreed their guilt! In the face of that decree there is no human guilt. Even marriage, that most hideous of all crimes, does not merit endless suffering——"

"You insist that all are damned; you rave. Nobody asserts that all are damned."

"'He hath chosen some to eternal life and foreordained the rest to dishonor and wrath.' Yet if there were but a single soul to suffer; if but one solitary creature of all the millions of men were doomed to dwell in hell forever— the knowledge that your child, Leonard, might be that lonely one—surely such knowledge——"

He ground his teeth. She drew texts from the source he had declared to be the living truth. He had no answer; there was no answer.

"Leave me," he whispered, in a tone that evidenced his fury better than a roar of rage. Again he hid his face in his hands. She often turned to look at him as she slowly withdrew, but he did not raise his head.

He wrestled fiercely with his emotions and with the problem that fate had raised. At times rage consumed his soul, and his thoughts rioted in brutal instigation, which even then he feared, and of which he was ashamed. At moments he hated, at moments he loved, but hating or loving, the seductive charms of the woman swayed before his eyes, mocking him as the mirage mocks the fainting pilgrim. Hours passed and he remained in the same attitude, striving to estimate the situation correctly, so that he could evolve a remedy. He could not deny her reasoning; he would not give up his faith. His mind, rigid from the training to which it had been subjected, was incapable of readily admitting new theories; and his best nourished and most vigorous attribute was involved. Whether his integrity could be bent or not, it was certain that his vanity would not submit. No! He would not deny his faith. He would enforce his rights.

But not without further effort at persuasion. He made a heroic and worthy resolve. He would be patient still, meanwhile using every gentle measure. He would enlist Mrs. Joe in his cause. She was a matron, shrewd and too well balanced to allow religious notions to carry her to fanatical extremes; and she did not hold his own views, apparently not even as to eternal punishment. Perhaps she would convince Natalie that there was no hell. It would be a lie, but better that his wife believe a lie than that hell reign in his house and in his bosom.

At the dinner hour the maid handed her mistress a note. It ran thus:

> "Dear Natalie—I have decided to leave home for a little time. I think we are better apart. If you will open your heart to Mrs. Joe she will explain that which you and I cannot discuss. I learn that you are in your own room, and think it better not to disturb you. Good-bye, for a little time. It may be that I shall not write.
>
> "LEONARD."

CHAPTER XXXII.

A PÆAN OF VICTORY HYMNED IN HELL.

On the day following that upon which Leonard and Natalie had last met in Leonard's study, there were two women in a room of a shabby New York house, evidently once a worthy residence, but now sadly fallen from that estate.

One of the two, half dressed, with a good deal of tarnished lace decorating such clothing as she had on, sat on the bed in an easy attitude, careless as to the display of a handsome person. Dark, heavy-browed, her first youth past, her haggard face was redeemed by deep, soft eyes, that now, however, from beneath their long lashes, looked out upon the face of the other woman with suspicious wariness.

This one, overfed, coarse, vile to look upon, with the face of a painted gargoyle, red and mottled, garishly dressed in a loose gown, stood with arms akimbo, her little eyes bent wickedly upon the woman on the bed.

"Ten days' board," croaked the fat one. "Ten days."

"Ten weeks, for all I care," was the reply.

The fat creature wheezed and snorted; she half lifted her great red hand as if to administer a blow.

"Try it," said the other, "and I'll stick this into you," holding threateningly the blade of a pair of scissors.

The fat one recoiled; there was enough recklessness in the eyes of the woman with the scissors to justify the movement. "Now, now, Frenchy," she remonstrated, "you won't be a fool. Possy bate, eh?"

"*Pas si bête*," laughed the other grimly. "Try it and see!"

"You know," said the rubicund one, "this ain't white, Berthe. Whose fault is it if you've no money?"

"Ah!" exclaimed Berthe. "You think me of your kind. I'm a lady; I was a fool to come here."

"Sure, you're a lady; and for that very reason ought to make a mint of money. I'll tell you what's the matter with you, Berthe—you're a mule. I swear," she exclaimed, suddenly conscious of wrong, "my boarders is the bane of my life. Mules—but there, nobody'd believe what I've borne."

"*Malheureuse!*" sneered Berthe.

"I tell you, missy, girls don't talk that way to me!" exclaimed the red-gowned dame, perhaps suspecting unseemly profanity veiled in a foreign tongue.

"I don't want to talk any way to you. Get out," replied Berthe.

"And the board bill?"

"I've had nothing to eat for two days."

"And won't have as long as you're a mule. If you have no money by this time to-morrow, out you go, and without your trunk; so Frenchy," concluded the woman, changing her tone to persuasion, "be reasonable. You shall have dinner if you'll promise to go out afterward. Think it over," and she waddled off.

Berthe lay back upon the pillow, her long arms stretched above her head, and thought it over.

She had left Mrs. Leon long ago, and since then her steps had been downward. For awhile a nursery governess, which, being amply capable, she might have long remained had it not been for her eyes. She was not altogether conscious of the capacity of her eyes, and was long innocent of the knowledge of the strife and hatred they had wrought in the family in which she served. Maltreated by an infuriated mistress, she had avenged herself amply, living for months in luxury, and on the money and caresses legally belonging to the other. But she had never cared for her sinner, and he had been glad to creep back to that which he had dishonored, not forgiven, but accepted as a hard necessity. Her luxuries and her money were soon spent— as for the rest, it is a dark tale that she recalls, lying there majestic, with her long arms above her black head and her dark eyes brooding.

The present was a problem. The move to this house was toward a deeper degradation than any she had known, and she recoiled from its demands. She knew its probable end, too. She was shrewd, dominant if she chose to be; in short, no fool. She could rise to prosperity and become like the gargoyle, but the prospect sickened her. All the inmates of the house were to her abhorrent, but the gargoyle was a loathsome, soulless, pitiless beast, only not a fool. The others were fools, and she knew, feeling the sparks of humanity within her, that she must even be a fool rather than a beast. And the end of the fool was misery, from which there was but one escape.

She was hungry. It was true that, except as to some slices of bread, smuggled to her by soft-hearted ones, she had eaten nothing for two days. She had long ago pawned her articles of jewelry. Her clothes were in the clutch of the beast. She would have to apply to her for garments for the street. She must surrender.

So she asked for her clothes and her dinner. The beast was gracious, but chary as to giving too many garments. The truth was, the beast hoped her boarder would not return. She had the trunk—she was sick of the mule.

Berthe wandered toward the lower part of the city. Plainly dressed, her carriage dignified, she was not molested, nor did she cast her eyes upon any passer-by. She walked straight on, yet not rapidly, for there was no purpose in her walk. Useless to seek that man upon whose wife she had avenged herself; he had been hurried off to do penance in the country; even if he had returned, she knew nothing of his present abode.

Mrs. Leon was a dweller in hotels, and at this season, not in town. Besides, Mrs. Leon could not be ignorant of what had been accomplished by the nursery governess she had herself recommended.

She wished now, for in truth, as she walked on, terror of possible starvation began to haunt her, that she had carried out an often neglected impulse to write to a man she knew, and who she believed could help her. She would have done so before this, but the man's wife was a friend of Mrs. Leon. This recollection had prevented her addressing him. Yet she knew he would have helped her. He was young, he was kind. Ah! he was adorable.

So she walked on, thinking of that adorable man, forgetting her fear of starvation. He had kissed her, or rather, and she smiled as she corrected herself, she had kissed him. He had been helpless. The innocent!

By this time she was in Fourteenth Street. A man seeing the smile upon her lips, stood in her path and addressed her. She moved aside and walked on; the smile had been born of a memory sweet to her. The man looked after her, astonished at the majestic ignoring of himself.

Suddenly the woman stopped, as if struck. Then she started, walking quickly, and entered a brilliantly lighted resort.

Leonard had passed a sleepless night in the train. In New York he went to a hotel which he had never before frequented. He desired to be alone. He had left home to think, not to seek acquaintance or distraction.

And he thought, walking the streets of the great city until he was footsore, and the more he thought, the less capable was he of reasoning, the more weary he grew of thought; finally, striding onward in a dream of incoherent fancies, that were not thoughts, but impotent efforts of a tired brain. All day long there swayed before his eyes visions inspired by objects seen but not noted and most incongruous. The passing glance upon a billboard, gay with motley figures, gave birth to a picture of living damsels, languishing in postures of inviting loveliness. He saw no stony streets, no squalid scenes, but wandered in a Moslem heaven in whose crystal streams Naiads bathed fair round limbs or sported in wanton frolic in silvery cascades, anon decking with lilies the roseate beauties of their queen. He took no heed of time or place, pacing street after street, along the wharves, seeing neither ship nor dray; in the Hebrew crowd of the East Side, noting nothing of the soft-eyed men with dirty beards, nor the women wearing wigs of jute, nor the children dancing in the streets to hand-organs, nor any of the sights of that crowded foreign city, full of strange interest. Of the things before his eyes he saw nothing; nor could he, being entranced by raptures which had tried the souls of saints a thousand years ago!

At ten o'clock at night, having eaten nothing since an early and neglected breakfast, he stood in the street, conscious that he must eat or faint. He entered a brilliantly lighted room where there were tables, but which was nearly empty.

Back of the room he saw another filled with people, decked with palms and artificial grottoes. He entered and sat down at the first unoccupied table.

"Bring me a sandwich," he said to the waiter, "and a drink."

The sandwich was brought and the drink. The latter Leonard supposed was wine. He remembered that he had scruples against wine-drinking; had, in fact, never tasted wine. He was too tired to care much for scruples, and besides, he was faint, and even his scruples permitted wine in case of illness. He swallowed the liquor, which was whiskey, at one gulp, and commenced to eat ravenously.

He ordered another sandwich and another drink, which was brought, this time with a carafe of water in addition. He drank greedily of the water, reserving his liquor, and, as ravenously as before, consumed his second sandwich.

Then he looked about him with more interest in his surroundings than he had known during all that day. He felt comfortable, happy in fact. He stretched out his legs and sipped his liquor, this time noting the strength of the beverage, which made him cough and brought the tears to his eyes, causing a woman to smile slyly. He smiled in return, then looked quickly away, abashed at his own temerity in thus answering the involuntary expression of a strange lady. This, as he looked about him, he thought must be one of those German beer-gardens he had heard about, but in this country had never seen. Evidently the people did not bring their children. That was well. Beer-drinking was a bad example for children. The women looked tired, he thought, though some were very rosy, remarkably so, and all were tawdry. The men were not a nice-looking set, though there were exceptions. Many were not much more than boys, and these affected brilliant, if somewhat dirty, neckwear. There were things about this place that offended him; principally, the tone of the men. They lolled a good deal and smoked in the women's faces; that was German, he supposed. The women, of whom a number were alone, were better behaved. He noticed a waiter order one to leave the place; that was singular, especially as she had slunk in very quietly and had seemed very humble. Suddenly the great orchestrion commenced to squeal and bang and clash, and soon the heads of the people were strangely bobbing, keeping time; now the strains grew soft and plaintive; a profound sadness crept over him as he listened to what seemed the requiem of a dying soul. He felt the tears rising in his eyes.

For a long time he had been eagerly watched by a woman. Berthe could not be sure if this were indeed the man she knew. What could he be doing here? Half hidden behind a curtain which draped a huge column, she watched the heaving breast of the man. Suddenly, she saw his head fall forward, smashing a tumbler, and a cry of agony broke from him. "Natalie, Natalie!"

It might have been the last despairing wail of the soul doomed thenceforward to darkness, whose requiem he had heard. To the obscene observers and the superintendent of the place it was the cry of a drunken man, who had no business there.

There was no hubbub. The habitués of the place comprehended that nothing of that sort was allowed. The man was quickly hustled into the front room by the manager.

"Get his hat," said this personage to a waiter. "Has he paid his bill?" he questioned as the man brought the hat.

"Yes, except the broken glass."

"Damn the glass!" replied the manager, who desired to get rid of the drunkard. "Come, young fellow, steady on your pins now and be off."

A woman slipped her arm under Leonard's. "I will take care of him," she said.

The manager looked at the pair as they made their way toward the street. "Do you know her?" he asked of an employee who had witnessed the departure.

"She's not a regular, sure."

"Nor he. Well, it's not our affair," and the manager returned to his duties.

The two wandered off, the man's unsteady steps supported tenderly by the woman. When the sun rose, his head rested on her bosom and her lips hovered lovingly above his own, and the hum of the waking city, borne to his ears, may, to him, have been the distant harmony of a pæan of victory hymned in hell.

CHAPTER XXXIII.

A DELECTABLE DISCUSSION, IN WHICH A SHAKSPERIAN MATRON IS ROUTED.

Natalie Claghorn had always nourished a sentiment, which with many is a conviction, with most a hope, that man is something more than the futile hero of a sorry comedy—not made to live merely that he may die. Hence, religion had been a need of her being, and, though unconsciously, she had developed a creed of her own, vague, no doubt, from the positive standpoint, but one which excluded those essential elements of the faith of her husband, Hell and the Devil; grim inventions these which, while imbibing wisdom at the paternal knee, she had learned were mere memories of ancient Oriental mythologies. This view, in so far as she had given the matter any thought, she had supposed the view commonly held, and universally held among the cultured. Recently, indeed, there had been a moment in which even with her bodily eyes she had, as she had then believed, beheld the terrors and the torments of the damned; but as many men and women, who believe not in ghosts, have nevertheless seen these dwellers of the shades, and yet in less receptive phases of the mind have been able to dismiss their visitants to the shadows from which they were evoked, so Natalie had been able to discard belief in the reality of her vision. Nevertheless, though incredulous, he who has seen a ghost remains impressed, and the memory of her experience naturally recurred with her theological studies, serving to emphasize the horrible, rather than the absurd, aspect of her acquirements.

Her desire to know had been honest, and she imputed honesty to others; hence, when Leonard, with pen and voice, asseverated his belief in a creed which must render paternity impossible to any being with a conscience, she had been confounded by the attitude he presented. She was not aware that between her husband and herself the sources of sympathy had always been shallow, and she was quite as ignorant of theological frenzy as she was of the knowledge of masculine passion. She had loved him; and she had loved Mrs. Joe, Paula, the Marquise, her maid Berthe; in fact, she had loved, and still loved, humanity, as far as she knew it, and it was thus that she had loved her husband, though, doubtless, in his case, this gentle flame had burned with more intensity than in others.

Though grieved that Leonard had left her without saying good-bye, yet she felt that he had acted wisely, in that he had given her time to think without the disturbing sense of his presence in his repellant mood. And during this period an incident occurred which aided her in finding the only solution of the problems which vexed her.

It was not to be expected of the Hampton matrons that they continue their tolerant attitude, with regard to Mrs. Leonard Claghorn. Her continued languid health after the birth of her child, the subsequent bereavement and absence, these had afforded an excuse for neglect; but now there was solicitude, and in a certain circle of dames, which met every fortnight to discuss Shakspere, but whereat other subjects, as possessing more of novelty, were occasionally considered, some rather severe strictures were made, in reference to Professor Claghorn's apparent inability to convert his wife—he who had so audaciously, if not successfully, coped with Brigston.

"Brilliancy is less effective than earnestness," opined Mrs. Waring, wife of Professor Waring, whose forte was Hebrew, and who was noted for great erudition, a large family and a feeble intellect.

"In the long run, no doubt," assented Mrs. Professor Flint. "But surely, she is not really unconverted!"

"She certainly hides her light. There are times—I hope I am not uncharitable—when I wonder, suppose she were a Jesuit!"

"Awful! She's French; her mother was noble—of the old nobility—and the old nobility are all Jesuits."

"And a Jesuit will stick at nothing in the way of deception. It's a terrible possibility!"

Natalie found apologists, notably Mrs. Tremaine, who maintained that there were no female Jesuits, and who defended the absent, partly because she was a spirited and generous woman, partly because, at this particular period, she experienced an unusually distinct impression of her own importance by reason of an acknowledged claim to the admiration of the other Shaksperians. Even Mrs. Waring, the mother of ten, was inclined to look with indulgence, if not with envy, upon this champion, though she whispered to Mrs. Flint that "after a half dozen, Mary Tremaine would change her note."

However that may be, Mrs. Tremaine's note remained on this occasion triumphant, and she glowed with victory, and also with good intentions; for she resolved to warn Natalie that the gossips were preparing for a feast, "and," said the lady to herself, "it must be stopped; never allow a tiger a taste of blood," which mental exclamation clearly indicates the exaltation of the lady's spirit.

In this spirit, as soon as the Shaksperian séance was over, she started for the Morley mansion, full of excellent intentions and the proud possessor of a secret already known to the wives of all the professors of the Seminary, except Natalie; and which, if confided to the latter, would indicate that friendly feeling by which she was really actuated, and thus pave the way to the warning she wished to give. She was also impelled by the pardonable desire to further impart the information already widely diffused; and which, in fact, could not remain much longer a secret, unless the complacent lady decided on complete seclusion for some months.

"Yes," she said, "I suppose it will be noticeable soon. Professor Tremaine is so proud; he actually struts. He hopes for a boy."

"Unfortunate woman!" exclaimed Natalie. "How can you smile?"

"Dear Mrs. Claghorn, I forgot your own recent loss. Believe me, time——"

"But, have I understood? You hope for a baby—you a Christian wife?"

"Why not I—a Christian wife, as you say?" was the answer of the visitor, who was both shocked and puzzled by the expression of her hostess.

"I do not understand," exclaimed Natalie hopelessly; then suddenly: "How can you dare? Have you no compassion, no fear? You can smile, believing that an awful calamity hangs over you!"

"Awful calamity!" echoed the bewildered visitor, perhaps a little alarmed by the speaker's energy.

"Is it not? Have I understood aright? Are you going to have a baby?"

"I have said so. Why the fact should affect you so strangely is a mystery to me."

"Do you believe this book?" and Natalie seized the well-known volume with its blue cover.

"Certainly, I believe the Confession."

"And your husband?"

"Does he not teach it?"

"And believing that this book is true, knowing that the furnaces of hell are choked with sinners—knowing this, you and your husband welcome the birth of a human being! God help me, and you, Mrs. Tremaine, forgive me, but I cannot understand these things. Why! you believe that your baby may be damned!"

"How dare you say such things? My child will not be damned. Ah! You poor woman, I see. You have brooded over your own baby's death, and have been dwelling on horrors. I have heard of such cases. Dear Mrs. Claghorn, dismiss such dreadful folly from your mind. Babies are not damned; nobody has believed that for years."

"*I* do not fear for my child, nor for yours. But you—you cannot be sure he will die. He may grow up—what then?"

"Then he must take his chance," said the would-be mother, though her face grew white. "We must all trust in God's grace."

"But he lends His grace to his Elect only. Unless your infant was chosen from before creation, he *must* be damned. You say this book is true, and yet you dare to have a child who may burn in hell! How can you commit such wickedness?" In her energy Natalie had arisen, and now stood before the unhappy matron in what to her seemed a threatening attitude.

"I—I—do not comprehend," she faltered. "You have no right to speak thus to me."

"No right! Have I not the right of humanity, the right of a child-bearing woman?"

"But——"

"I had some excuse, I did not know. But you knew—and yet you dared!"

"I didn't," whimpered the lady. "It was the Professor—it was God's work. You talk horribly."

"God's work! And you lend yourself to God's work! You could have died—anything, rather than be an instrument of wickedness in God's hands!"

Mrs. Tremaine breathed a great sigh of relief when she found herself safely on the outside of the Morley mansion. She sat for awhile on a bench in the Square, and when she had in part recovered her equanimity, she went slowly homeward, pondering over the difficulties which present themselves to those who try to do good in secret.

Yet she had done good; for when Natalie beheld this matron in all the pride and joy of approaching maternity, she saw in the spectacle a living denial of the frightful dogma which, if believed, must have turned the woman's triumph to despair. The orthodox lady served to demonstrate the fact that the upholders of hell do not believe in hell; for the conclusion to which Natalie had arrived was sound: The woman that believes in hell dare not bear a child.

Leonard's continuing absence afforded time for contemplation of this discovery and its consequences; among others the gradual conviction which subjected Leonard, with thousands of others, to the accusation of maintaining palpable falsehood as the living truth. No other conclusion was possible in the face of the fact that humanity can judge only by the aid of human faculties, and that these must, perforce, pronounce eternal punishment incompatible with justice, and preordination to everlasting misery as impossible to a God of mercy. Her training made it difficult for her to understand the palliation of the offense of those who maintained the paradoxes which denied their actions. She was not aware that the minds of such as Leonard had, from infancy, been receptacles into which had been emptied all the follies bred from the meditations of those who profess the mission of being interpreters of Omniscience; nor could she fairly estimate the partisan rage which carried such men, engaged in controversy, even beyond their convictions. She did, however, gather some comprehension of these extenuating forces from the further researches offered by Leonard's table, on which were strewn numerous pamphlets referring to the late theological war. The tone of rancor which pervaded the effusions of the religious antagonists was repellant, but she was shrewd enough to see in so much sound and fury evidences of weakness; and when she came to the theologian who lauded the "beautiful faith" of that Christian father who demolished his pagan adversary with the words, "I believe, *because* it is impossible," she closed the book, and thenceforth avoided further contemplation of the high mysteries of theology.

She could not but condemn Leonard, though she would not dwell upon the thought. To her, as to Dr. Stanley, belief in the impossible was impossible, and, therefore, pretense of such belief dishonest; yet, since these pretenders were not otherwise dishonest, there must be some ground for their attitude, which to her must remain a mystery, but which ought to cause her to hesitate in judging. So, she would not blame Leonard; she perceived now, that her own conduct merited reproach. She was ignorant of her own cruelty and her own absurdity, and would have resented those terms as applied to her attitude; but she acknowledged with sorrow that she had not been kind, and for her unkindness she craved forgiveness.

Very early one morning she started to walk to the cemetery, going by way of the shore, and glorying in the grandeur of the ocean and the breeze that came, health-laden, from its bosom. She stood and looked upon the broad expanse of blue, recalling the day when Leonard had plunged into the raging waters to rescue the boy. That effort had been in vain, as to its intended object, but had it never been made she would not be walking here a wife. She had loved him before, but not with a love that would have urged her to grant him the boon of kisses; but, fresh from that brave deed he was a hero, had taken the hero's meed from her lips, and in that act had sealed the mastery which his courage had won. She gazed long upon the waters, listening to the surge and noting the glint of the sun, tinting with rose the billows rolling toward her. She sighed and, pressing her lips together, turned her back upon the waves and hurried on. It was as though she had resolved not to see some fair vision suggested by the rose-tint in the feathery edging of the billows.

When she entered the beautiful cemetery the birds were chirping in the trees, only their joyous trills breaking the silence of the city of the dead. She sat down beside the grave of her boy.

And here, recalling her recent thoughts and her condemnation of others who were dishonest in their attitude toward God, she saw the need of honesty for herself in all things. If there were facts in her life which she had been willing to ignore, she must look them in the face and deal with them as best she might, being honest always. If, in marrying Leonard, she had striven to escape the longing for a love denied her, and in so doing had cheated her husband, she must admit her fault and resolve to make every reparation in her power. If she had chosen to believe that she had craved religion, and in her husband had seen its embodiment, while in truth she had craved an earthly love, and had in marriage weakly sought refuge from her shame, she must even admit her fault and do what might be in her power to avert its consequences. Not in the futile attempt to deny hearing to her conscience, to murder her reason, but in every wifely allegiance. Thus far she had wofully failed in such allegiance. Even before the last sad breach between her husband and herself she had allowed estrangement to come between them, and had so exclusively devoted herself to her child that Leonard had been secondary. It was true that she had not consciously intended this, but she had been willing that it be so. Her consciousness of wrong warmed her heart toward her absent husband, and filled it with longing to reconsecrate herself to him. He would surely come to-day! As she sped homeward she was more and more persuaded of it, and, finally, believed that on her arrival she would find him waiting for her. As she neared the house she trembled with expectation; she longed to clasp her arms about his neck and falter her prayer for pardon, and assure him of her love. There should be no shadows between them in future. She had dared to look truth in the face, and, lo! it was no longer truth. All the foolish, sinful longings of the past, persistent because she had refused to recognize them, had been dissipated by the light of day. The present moment was to live forever. Henceforth, Leonard, and only he, should dwell in her heart of hearts.

In her agitation she fumbled at the door-lock, then desisted, for from the hallway she heard the firm step of a man coming to the door. Her heart beat wildly; another moment and she would be forgiven.

The door was suddenly opened. With a glad cry Natalie spread wide her own, and in the same instant was clasped in the arms of Mark Claghorn.

CHAPTER XXXIV.

WHEN MANHOOD IS LOST WOMAN'S TIME IS COME.

In the misery of awakening to a consciousness of existing facts, Leonard could see no possibility of extrication from the bog of degradation into which he had fallen. With excellent intentions on the part of his pastors and masters, he had been trained to dishonest depreciation of his own strength, and he was now without confidence or courage. His days had been without guile, and the unaccustomed aspect of guilt overwhelmed him with hopeless terror. The precepts instilled from infancy thundered direful threats, dwelling lingeringly on the curses of Omnipotence; and in the moment of the acquirement of the dread knowledge that he had been self-deceived, that the Grace of God had not been his, that he, like other doomed and defrauded sinners, had mistaken those "common operations of the spirit," that even non-elect may have, for the effectual call addressed only to the few chosen from eternity, and which to all others is a monstrous mockery—in the moment of this awful revelation he felt all the suffocating horror of that which he had taught as truth: that for the weak there is no Father, no path but the path of evil.

The woman looked upon the exhibition of misery thus presented with compassion tinged with scorn, yet with bewilderment. She had never seen a sinner like this before; but instinctively she felt that when manhood is lost woman's time has come.

"*Voyons, chéri,*" she said, "what is it all about?" and she drew his head to her bosom.

He grasped at the offered sympathy as a starving man may grasp a loaf. The picture he presented was not adorable, but there was truth in it, if, also, some unconscious comedy; and her compassion was not without sincerity, though his broken story was of less interest to her than the simplicity of the narrator. She felt that she had been fashioned fit for this man's needs; and while she soothed him, his spirits rose a little, and he experienced a sort of satisfaction that, since he had taken this direction, he had gone amazingly far. See, now, what Natalie had done!

They rescued Berthe's clothes and left the boarding-house, and were soon quartered in a small French hotel, bathed and well dressed. The surroundings were cheerful; the lunch table, with its bright glassware and silver, white napery and bottle of champagne in its bucket of ice, was inviting; the woman was gay, yet still compassionate and tender. With the first glass of wine Leonard felt actually happy; and as he sat opposite the well-clad woman with the great dark eyes, now languid and inviting, now bright with challenge, and listened to the prattle, which women of her nation can make so engaging, he, looking back upon the past week, was enraptured by the contrast. Of such as she really was he had no perception; he could no more estimate her character than could the veriest college freshman, weary with knowledge of the world. Her brightness of intellect was apparent, and there was neither coarseness nor ignorance of amenities in her bearing. She had said to the mistress of the boarding-house that she was a "lady," and she fitted sufficiently the ordinary acceptation of a much-abused term. She told her story (with the essential suppressions and variations), and he saw in her one who had suffered from the injustice of the world. She admitted being in the last stress of poverty, and confessed to having suffered actual hunger, thanking him, with the first sheen of tears in her eyes, for rescuing her clothes from the clutches of the hawk landlady.

All these confidences, sweetened by moderate draughts of champagne—for Berthe preached moderation, and economy as well—insensibly disposed the man to further confidences of his own, and she listened eagerly to the tale, of which she had heard disjointed fragments in his first outbreak of despair.

"It is all plain, *chéri*" was her comment. "Mademoiselle—I mean your wife— never loved you."

"I know that," was the gloomy answer.

"Ah, but why not? You so beautiful a man, so good!" and she knelt beside him and put her arms about his neck.

"So beautiful! That is a matter of taste. So good!" he sighed, but let his head droop on her shoulder all the same.

"Any woman must love you," she murmured. "But one thing could hinder."

"And that thing?"

"That she first loved another," she whispered.

He was silent.

"We all knew it in France," she said.

"The Marquise?" he asked huskily.

"The Marquise, assuredly. Why, we ran away from her because of it."

"Tell me all you know," he said, after awhile.

The woman's heart fluttered; here were her tools. She could keep him, and she would. Kneeling thus beside him, her arms about him, her body close to his, his cheek against her own, he was hers. No woman should take him from her. Rights? Bah! Hers were the rights of conquest, and of the fierce demands which bade her hold what she had gained. There were no other rights.

"She loved him always," she murmured. "It is all told in that." Yet she told much more; of how the Marquise had always suspected, of wanderings in Paris with no other chaperone than herself; on which occasions, knowing what was expected of her, and unwilling to spoil the pretty game she watched, she had discreetly remained as much as possible in the background. "He was generous and gave me presents—but, *ciel!* Why shouldn't he with a gold mine?" They had especially affected churches, and picture galleries where they could sit in secluded nooks, and where Natalie's attendant could easily lose herself temporarily. "The Marquise raved furiously," added the narrator, "but she would have raved more furiously still had she known all I knew."

"She never loved me," faltered Leonard.

"But I loved you the moment I saw you. It was hard to have you leave me after that kiss. Tell me it was hard for you."

"It was hard; better had I never left you."

"And now you never will. You have made me love you; and I,—I have made you love me; is it not so? Is it wicked? Ah, no; it is good, it is good."

To him who heard the murmured words and was enveloped in the tenderness she shed upon him; who felt her lips upon his own, and who, in the contact, found sweet content—to him, this was a foretaste of the life that might be, if he had the courage to embrace it. He was like some worn and weary pilgrim in arid sands who, visioning an oasis, lies him down by a green brookside, rests in the fresh breezes, listens to the rippling waters, sees their sparkle and inhales the fragrance of the flowers, and so is lulled to fatal languor, unconscious that all is a mere mirage.

To her he was no mere wayside victim, but in his resemblance to him whose picture she had held toward heaven in the church, a reminder of the happy days when first she had known love. She longed desperately to retain him, and though she feared the dark gulf of misery in which he had found her, with him she would have even faced it again, rather than safety with another; so that her cajolements had the grace of sincerity, though the parting, which he knew must come, remained constantly the dark background of the present. It may seem that to leave the woman required little heroism; that whatever charms she might possess for him, that those of dignity, of worthy citizenship, of respect, of all that even worldly men hold dear, would allure him with greater power. All of which is reasonable, and, no doubt, such considerations do often operate in cases where discreet sinners, having sinned in secret, quietly emerge from the bog of evil-doing, cleanse their garments and, animated by good resolutions, go forth among their fellows, keeping their own counsel; but these are sinners of experience. The innocent man, like the innocent woman, falls far when he falls; such men sacrifice present respect and hope for the future, choosing ruin; and while there are numerous roads to that goal, the most frequented is that one where woman roams.

But whatever heroism may have been necessary, this man possessed it. He turned his face resolutely from the allurements of the present, and, if trembling, faced the future.

"It cannot be otherwise," he said, falteringly. "I do not leave you to return to happiness. I might find that with you. I go because both for you and for me it is right. We may have years of life before us; let us use them for repentance. In this lies our only hope."

"Do you know what my life must be?"

"One of better deeds. It is not for me," he said, sorrowfully, "to try to win you to high thoughts. That would seem impious, and would inspire you with just contempt for me and for those teachings I have disgraced. But I urge you to consider these things. Seek counsel; I can give you the means; or, if you prefer, go to a priest of your own church."

She smiled bitterly. Knowing his own deadly depression, he could read her thoughts; he implored her not to despair, pointing out that that which was a solemn obligation, her temporal welfare, would be surely fulfilled by him. "Our unholy union," he said, with sad simplicity, "entails upon me the duty of making due provision for you. This will be a matter for immediate attention; promise me to remain quietly here until you hear from me."

And so it was arranged, he giving her money for present needs. He watched her while she packed his valise, touched by wifely attentions, the lack of which, he told himself, had long been a grievance, of which now he knew the cause. He looked about him, noting the embellishments which her taste and her training had enabled her to add to the room, even in the short period of their occupancy, and the sense of a justifying grievance grew stronger.

"There's room for this," she said, holding up a bottle of champagne, the last of a series, and unused because she had insisted upon moderation. He watched her place it in the bag. He had resolved never again to drink wine, but he would not refuse what she gave him, denying herself.

They said good-bye. He left her, promising soon to see her, and in his heart solemnly resolving that they should never meet again. The lie was but one more added to his catalogue of sins, and had been necessary. As to that provision for her needs, he would make it generously. He could not as yet see how details were to be arranged, but for the present there were other things to think of. A man cannot suddenly make the acquaintance of himself without paying some attention to the stranger.

He remained a day longer in the city, and then, absolutely unable to bear solitude, and with a manful struggle to avoid returning to the beckoning comfort he had left, he started on the dreaded journey homeward.

CHAPTER XXXV.

A BOTTLE OF CHAMPAGNE.

As he left the train in the early morning and crossed the Square toward his house he was, notwithstanding a half-defiant carriage, assumed to hide the cringing of his heart, probably the most miserable man in Hampton. He sat down upon the bench where he had rested after his first meeting with Berthe and, recalling that meeting, remembered how he had striven to give a jaunty trend to his thoughts, and had tried to persuade himself that the kissing episode was but a venial misstep, having indeed little of dignity, but even less of sin. Behold, now, to what it had led him!—that deed in which he had actually gloried, seeing himself, because of it, somewhat more a man of the world than was suspected, with experiences concerning which honor bound him to secrecy as it did men of experience; wherefore he had despised the blabbers of his college days, who either kissed not at all, yet boasted of such kissing, or, displaying equal ingenuousness and greater meanness, bragged of actual kisses. He recalled all this with real sorrow, not unmingled with contempt for the callow youth who had sat here indulging in boyish fancies, the wickedness whereof was surpassed only by their shallowness. It was then, he thought, that his unconscious yet diabolical arts upon the woman, destined to be his victim, had commenced. Though his present misery was as great as he could bear and his penitence sincere, nevertheless, there was an underlying consciousness, and pride in the fact, of more than ordinary fascinating powers, in respect of women. She had loved him from the moment she had seen him, and had loved him to her own destruction! Though he regarded with horror that which he believed himself to have compassed, yet the underlying complacency was there. All these years she had been faithful to his memory. Alas for her weakness! alas for the fate which had made him, in respect to her, a villain! He truly repented,—was he not bowed to the ground in humiliation and sorrow for his sin? Yet, was he wholly responsible, he who had, in ignorance, exercised seductive powers, possessed in ignorance?

The inner being of this man, of noble outward form, was not cast in heroic mould, such moulds being seldom used in the fashioning of our neighbors; yet he was no unusual product, being the inevitable result of various influences, for most of which he was not responsible. An idolized child, a boy of wondrous promise as of wondrous beauty, a youth completely filling all promises of boyhood, early called to the service of Heaven, and so, somewhat set apart and cherished with a care befitting a sacred vessel, to be guarded from every rude touch lest its perfection be endangered,—thus he had been fitted for the world. Every natural healthy instinct had been bent and distorted by the loving hands of ignorance, while equally natural impulses had been ignored as unwholesome weeds, which would find no place in a nature dedicated and cultivated for Heaven. He had been esteemed as somewhat higher than ordinary humanity, while human vices had been nourished in him so that they bore blossoms so fair to look upon that they were as virtues. His innate vanity had been so fostered that it had become the central product of his moral being, permeating every thought, mingled with every act. His most patent and engaging graces had been developed by this vice. His frankness, his amiability, his generosity, his mental aptitude, were all means for winning the esteem he craved, and had been employed, in fact, to that end. They were real virtues. He was in goodness all he seemed to be. The kindness of heart for which he was praised and loved, even this excellence aided in the nurture of that self-complacency which led him to ascribe the woman's undoing to his witchery, rather than to her willingness.

As he raised his eyes and caught sight of his home, and knew that he must enter the house, the subtle consolation which had formed the undercurrent of his despondency was forgotten, or, perhaps, its utter worthlessness for the moment recognized. The whole horrible load of regret weighed again upon him, crushing his spirit. There was no comfort now in any phase of his reflections. He had gone forth from the home of his innocent boyhood, as of his worthy manhood, unhappy, indeed, but claiming and receiving the respect of all his fellows. Now, he must creep back, so vile a creature that he dreaded to meet the eyes even of his servants.

As to his wife, though he had left her without good-bye, and though there had been estrangement between them, he knew that he must meet her face to face, and while he dreaded the meeting, still he longed for it and longed to throw himself upon his knees before her and confess. As to that which had estranged them, it seemed a trifle to him now. Let her have her will; if therein there was to be punishment for him, was he not willing to do penance all his days? As to those confidences made by Berthe, while he believed them, he believed only what he had been told. As to seriously thinking of actual guilt in connection with Natalie, she was too truly estimated by him, and he too truly innocent, still, to harbor base suspicions. But he knew that she had not loved him, and in the dismal oppression caused by his own misdeeds this conviction created a distinct and sharp pain, and yet it had its own alleviation. He, too, had something to forgive, and did forgive, even now, before forgiveness had been granted him. Yes, he would meet her face to face, and there should be repentance between them and, as each had done wrong, so each would do all that could be done in reparation, and if the sacrifice she had demanded of him be still required, he would make it.

And thus, while Natalie, in the cemetery, had seen the way to reconciliation with her husband, and had recognized that she had wronged him, and in that recognition had found in her heart a greater love for him than she had known before, so he with similar thoughts, though more confusedly and with less honesty, though not consciously dishonest, slowly made his way toward the house. He entered by means of his latchkey, meeting nobody, and went at once to the library. It was still early: doubtless Natalie was in her room. He was not sorry for a respite.

He was faint and felt the need of refreshment. No doubt, the maids were about, so he went toward the bell, then drew back, recognizing in his action his dread of meeting any occupant of the house. Then he remembered that in his valise was a small bottle of champagne. He was not sorry, now, for Berthe's foresight, and in his heart thanked her. He recalled how pleasantly this wine had affected him, how it had given him courage, and how his horrible depression had vanished under its influence. Notwithstanding his resolve to resume his old practice of abstinence in regard to wine, he was glad that he had this chance bottle, for he had never needed courage more than now. He wished he had some food, for he had eaten but little for many hours; the wine would serve until he had the courage to ask for food.

While he was opening his bottle the front-door bell rang. The library, its doorway hung with heavy curtains, faced the entrance to the house. Leonard, peeping between the curtains, saw Mark Claghorn admitted and ushered by the servant into the drawing-room.

The sight of Mark, whom he had supposed in Europe, aroused his anger. He hated Mark as one who had gained a love that should have been his own. Under the circumstances he was not sorry that his presence in the house was unknown. Mark, who was noted as an early riser, had probably ridden over from Stormpoint on some trifling errand, and, soon after Natalie appeared, would doubtless leave the house.

And so he waited, thirstily quaffing the champagne and wishing he had a biscuit. He tried not to think of the visitor in the drawing-room, but found that effort vain, thinking of him, in fact, with fast-rising anger, until he was on the point of seeking the man to force a quarrel on him which should banish the intruder from the house forever.

He was arrested in this intention by hearing Mark emerge from the drawing-room and walk quickly to the front door. Leonard peeped through the curtains and saw his wife, with her arms outspread, fall upon Mark's breast, and heard her cry aloud:

"My darling, my darling, welcome home!" and with upturned face she drew Mark's downward, kissing his lips as she had never kissed the watcher.

Who staggered backward, sinking into a chair, dazed as by a blow.

Her face had been illumined, glowing with happiness. Her dancing eyes, her outspread arms, her lips upturned, her gladness unrestrained, so impatient in her longing that she could not wait for greater privacy than the hall—in these he had seen a woman never seen by him before. This was Mark's welcome home. What was his to be?

Great tears streamed down his face; of wounded vanity, of love and trust betrayed, of growing fury. His moods followed fast one upon another. Now sunk in profounder depths of sorrow than any yet sounded, now raging with frantic lust for vengeance upon the woman and her lover.

Even while chaotic fancies whirled in his brain he could hear the murmur of their talk, ecstatic dalliance which he would interrupt.

Yes, he would disconcert their cooing, cover the pair with humiliation, eject the glib intruder and bring the woman to her knees.

But he could not move. He was chained to his chair. A horrible fluttering of his heart made him gasp for breath, his head fell back, his face and lips were white. The want of food, the nervous depression, the rage and exhaustion, all intensified by the sharp and unaccustomed fillip of the wine, had done their work. At first it was fainting, then came slumber.

CHAPTER XXXVI.

SHE CRIED ALOUD SHE WAS A GUILTY CREATURE.

For a moment Mark had yielded to the rapture of the first pure pressure of lips he had ever known. From the window he had seen Natalie advancing toward the house, and had involuntarily gone to meet her. The sight of her had quickened his blood, but if, for an instant, he had reveled in the bliss of the welcome she had granted him, almost in the same instant he recognized and regretted that he had dishonored her in accepting caresses not intended for him.

He drew her somewhat hastily into the drawing-room. Before he could say a word she had recognized him.

"Mark," she exclaimed, amazed, and then a rosy blush spread over her face.

"I startled you," he said. "It was absurd in me, unpardonable."

"I thought it was——" her voice faltered.

"Leonard, of course. Now welcome me for myself," and he took her hand and shook it warmly, after a proper, cousinly fashion, perhaps sadly noting the contrast, but striving to shield her embarrassment.

He succeeded, as far as appearances went. But both were conscious of emotion, though each strove gallantly to hide it.

"I am so surprised," she faltered. "You must have made a remarkable passage. Your mother did not expect you yet. In fact, Paula——"

"I took an earlier steamer than I had originally intended, and had a quick passage besides."

"How glad they must have been at Stormpoint!"

"They seemed so. I arrived last night."

"I am sorry Leonard is not home yet. I expected him this morning. He has been in New York."

"So the maid told me. Of course, I should not have disturbed you at this hour had I been aware of his absence. I rode over, and knowing that Leonard is, like myself, an early bird, thought I would say good-morning."

"I am very glad you did, Mark."

"Yet, it is always foolish to run outside of conventional grooves. The maid told me you were gone for a walk, and so I waited."

"Which was right. I am glad you waited."

Plainly she was uneasy and so, feeling rather foolish, he explained that in order to fulfil the duty of breakfasting at Stormpoint he must be going. Her suggestion that he remain and breakfast with her was made rather faintly. "Good-bye, Natalie," he said. "Remember me to Leonard. Next time I shall call in proper form."

And so he rode away, watched a little while by her, who then went to her own now belated breakfast. She sat at the table, eating hardly at all, seemingly lost in thought. Then she went slowly upstairs to her own room.

She sat down upon the bed, suddenly catching her breath, as one stifling a sob. Then she twitched her body with an impatient shake, like a naughty child. Then she rose quickly and began to rectify or complete various small duties, neglected by the maid, who had arranged the chamber while she had been out. Ornaments were to be lifted and dusted, pillows more carefully smoothed, chairs to be moved an inch forward then replaced. Mirrors to be wiped clear of invisible dust, but not, for some inscrutable reason, to be looked into; in short, pretended duty must be indulged in—a poor pretense, which died away as she sank into a chair and, with listless hands lying in her lap, permitted thought to have its way.

Had she known him or not? Of course she had not known him. Not even when (here she blushed and her lips parted slightly)——She was angry at her impetuosity, honestly angry. It was silly, but she had no other reproach to make to herself. It had not been her fault, coming from the sunny street, that she had not recognized the man who had advanced so eagerly to meet her,— the last person she could have expected to see in her own house. It would be absurd to feel more than passing annoyance at such a contretemps. Only a morbid conscience could find reproach for an episode in which there was no fault, which naturally she regretted——

No! She did *not* regret. Had her heart not fluttered with joy every moment since it had happened? Was it true or was it not—she did not know, but, alas, she wished it true—that for one brief instant, ere he had released her, she had known him and had been happy? Happy! What a barren word was "happy."

Her thoughts wandered far—farther than ever before. The secret casket in her heart, wherein heretofore they had been hidden, was opened, and they rushed forth, to roam in regions forbidden, yet so fair that her feeble protests were unheeded; and she smiled upon them, these bright children of fancy, wandering with them in the paradise where Love has made his home. She closed her eyes and strove to realize again the brief ecstasy of an hour ago. She knew—she must have known—in whose arms she had been enfolded. She wished it so; it must be so. Again she felt his beating heart against her own, his arms once more about her, his breast pressed close to hers. "Mark," she whispered, stretching forth her arms and pouting lips as one prepares for meeting other lips——

The morning grew old, and she still sat thinking of many things. She knew that she loved the man that had left her, with a love that must be his, and his only, shared by no other. She had known it as she had that morning stood upon the strand, seeing in the fleeting rainbows of the spray pictures of a life that might have been, but which could never be. She had turned her back upon the vision, well knowing why she turned away. She had seen it again in the cemetery and had denied it, bidding it begone forever; and she had met it on the threshold of her home, no longer a vision, but a fact so rapturous and so mighty that she dared no longer deny the truth. She loved him; she had always loved him.

She sat long, dreaming her pleasant dreams, which only slowly merged with the facts with which she was environed. Very gradually the full import of her thoughts came home to her, but it came surely, disclosing an abyss so evil and so deep that she was appalled, and sinking upon her knees she cried aloud that she was a guilty creature, and prayed fervently and long for aid to be that which she had only that morning resolved to be, a faithful wife in thought as in deed.

At last she went downstairs. Entering the library, she discovered her husband.

He still slept, the deep sleep of exhaustion. She watched him, noting the careworn face, the disheveled dress. To her he looked like a man who had passed through a crisis of illness, he was so changed.

And now the regret and penitence for all the wrong she had done him pressed upon her as a heavy weight. She was his wife, yet had driven him from her side. She was his wife, yet had, within an hour, dreamed her dreams of love and happiness in which he had no share.

CHAPTER XXXVII.

A GOLDEN BRIDGE ACROSS AN ABYSS OF SHAME.

When Leonard awoke to find her bending over him, the anxiety in her eyes looked to him like fear. He had no perception of the fact that hours had passed since in the meeting in the hall he had seen the same eyes dancing with the light of joy, and had heard from the drawing-room the fond murmurs of forbidden love. In his first awakening the scene he had witnessed and the murmurs he had heard swayed before his eyes and sounded still in his ears. Fresh from dalliance with her lover, she might well tremble to find her husband here! With this thought uppermost, he staggered to his feet.

She started back. He glared upon her with a gaze so furious that she was in truth afraid.

For the burden of her guilty dream weighed heavily upon her, justifying the hatred in his eyes, a hatred born of the ascription of all his woes to her, and while she saw abhorrence, the suffering he had endured was no less plainly written in his haggard face, accusing her even as she accused herself. Her sins against this man, her husband, the father of her dead child, crushed her with the burden of the humiliation born of them.

"My husband!" In her self-abasement she sank upon her knees. The action was instinctive in her of Gallic training; to Leonard, bred to less dramatic display of emotion, it was proof of guilt far deeper than he had until now suspected.

"Get up," he said harshly, and taking her by the arm he led her to the doorway, pushing her from the room and, with unconscious violence, almost throwing her against the opposite wall. He returned to the room and rang the bell. His rudeness had given him a sense of mastery in his own house, and had dissipated his dread of meeting the servants. He asked the maid if breakfast would soon be ready, and was surprised to learn that it was long past noon.

Ordering a meal to be prepared he went upstairs, boldly and with something not unlike a swagger in the perception that there were sinners as bad as he, and having bathed, being clothed in fresh garments, and having eaten almost ravenously, he felt, he said to himself, like a new man.

Which indeed he was, if new thoughts make a new man. That dreadful load of regret for his own misdeeds had been lifted from his shoulders. His violence toward his wife had somewhat shocked himself, and while attending to his physical needs, he had had time to regret his hasty outbreak; and this fact led him to resolve to consider the situation calmly and judicially.

To know all is, if the French adage be true, to pardon all, which is perhaps the reason why we find it easier to forgive our own sins than those of others. We presumably know what motives actuated us in evil-doing, and being aware of the strength of the force that drove us, we are conscious of the fact that had the incentive to sin been less powerful than our rectitude we would not have been guilty. In other words, we sin because we can't help sinning, a logical and soothing conclusion, converting our wickedness into misfortune and rendering us objects of self-commiseration rather than of self-condemnation.

But in that contemplation of the iniquity of others, to which circumstances sometimes impel us, and which is always so painful, the strength of temptation which we have not personally experienced is less obvious, while at the same time the sense of our own rectitude is naturally in the ascendant. And as, in such contemplation, our judgment is inevitably swayed by our morality in its sternest mood, especially if the crimes under consideration have wronged ourselves, our indignation is naturally fervent. It is also true that our vision is clarified, our memory sharpened, and we recall incidents, now corroborative of guilt, though heretofore unremarked, or regarded as innocent.

Leonard recalled so many of such incidents that at last nearly every remembered act of his wife assumed a semblance of guilt. There were those visits to churches mentioned by Berthe, the woman who truly loved him, and who, doubtless, had minimized the truth to spare him, and the same habit had been indulged in after marriage. It was not to pray that she went to the churches; he remembered that she had herself said so. No; it was to dream of the old unhallowed meetings in the hallowed precincts. To dream! Why not to meet her lover? During much of their sojourn in Paris, Mark had been supposed to be in London—what was a passage between London and Paris to Mark? He remembered now that in Natalie's bearing toward himself there had always been a vague and undescribable something which he could not define, but which he had felt. It was easy now to fix the date of the commencement of this aloofness (he had found this word for it); it had been during the visit in Paris. He recalled a thousand instances with which to torture his mind and prove his suspicions true. The aloofness had increased; after the birth of the child it had even been noticed by others—and then as a blow came the conviction that the inferences she had drawn from his belief in hell and her consequent resolve to live a celibate life were all pretense, a ghastly role played in obedience to her lover's command.

As this hideous thought took possession of him all semblance of judicial summing up was put aside. He laid his head between his hands and wept aloud in his great misery. He had loved her; she had been the light of his life. He remembered her now (and the vision he recalled was strangely clear and vivid) as she had stood at the entrance to the cave where dwelt the echo of Forellenbach; she laughing a little at the strange American boy who thought wine-drinking an evil; he standing within the cave, half shy, half proud, and longing to wake the echoes with the pretty name, on that day first heard by him. Yes; he had loved her then and always, while she,—and he groaned and his hot tears fell fast as he remembered that Berthe had said—Berthe who knew—that his wife had never loved him!

The thoughts that racked him were base and unworthy, but he believed them. It may be that at the bottom of his heart he wished to believe, even while the belief rent him with actual anguish. He needed justification for his own sins, and true to his human nature, found it where he could. Again, perhaps dim as yet, but only dim because he closed his eyes, was the desire to be driven to a step which he had hardly dared contemplate, which he had refused to contemplate when it had been suggested to him, but toward which now he was making his way as certainly as he who, lost in the gloom of some dark forest, makes his way toward a rift of light.

He took Mrs. Joe's cheque from his pocket and looked at it. He recalled a suggestion of Berthe that they cash it and go to France together. The suggestion had startled, yet had fascinated him. He had put it aside. Now its fascination returned with tenfold power—to put the ocean between him and the past; to be a denizen of that land where man can be free; to be one of those who, being damned, refuse to accept misery in this life as well—he had recognized it then as a picture painted by the devil; it now assumed a worthier aspect. There would be boldness in such a step, a certain picturesqueness as well, and a dramatic ending to the play in which he had enacted the role of dupe. The curtain would be rung down upon a scene not contemplated by the authors of the drama—a scene in which he alone would retain some dignity, to the discomfiture of those whose puppet he had been.

No thought of financial dishonesty was in his mind. The peculiar fascination in the cheque was the facility it afforded for complete and sudden rupture of every tie. He could secure the maker of the cheque against loss; that could be done at his leisure; meanwhile, there it lay, a golden bridge for passage across an abyss of shame, beyond which lay a region of beauty and content.

Yet even while he mused, finding a balm for wounded pride and love betrayed in visions, of which the central figure was the woman who had parted from him in despair, and whose pleading eyes even now besought him, while his own lonely heart called out to her—even now, when despair on the one hand, and passion on the other, strove for mastery, even now he turned from the devil's beckoning finger, resolving to be just.

Yes; the accused should have a hearing. He would confront his wife and demand an explanation of that meeting in the hall. She was probably aware that he had witnessed it, for she had crouched in fear before him when she had unexpectedly found him in the library. If she had not known of his presence he would inform her and warily watch her, and carefully weigh whatever she had to offer in explanation. He would not be deceived, but she should meet the accusation face to face, himself accuser, judge and witness. He looked at his watch. It was after nine o'clock. Natalie could hardly be in bed. He would see her now in her own room, away from the chance of eavesdropping servants.

He prepared to put his intention into effect and was already in the hall, when a maid handed him a sealed note.

He read the letter. It commenced abruptly, without address:

> "Your violence has so agitated me that it has only been after a long struggle that I have brought myself to write you. But I persuade myself, as indeed I must, that you were unconscious of your harshness. I will not, therefore, offer you my forgiveness for an offense which was unintentional. But I think it better that we do not meet immediately. I am the more urgent in this because I wish your spirit to be soothed and your anger against me to be mitigated, so that you shall hear me calmly. For, I have much to say to you— a sad confession to make which may be even harder for you to bear than the sorrow you have already borne. But I have hope that if you will hear it calmly you will recognize that if I did not love you I could not open my heart to you, as I shall do. My husband, I have not been that which I so long to be in future, a true wife to you. But I know, for I know your goodness of heart, that when you have heard all you will pardon all, and that our future shall be cloudless; that your love shall help me to be that which I have failed in being—your faithful wife."

No need now, having read this confession, to consider his future course. It was fixed. He looked at his watch. The train left at midnight. He would write the necessary answer to the letter at once.

He wrote swiftly and without pause. His brain had never been clearer, his heart never lighter.

A few minutes before midnight he quietly left the house. When he had crossed the street to the Square he looked back at the only home he had ever known. For good or for evil he was about to leave it, never to return the husband of the woman who watched in the dimly lighted chamber. A sob shook him as he turned from the light toward the darkness.

CHAPTER XXXVIII.

THE RUINS OF HER AIR-CASTLE LAY AROUND HER.

Father Cameril laid down the "Life of St. Dunstan" and sighed. "He was strong, he was faithful," muttered the good Father. "Alas!" and he sighed again.

He took a photograph from his pocket and gazed long upon the pictured features. "Dr. Hicks did it," he murmured. Then he replaced the photograph and went forth, going toward the sea, until at last, by many a devious way, he came into the grounds of Stormpoint, and there, by Eliphalet's Tomb, he saw a woman. "'Tis fate," he muttered. The woman turned; Father Cameril started. He was face to face with Natalie.

He stammered awkwardly, being wholly taken by surprise, that he had thought she was Miss Lynford; then, after some conventional references to the weather, he escaped. Natalie watched him as he walked away, then fell into bitter musings, in which he had no part.

Two years had passed since Leonard's flight. With the fall of her hero, the light of the life of Miss Claghorn had been extinguished, and though, with grim courage, she had striven to bear the heavy hand of the Lord, laid thus upon the House of Claghorn, the knowledge that another of the race, the brightest and the best, was doomed, was too heavy a burden. Other Claghorns would be born and would live their little day, but for whom could hope be cherished after such a fall as this? She passed from life sure of her own salvation, but with the knowledge that the elect race was no more to be reckoned as of the favored minority. She refused to leave any message for Leonard; since the Lord had closed the gates of glory upon him, it was for her to close her heart. She charged her estate with a liberal annuity for Tabitha Cone, leaving her fortune, otherwise unincumbered, to Natalie, who, with Tabitha, continued to reside at the White House.

A further untoward result of the catastrophe was the derangement of the political plans of Mrs. Joe. The use of her cheque, given to Leonard, as trustee, his unfulfilled promise of a large donation from an anonymous lady (who could be no other than the lady of Stormpoint), his curt resignation sent to the Seminary authorities from New York, the separation from his wife, her seclusion, the crushing grief of Miss Claghorn, the perturbation of Mrs. Joe, shared by Mark—these were all parts of a puzzle eagerly put together, and so far successfully, that the fact of the misuse of the cheque was established, at least to the satisfaction of the multitude. And this involved an explanation from Mrs. Joe, and the making known of her change of mind in respect of the donation, which again involved some reflection upon the god and the Confession revered by the Seminary, wherefrom was emitted a spark of resentment, not allayed by Mark's openly expressed indignation with those who professed to discover something parlous with regard to the change of mind of his mother, in respect to the once-intended bounty. The upshot of all this confusion was the lassitude, not to say, disgust, evinced by Mark for the political prospects held out by Hampton, and Mrs. Joe's recognition of the need of acting upon the shrewd advice of Mr. Hacket, which was to "lie low till the pot stopped boiling," a consummation not fervently hoped for by the adviser.

With eyes fixed upon where the sun, a fiery ball, fast sank in the distant waters, Natalie, standing where Father Cameril had left her, recalled the days of her girlhood and their dreams. Her life, short as it had been as yet, had been full of trouble. Were all lives thus? Her glance fell upon the tomb; she wondered if the man at rest these two centuries and more had in death resolved the deep mystery of living; or was he, in fact, not yet at rest, but wandering still in other spheres, the toy of a destiny he could neither shape nor fathom? She recalled the day upon which she had seen the handsome American boy in the Odenwald, and she thought of the ruin of his life with unutterable sadness. She remembered how she had prattled with her father as the two dusty travelers had entered the garden, and she recalled her bright visions of the days to come. The days were here! The crumbling ruins of her air-castles lay about her, and in the great upheaval that had caused their fall a life had been wrecked. She looked out upon the waters, hearing the ceaseless moan of the surge, and remembered how the kindly fury of the waves had striven to rescue that life from shame and degradation. Better, ah! how much better, had Leonard never returned from that desperate plunge, but had gone a hero to whatever lay beyond!

She remembered the day—it was not a day to be forgotten—that she had taken the early walk to the cemetery; and how, as she had then looked out upon the waves, a truth that during all the days of her wedded life had lain at the bottom of her heart, had confronted her unbidden, demanding recognition. She had refused to see it, until in the awakening that had come to her in the cemetery she had, with high resolve, determined to defy it and make of it a lie—and within an hour had forgotten her resolution, and had dreamed her dreams which had their birth in the pressure of lips to which she had no right. On the morrow of that darkest day of her life she had found her husband's letter to herself, a letter whose words were burned in upon her memory: "Natalie, in your heart you never loved me." He had added more, the justification of the wretched confession, now defiant, now maudlin, which followed; much of it sadly false; but she remembered it all, and the true text of his miserable story stood out before her as though lettered in the air. The words condemned her. It was not true, and she made a gesture as though repelling an accusation—it was not true that in the truth of Leonard's words lay the underlying motive of the course of life she had resolved upon. She denied this in her thoughts with almost frantic vehemence; yet, urgent in her wish to find palliation for her husband's sin, and seeing with clear vision the folly of the frightful dogma which she now knew that in very truth he could not have believed, but which, if believed, must of her own wrong have made a virtue, she grew confused, and could find but one utterance to express the truth—"I have sinned."

She drew from the bosom of her dress a letter which she had received but a few hours before. It was from Leonard, written from New York, and repeating that accusation which she confessed as true. In the letter the writer expressed his surprise that he had not found, on his return to America, that she had taken steps to rid herself of ties which must be hateful to her. This, he claimed, was an added injury to him, since it prevented the course which his conscience required, and which he was in honor bound to take for the sake of one who had loved him sufficiently to sacrifice herself for him (meaning, though Natalie was ignorant of the fact, Mademoiselle Berthe). He had added that if, within a given time, his wife did not avail herself of the legal right to secure her freedom, he would, actuated by the high considerations suggested, be compelled to take measures to satisfy his conscience and his sense of honor. And he concluded the epistle by setting forth with sufficient distinctness the fact, that the law would recognize the validity of the grounds on which he would, if it became necessary, base his application for divorce.

Heretofore she had resented the urgency of every friend (except one who refrained from advice) to take the step to which she saw now she would be driven. Mark alone had been silent, and her heart had often fluttered, knowing his reason. But she had not dwelt upon a thought upon which she knew she must not linger; rather had she prayed that Leonard might return, and she be enabled to carry out the resolve she had so often made, and in which she had so often failed, to be in all things a true wife; thus earning the forgiveness which she craved by according that which was due from her. Perhaps she had persuaded herself that such a course would be possible— even so—she knew that in the letter she held in her hand, she saw not the insult to herself, not the base attitude of its writer, but the dawning of another day, and the promise of a happiness which hitherto she had not dared contemplate, and which she tried hard not to contemplate now.

CHAPTER XXXIX.

VOIDABLE VOWS OF TURKS (AND OTHERS).

When Father Cameril had found Natalie at Eliphalet's tomb, expecting to find Paula, he had received a greater shock than the incident would seem to have required.

He had said to himself it was Fate; but had found that it was not fate that determined a step which he desired to be compelled to take.

That vow of celibacy had been made in ignorance. He was sure, having examined the authorities closely as to this, that a vow taken in ignorance was not binding. Turks were in the habit of vowing enmity to the truth, yet could a Turk do a more praiseworthy deed than break such a vow? He had supposed that celibacy was a good things for priests. He had been wrong. It was a very bad thing. Ought he to continue a wrong course in deference to a vow taken under a misconception? The underlying motive of the vow was the desire to live worthily; since life lived in accordance therewith would be passed less worthily than in opposition to it, the only honest course was to disregard the vow. So argued Father Cameril, unaided by fate, and hence, compelled to fall back on logic.

But fate was to be more propitious than he had feared. Seated on a rock in a distant portion of the grounds, gazing out upon the setting sun, he came upon Paula.

He took the hand she offered and which, as had lately been the case, lingered a little within his own. Then he sat down beside her.

"How beautiful it is," she observed.

"Paula," he said, "I love you. Will you be my wife?"

"Oh!" exclaimed Paula.

Perhaps it was not very reassuring. But it was not a refusal. Her face was rosier than he had ever seen it. Her heart was beating wildly.

"I wanted to be a nun," she faltered.

"I know it," he replied; "and I——"

"Vowed celibacy."

"It is true," he admitted.

And then they sat and looked at where the sun had been.

After awhile Paula arose and said she must go to the house.

He offered his hand.

"May I kiss you?" he said, in a low tone, his face very pale.

"Father Cameril!"

He hung his head. "You despise me," he said, after awhile. "You are right. I despise myself. It is very hard."

"I don't despise you; and you are not to despise yourself," she stammered. "You perplex and confuse me. You astonish me."

"I knew I would," he answered hopelessly. "It is very natural. I wish I had not been born."

"I beg you not to say dreadful things, not to have dreadful thoughts," she exclaimed.

"But I can't help them. If you knew how awful they are sometimes. Dr. Hicks did it, Paula."

"Don't let us talk of it."

"Let us think about it."

"I couldn't."

"Don't you love me?"

"I love everybody. You, and everybody."

"Yes, you are a saint. I am not. I only love you. I only think of you. Morning, noon and night. At Mass; everywhere——"

"Do you, really?" she interrupted.

"I do, really."

She looked at him curiously. It was very nice, indeed, to know that a good man was in the habit of thinking of her so continuously. But——

"You should not think of me in church," she said.

"Of course not. I wouldn't if you were my wife. As it is, you creep into all my thoughts. You are in the prayer-book, in the Bible, in the Life of St. Dunstan, and of St. Thomas (of Canterbury), too. You are everywhere."

"Oh!" said Paula again. This was love indeed.

"But your vow?"

"I can explain that. Vowing under a misconception is not binding. That was the way I vowed."

"On purpose?" she asked, horrified.

"Oh, no. I thought I was doing right."

"Perhaps you were," she said. "If you were, this must be wrong."

"I have examined my own heart closely, very closely."

"Have you been to confession?"

"To whom can I go? The Bishop would not hear me. He is benighted———"

"There's your friend, Father Gordon."

"Oh, Paula, he's only twenty-three."

"But he's a priest."

"But *he's* under a vow. How can he understand?"

A rapid footstep was heard. "There's Mark!" exclaimed Paula.

Father Cameril tripped quickly away. "You here!" exclaimed Mark, as he came upon Paula. "Isn't it dinner time?"

"It must be," she said, slipping her hand into the arm he offered.

"It was Father Cameril, Mark," she said, after a pause.

"Of course," he replied.

"Why, of course?" she asked, with slow utterance.

He looked down into her face a little quizzically. "Is it not of course?" he asked.
"I—don't—think so," she answered slowly.
"Paula!" He stood confronting her suddenly.
"Well, Mark?"
He laughed, yet looked at her rather seriously. "I thought you were going to be a nun?"
"I am; do you object?"
"I shall be sorry to see it. But———"

"But what?"

"There are other things I would regret more."

She looked into his face. It was a quick, questioning glance, but long enough for him to note her beauty. They went on to the house in silence, but Paula's heart fluttered.

CHAPTER XL.

HER FACE WAS THE MIRROR OF HER PLEASANT DREAMS.

In Hampton Cemetery there stands, and will stand for the sympathetic admiration of future ages, an imposing monument, which apprises him who meditates among the tombs that it was "Erected to the Memory of Jeremiah Morley, by his Sorrowing Widow." At the date of the construction of this expensive evidence of grief, the cost whereof had been provided by testamentary direction—for the late Jeremiah had not been the man to stake a testimonial to his worth upon anything less binding—the stone-cutter, as one versed in the prevailing fashion of monumental inscriptions, had suggested the conventional reference to the usual "Hope of a Joyful Resurrection"; but the widow, her conscience already strained by the legend agreed upon, had objected. Yet the inscription which strained her conscience had the merit of truth; for the man beneath the stone had left her sorrowing, as she had sorrowed nearly every day since she had been pronounced his wife; but, being strictly Hamptonian in her views, her long intimacy with the deceased had rendered her incredulous of his joyous resurrection.

Years before the erection of the monument, while Easthampton was still a port known to mariners, the warehouses since pulled down by Mrs. Joe having hardly commenced to rot, a certain Jerry Morley who, so far as he or anybody else knew, had no legitimate right to name or existence, had sailed from the harbor in the capacity of third mate of the barque "Griselda," a trim vessel manned by a crew of blackguards, not one of whom could approach the mate either in hardihood or in villainy. At that time Mate Jerry had been scarcely more than a boy, ragged, unkempt and fierce-eyed; when he returned, which he did by stage (for the barque had disappeared from the ken of man), he was a smooth-shaven, portly gentleman, hard and domineering; but strict in his walk (to all appearance), and rich. The voice of detraction is never absolutely silent, and though Mr. Morley possessed all the ingredients which go to the making of a "Prominent Citizen," and played that role successfully for many years; yet occasional whispers were heard as to mutiny, murder, seizure of the "Griselda," and a subsequent career as a slaver; whispers, confined mostly to the ancient mariners who smoked and basked about the decaying docks of Easthampton, and which, in due time, were heard no more. Mr. Morley purchased a fine residence in Hampton, was munificent to the Seminary, married the fair daughter of a prominent theologian, and, in short, appeared to the eyes of the world as a clean, pompous, very wealthy and highly respected citizen and church member. Few beside his wife knew that, in fact, he was a brute, given over to secret vices. He had possessed a brain incapable of either excitation or ache. Never sober, no man had ever seen him (to the observer's knowledge) drunk. Few suspected his secret indulgence, but at the age of sixty, liquor, aided by other sly excesses known only to himself, struck him down, as a bullet might have done, relieving a once rarely beautiful woman of a great load, and granting her a few years of comfort as a set-off against many years of hidden misery.

From this grandfather Leonard had inherited more than one unsuspected trait, but not the iron constitution which had succumbed only after years of abuse. Berthe still had her adorable one, but her adoration was gone; her man had become an object of compassionate disgust. The brilliant theologian was a sot.

His fall had been from so great a height to so low a depth, that in his own eyes his ruin was accomplished before his case was hopeless. He was not hurried to his doom by late awakened appetites alone; he had hardly abandoned his home before regret, if not repentance, became a burden too heavy for endurance. The mournful echoes of his days of virtue, the visions of his past of honor, were ever in his ears and before his eyes. Remorse, the hell of sinners, was ever present; and from its constant pangs was no relief except in plunging deeper into sin, inviting greater horrors, and ever beckoned by them. To such miseries were added the fear of that unending life beyond the grave; the life of torment, which all his days he had been taught to contemplate as the doom of souls abandoned by their Maker. The knowledge that he was one of those "passed by" and left for the fires of hell—this knowledge hourly increased the anguish of his spirit. Who among men shall too hardly judge a ruined fellow-creature, abandoned by his God, who in debauchery can find forgetfulness; or who, in the hazy mists of drunkenness alone, can see some rays to cheer the gloom of ruin?

They had at first gone to Paris, and there he had plunged into dissipation with an ardor that had startled and angered his companion, whose good sense had been revolted. True, she had shown him the way, recognizing his need of distraction; but she had not counted on reckless excess, and had at first welcomed the change when he showed a disposition to concentrate his attention upon liquor alone. She was to learn that this slavery was the most debasing of all.

The woman had loved her victim in her own way, and for awhile she honestly strove to raise him from the foul abyss in which he seemed doomed to settle, but her efforts had been vain. She had long been possessed of the common purse, and though her prudence had husbanded the proceeds of Mrs. Joe's cheque, she saw the necessity of reasonable economy; so she got her man to London, where he, by this time, exhausted from dissipation, was content to live frugally, so long as his decanter of gin was kept supplied. The woman often gazed furtively at him, and was troubled. She commenced to consider the future. "Leonard," she said one day, "you ought to marry me."

He was neither startled nor repelled. "It would be the first step in the right direction," he answered. "Perhaps then I could overcome the craving for drink." She was touched by the hope which for one moment gleamed in his dull eyes. It aroused an answering hope in her bosom. Ah! If it could be! If she could become his lawful wife, an honest woman; and he the man he had been before she had led him to ruin! The passing vision of purer days lured both.

A nobler desire than mere acquisitiveness was awakened in her. She knew that probably no such marriage would be legal; it might even be dangerous. But, it would bind him to her so that there could be no escape. And so the matter came to be discussed between the two. Both were aware of the possible criminality of the act, though both hoped that Leonard's wife had procured a divorce; but, notwithstanding some misgiving, the marriage was finally accomplished. Berthe had her own reasons for not waiting until they could revisit America; and perhaps in the loneliness of his wrecked life, Leonard's object was like the woman's, to bind her to himself with hooks of steel. Perhaps it was but the result of influence of a stronger will upon a fast decaying mind.

Thus it had come about that the two had returned to America, and, on their arrival, had concocted the letter to Natalie, by whom it had been submitted to Mr. Ellis Winter. That gentleman advised that Natalie take up her residence in New York, and he engaged to notify Leonard that his demand for divorce would be accorded, as soon as the needful legal requisites could be complied with. Natalie was to make her application on the ground of abandonment, and to refuse to ask for alimony.

And now, alone with Tabitha in a big hotel, without occupation, except such as was afforded by recollections which could not be other than bitter; in the gloom of the days and the miserable object of her present existence, Natalie allowed herself to see the rays of hope illumining a future upon which she looked, shyly, and with a sense of guilt. Yet who would not contemplate the alluring tint of fruit as yet forbidden, but ripening for us before our eyes?

During this period of isolation she saw Mark once, his visit having the ostensible excuse of business. Leonard had, by the hand of his legal adviser, written to Mrs. Joe, suggesting that she purchase the Morley mansion, so that out of the proceeds of the sale he could repay his debt. While the lady would have been as well content that the debt remain unpaid, it was believed by all who still hoped that Leonard might be won back to respectability, that the suggestion was a good one. To carry it into effect the consent of Natalie was, of course, necessary, and also that the transfer be effected before the institution of divorce proceedings. The consent was immediately given.

"And, Mark," said Natalie, as she handed him the deed, "if you see Leonard, say to him that I hope for his forgiveness."

"His forgiveness!"

"Ah, Mark! I wronged him; I ought never——"

He knew what was on her lips, but which she could not say to him—that she ought never to have married Leonard. He took her hand and drew her, unresisting, toward himself; her head drooped upon his shoulder. They stood thus, for a moment, and then he left her. Words of love remained unspoken, but the heart of each was full of that which was unsaid.

There was a long and dreary interval, but at length came the day when Natalie was made free. She learned the fact in the afternoon, but concealed it from Tabitha. That evening she was melancholy, and Tabitha essayed in vain to cheer her; and so the next day passed. But the day after that Tabitha noticed a change; a tremulous fluttering, some tendency to tears, but more to smiles. And Tabitha discovered that she was being petted. She must have a drive— and had it; special delicacies at luncheon were ordered for her delectation, including a share of a pint of champagne, which Tabitha averred was sinful, though she sinned with satisfaction. A beautiful gold watch was given her to replace the fat-faced silver bulb, precious in Miss Cone's eyes as once the property of the long-drowned mariner, but which of late years had acquired the eccentric characteristics of the famous time-piece of the elder Weller; and at last when the time came to say "good-night," Tabitha must be kissed and hugged. But the last proceeding was too much for the maiden's discretion. "What is it?" she asked.

"Oh, Tabby, I'm so happy." And then, ashamed, and afraid of having said too much, Natalie escaped to her own room.

And there read again the letter which she had received that morning, and which she had furtively read many times during the day. She knew it by heart, but she liked to read the words written by her lover's hand.

> "Dear Natalie—The decree is granted. The words, 'I love
> you' have been on my lips so long, that they must find
> utterance. I repeat them, if not with lips, yet in my heart
> every moment of the day. Write or telegraph me the date of
> your arrival at the White House. I would rather have a letter;
> in a letter you can say that you love me. Shall it be a letter?
>
> "MARK."

To this she had answered by telegraph: "I write to-night." He was in Philadelphia, and until the evening of the following day she would be unable to leave for home. He would receive her letter in time to get to Stormpoint soon after her arrival in Easthampton. He desired a letter; he should have a letter.

Yet it was hard to write. It had been easy to whisper to herself such phrases as "Mark, dear Mark, I love you, I love you"; but it was less easy to set those words down on paper, though there was a joy in it, too. The difficulty of writing them vanished when they were for her own eye only, not to be mailed. And so she scribbled over sheet after sheet of paper: "Mark, Dear Mark, My Love, My Own, My Lover"—such words and many others she wrote, blushing, smiling; at times not seeing what she wrote for the tears in her eyes. At last she roused herself from this foolish play and wrote a proper letter.

> "Dear Mark—How good you have always been! I shall
> arrive home on Saturday morning. I long to see you. Dear
> Mark, I love you."

The last phrase was hurriedly written and had required resolution, but she was happier for having written it. She sealed the letter that she might not be tempted in the morning to substitute another. Then she went to bed, and all the night through her face was the mirror of her pleasant dreams. No shadow of the future was upon her as she slept smiling.

And awoke with the smile upon her face, and in a low voice sang while dressing. Her toilet concluded, she took her letter from the table, kissed it shyly, and placed it in her bosom. She would mail it as she went downstairs.

A knock at her door and the announcement of a visitor—a lady who had business of importance. Natalie ordered that the lady be shown into her sitting-room.

On entering the sitting-room she found Berthe.

CHAPTER XLI.

HER GUILTY CONSCIENCE CRIED: "BEHOLD YOUR HANDIWORK."

Natalie saw all things through the halo of the rosy hopes that now encompassed her. "Berthe!" she exclaimed, both hands extended in welcome, "I thought you had gone to France. Mrs. Leon told me so—but, how is this? You look pale and ill?"

Pale and ill she was, but no illness would have deterred her from making the appeal she had come to make.

Since his return to America, Leonard had indulged in drink more recklessly than ever, and Berthe, though conscious of the value to herself of the divorce, had dreaded the granting of the decree. For the prospect of being bound to this lost creature filled her with aversion.

Conscience makes cowards of us all, and Berthe feared the man. Not that he had shown any inclination for violence toward her, though he had long been irritable and disposed to quarrel on slight provocation. She did not fear his hand; it was his presence. The sodden spectacle was becoming a weight upon her soul, an accusation beyond her strength to bear. She had loved him, loved him even now, and her guilty conscience cried incessantly, "Behold your handiwork!"

On the day when Natalie had petted Tabitha, she had for the first time lived in fear, even of his hand. Early that morning she had noticed that his speech was tremulous and uncertain, though he drank less than usual. He dozed constantly, often waking with a cry of terror; and then his whole frame would tremble as he gazed with eyes of hate and horror at herself, or at some invisible yet dreadful object near her, muttering incoherent phrases indicating fear. Again he would doze, again awake and the scene would be repeated. With each new seizure his action became more violent, while the nameless horror that was upon him communicated itself to her. At last she sent for a physician, but not until there had been a wild outbreak. He had clutched her by the throat: "Devil!" he shouted, "you shall not take me to hell; I am of the elect, a Claghorn! Down, fiend!" She had cowered in fear, and he had saved her life by fainting.

The doctor easily diagnosed the case. Berthe's willingness to pay for the services of two male nurses, and the fear that any disturbance might entail a frantic outbreak and death, were the considerations that restrained the physician from ordering the patient's removal to a hospital.

The convulsions of the stricken man were frightful; his shrieks, his wailing prayers for deliverance from hell—these appalled the woman, filling her with apprehension akin to that of the raving victim. His calls for Natalie were most piteous, wails of anguish that pierced the heart of the woman that had loved him, and whose moans answered his incessant repetition of the name of one, lacking whose forgiveness he must face the horrors of the damned. The unending utterance of the name, never ceasing even when at last he sank into the stupor of exhaustion and of opiates, attracted the attention of the physician, who told Berthe that while he believed the case hopeless, possible good might be effected by the presence of the person without whom it seemed as though the man could not even die.

The awful fear that he would die, his last wish ungratified, wherefore, in her belief, his restless soul would haunt all her future days; this, added to the pity for the man she still loved, who had rescued her from misery, whose head had lain upon her bosom, nerved her to carry out the resolve she had taken. She knew that no messenger could effect the purpose; she must assume the task herself. It was not without a pang that she determined upon a mission which, if successful, must involve her desertion of the dying man; but, though she did not forget such jewels as she possessed or to collect all the money that remained, her flight was nevertheless intended as such expiation as she could make.

She hoped, though she could not be sure, that her identity as Leonard's companion was not known to Natalie; but she assumed that Mrs. Leon had given information as to other misconduct, and she expected to be met with cold disapproval, if, indeed, she were received at all. But instead of disapproval she was encountered with outstretched hands and their friendly pressure; and, as with this reception there came upon her the recollection of the sweet graciousness of her former mistress, and with it the consciousness of her requital of the kindness of past days, her heart was like to fail.

"I bring you a message," she gasped, "from your husband."

"My husband!" For the moment Natalie forgot that she had no husband. Then the recollection came upon her, and with it a premonition of evil. She was as pale as Berthe, as she stood, looking at her visitor, bewildered and afraid.

"Stop!" she exclaimed, as Berthe was about to speak. "What can you know of him you call my husband? He left me, abandoned me for a wicked woman. He wrote me confessing his shame, but not his fault. Again he wrote, insinuating wicked deeds of me, and threatening me. Since two days he is no more my husband; I can receive no message."

"He is dying!"

The red flush which had displaced the pallor of Natalie's cheek disappeared. Again her face grew pale; she stared at Berthe.

"Listen," faltered the Frenchwoman. "He wronged you, yet he loved you always, has loved you till this hour, and cannot die without your forgiveness."

"Take it to him——Dying! Leonard, Leonard!" She covered her face.

"I was maid to the woman he went away with," continued Berthe, "and so I came to know his story. The woman has been kind to him—let her pass, then"—seeing that her listener shuddered. "The man is dying. He moans and wails for you—for you. The woman herself begged me to come for you. He fears" (her face grew whiter) "he fears the fires of hell, but he will not have a priest. Only you can rescue him—your pardon—he cannot die without it." She broke down. All else she might have borne upon her conscience; but she could not bear that he should go unshriven.

At the mention of the fires of hell Natalie was conquered. "Take me to him," she said.

"Follow me in half an hour," Berthe rose as she spoke, handing a written address to Natalie.

"But no time must be lost——"

"In half an hour," repeated Berthe. "Give her—the woman—time to get away." And then she passed out of the room.

CHAPTER XLII.

"I WILL NEVER LEAVE HIM, SO HELP ME GOD IN HEAVEN."

"Natalie." He stirred uneasily, muttering the word, which since her coming he had not uttered; then, as she lightly pressed the hand she held, he slept again. So she had sat for hours beside his bed.

The physician had prepared her for the sight that had met her eyes. From Tabitha, who was with her, he had gleaned some knowledge of the facts. Tabitha, still ignorant of the granting of the decree, had assured him that the visitor was the wife of Leonard Claghorn.

"Poor woman, she will need her courage," he said. "The other one has gone. As for the wife, if she can bear it, I would have her sit beside him so that he can see her when he wakes."

So there she had taken her place, beside the man whom the law had decreed was no more to her than any other. But death mocks law. Dying, he was so much to her that no hand but hers should smooth his pillow.

Perhaps the nature of the disease, perhaps the deep exhaustion, had made a great change in his appearance. The bloated aspect of his face was gone, and even a greater beauty than the beauty of his youth and innocence was apparent. But it was the beauty of ruin. The face was marble, yet lined with the deep furrows of sorrow and remorse. The hair was gray at the temples, the cheeks were hollow and the mouth was drawn. It was Leonard, the man whose head had lain upon her bosom, the father of her child—the same, yet oh, how changed!

"Natalie!"

She bent toward him. He essayed to lift her hand to his lips; she placed it on his brow.

"I have had a dream," he whispered, "a dreadful dream!"

"Hush, Leonard. You must sleep."

He feebly raised his arm and tried to draw her to him. Slowly she bent toward him, falling on her knees beside the bed. His arm was now about her neck; he drew her cheek to his.

"My wife!" He uttered the words with a long-drawn sigh, of such sweet content that in that sigh she believed he had breathed his life out. Soon he spoke again. "Now I can sleep," he said, and freed her from his embrace. She rose gently and stood watching him; he slept without the stertorous breathing of before. Looking up, she saw the physician in the doorway. He beckoned to her. She rose and quietly left the room.

"Madam," said the doctor, "this is wonderful. That natural sleep may portend recovery."

"Then I can go," she said.

The doctor looked at her gravely, not approvingly. But it was not as he supposed; she was not hard-hearted; but the woman! Leonard had written that his conscience and his honor demanded that he marry the woman. If he were to live, there was no place at his bedside for her, who had once been his wife.

"Mrs. Claghorn," said the doctor, "your companion, Miss—ah—Miss Cone, has informed me of the existing relations between you and your husband. As a stranger I can give no advice, can only tell you that the woman who has been his companion has left your husband forever."

"Left him to die!" she exclaimed.

"Precisely. It need not surprise you. It is barbarous; but such women are barbarous. I shall be surprised if one who has displayed so much magnanimity should fail now. Pardon me, Mrs. Claghorn, but your place is by your husband's side. One woman has basely left him to die. Should you leave him now, you repeat the act."

The doctor silently withdrew. Natalie sank into a chair. Her mind was confused. Her place by her husband's side! Had she then a husband? The scenes in which she had been an actor had numbed her faculties, strained by the long watch by the bedside she had left. A feeling of suffocation was stealing over her; instinctively she loosened her dress at the throat. The letter she had written to Mark fell upon the floor, and she sat staring at it, dumb.

It became evident that her husband, as all in the house believed him to be, would live. Over and over again the doctor congratulated her on the wonderful influence of her presence upon the sick man. Naturally, he was glad to have rescued a patient from the very jaws of death; and though, since he had learned more of her history from Tabitha Cone, he had slight sympathy for the man, yet he believed that even under the untoward circumstances existing, forgiveness and reconciliation was the course which promised most for future happiness.

"It is the best thing for her," he said to Tabitha. "She will withdraw the divorce proceedings and forgive him. She can never be happy unless she does."

Tabitha, though sure that she herself would never have forgiven her mariner under similar circumstances, which, however, she admitted were unthinkable in that connection, agreed with the physician.

"He will be long in getting well," said the physician; "if, indeed, he ever recovers completely. If he has the heart of a man he must appreciate what she has done for him; literally brought him back to life."

"He was a good man, once," observed Tabitha, her eyes filling. "Oh, Doctor! The most beautiful, the sweetest; the most frank and loving boy——"

"And a brilliant theologian, you tell me. Well, well, Miss Cone, in my profession we learn charity. It is astounding what an evil influence some women can gain over men. And this one was not even beautiful."

"The hussy!"

"Quite so. Ah, Miss Cone, our sex must ever be on guard," and the doctor laughed a little. He was feeling triumphant over the recovery of his patient.

Yet in watching that recovery his face was often very grave. Natalie was sharp-eyed. "Is your patient getting well?" she asked.

"He improves hourly," was the answer, but the tone was not cheerful. He looked at Natalie anxiously.

"Physically, yes. His mind, Doctor?"

"His mental faculties are failing fast."

"How long has this been going on?" He was surprised at her equable tones. Evidently she had nerved herself for this disclosure.

"A brave woman," he thought.

"That is a hard question to answer."

"Do you think it the result of drink? He had never touched liquor two years since."

"I should hardly ascribe it to liquor entirely. Doubtless, over-indulgence of that nature has been a force, a great force. The delirium in which you found him may be directly ascribed to drink."

"If he had been greatly harassed, say two years since, having been up to that time a good man—if then he had suddenly fallen into evil—would you ascribe such a fall to the mental strain consequent upon the worry I have suggested?"

"She seeks every palliation for him," thought the doctor. "Madam, I should say that in the case of a man, such as you have pictured, a sudden lapse into evil courses, courses which belied his training and previous life——"

"Yes?" She was looking steadfastly at him. He little knew the resolve that hung upon his words.

"I should say he was not wholly responsible. I should attribute much to the worry, the vexations, to which you have alluded."

With all her firmness she shrank as from a blow. Thinking to comfort her, he had driven a knife into her heart.

"And now, my dear Mrs. Claghorn, since we are upon this subject—a subject from which I admit I have shrunk—let me tender you some advice. You have saved your husband's life; let that be your solace. It will not be for his happiness that you sacrifice your own."

"Go on," she said, seeing that he hesitated.

"After awhile—not now," he said, "but after your presence is less necessary to him, you must let me aid you to place him in an establishment where he will have every care——"

"An asylum?"

The doctor nodded.

"I will never leave him, so help me God in heaven! Never, never, Mark, my darling, for I, and only I, brought him to this pass!" She cried these words aloud, her hand upraised to heaven.

CHAPTER XLIII.

MONEY, HEAPS OF MONEY.

Mark Claghorn, standing by the window of that room at Stormpoint which was especially set aside as his own, but which, in its luxurious fittings, bore rather the traces of the all-swaying hand of the mistress of the mansion, gazed moodily out toward the tomb, speculating, perhaps, as to the present occupation of the soul that had once been caged in the bones that crumbled there.

To whom entered Mrs. Joe, who silently contemplated him awhile, and then, approaching, touched his shoulder. He turned and smiled, an act becoming rare with him. "Mark," she said, "I am getting old."

"You look as young as my sister might," he said.

"That's nonsense," but she smiled, too. Barring some exaggeration, she knew that his words were true.

"Even so," she urged seriously, "you have wandered enough. You might stay here for my sake."

"Mother, I will stay here for your sake."

"Only that, my son? You know I want more than that."

"Yes," he said, "you want too much. Let us have it out. Believe me, your pleasant dream of a political career for me is hopeless. Granted that I could buy my way to high office—though I do not think so—could I ever respect myself, or command respect? Where, then, would be the honor?"

"I never thought of buying."

"No, not in plain terms. But at my age, together with the fact that I am a stranger, at least a newcomer, in this State, money would be my only resource—perhaps a hopeless one, in any case. The rich man must learn his lesson, which is, that wealth bars the way to honor."

"Our senior Senator is rich."

"I do not speak of moderately rich men. Suspicion is even directed (unjustly, I believe) against such men. But the whole State knows that, politically, our Senator has risen from the ranks. Perhaps he has been compelled to buy that which is his due—who can tell? But all know that at least he has earned the distinction he has won."

"And could you not earn it?"

"No. I am not merely moderately rich. I should be 'held up' by every rogue that glories in the name of politician. If I refused to buy, and refuse I must, I should have no chance whatever. Gold besmirches many things. A rich man is of necessity defiled, let him keep his hands as clean as he can."

Mrs. Joe sighed.

"You have not been willing to realize the facts which influence my life," he went on. "We must look facts in the face. Political distinction is not for me. For your sake I would try, were I not assured that your disappointment would be inevitable. He laid his hand upon her shoulder. He spoke very kindly.

"Mark," she said—there were tears in her eyes—"I wish you were happy."

"If I am content——"

"But you are not. Oh, Mark, seek happiness. Marry."

He smiled grimly. "I wish I could," he said.

"Mark, you say my dream is hopeless. I surrender it. Is yours less hopeless? You wear your life away. Is it worthy to wait for a man to die?"

He made no answer.

"Dear," she said, and the word moved him deeply, for though he knew how much he was beloved of his mother, a term of tenderness was rare from her lips—"Dear, you know what she wrote me."

"You showed me the letter. She gave me the same advice long ago."

"It is the right thing to do. Paula loves you. Natalie is lost to you. You do not know where she is; she does not intend that you shall know. She will not marry you now, even though death were to free her from the bonds she has assumed. She is right. Mind, Mark, I say no word of censure. I believe in her purity as I do in Paula's—but the world will talk. That which she has done cannot be kept secret, but her motive must remain a secret. Had the man died——"

"Enough!" he said sternly. "You say you believe in her as you do in Paula. No shadow of suspicion can ever cross my mind or yours. We need not consider the world——"

"But, my son, she will consider it. She does consider it. Her letter to me shows it. That letter was no easy one for a woman to write. Do you think she would even indirectly have disclosed your secret to me, except that she believed it necessary for your good? I do not doubt, Mark, that she has renounced your love even to you. Is it not unworthy to——"

"To love without hope? Perhaps it is. But since the fact is not generally known—here, as in some other things, the sin consists in being found out." He laughed. "You know you didn't find out; you were told."

"Yes; in the hope, I verily believe, that the disclosure would wound you and so kill your love."

"It wounded, certainly," he said bitterly. "Perhaps, if you give it time, the wound may yet be as fatal as you wish—as she wished." He laughed again very grimly. "Strange creatures, women," he said. "Their self-sacrifice includes the sacrifice of every one but self."

"That is cruel! From no possible point of view can her life be a happy one."

"How you quarrel about a man and cling together against a man!" he said, smiling down upon the lady, who had no other answer than the shrug which, when it moves feminine shoulders, implies that masculine density is impenetrable. His smile broke into laughter.

It aroused her secret indignation; but encouraged her, too. If he could laugh, her case was not hopeless.

"Mark, let us be sensible. You should marry and have children. What else is open to you, the rich man? You have no faith in the world, none in friendship, none in love. Consider what your life must be if, at this age, all purer sources of feeling are dried up! In marriage you will find them all reopened. Your family will be your world. You need children. I need them. We are rich; yes, horribly rich. What is all this worth to us? You are the last of a race, honorable since the tenant of yonder grave first set foot upon this soil; honorable before that time. Shall that race die in you? My son, that old-world notion of Family is estimable. This country needs that it be cherished. The wealth will not be so new in the next generation. Your sons will not be strangers in the land of their fathers. You shall so train them that in them you shall reap the distinction denied to you. You say I am yet young. I am not old, and may still live to see my grandsons honored by their fellow men. By your own confession nothing remains to you but marriage. Love is offered you daily, by one most sweet and most lovable. Paula——"

He stopped her by a gesture. Her unwonted energy had impressed him. She had spoken well. "You have uttered many truths," he said, "but what you say of Paula is not kind, nor do you know——"

"Mark! on my honor as a woman, I believe that Paula loves you." Then she left him.

He remained long musing. Why should he not make his mother happy? It was true, waiting for a man to die was a pitiful occupation. And even should the man die there would be no hope for him. It was a year since Natalie had hidden herself with her burden and Tabitha Cone. Hidden herself, as he well knew, from him. She had written both him and his mother. She had not feared to again acknowledge her love; but she had prayed him to forget her. And she had told him that Paula loved him; she had shown him that his duty required him to love Paula in return; finally, she had, almost sternly, bade him cease to hope.

Perhaps his mother was right. Perhaps Paula loved him—as much as she could love. He loved her in the same cool fashion. He was used to her. She was very beautiful, completely amiable, kind and gentle. Not very brilliant, yet if simple-minded, not a fool. Marriage would bring out all there was of Paula, and that might be much more than was generally suspected. And whatever it was it would be lovable. He knew he was living the life of a fool. Why live that life consciously? Why not make his mother completely happy; Paula and himself happier; as happy as they could be?

He turned to his desk and opened a hidden drawer therein. From this he took a small packet of papers. "A man about to die or marry should set his house in order," he muttered, as he spread the papers open. There was the first letter Natalie had ever written him; a reply to his letter of condolence concerning her father's death. He glanced over it and slowly tore it into fragments. He did the same with the few others written by her, all except the last he had received. This was in answer to a letter into which he had thrown all the strength of his soul, lowering, if not completely breaking down, the last barriers of reserve behind which those who feel deeply hide their hearts.

He could not complain that in her answer she had not been equally frank. "From the innermost depths of my soul I love you, and if more can be, I honor you still more—and because I so love and honor you I must not see you again. I have loved you since the day I first saw you in the Odenwald. I loved you when I became the betrothed of another. I hoped then you would find a way to free me from the promise I had given. I aver before Heaven that I tried with all my strength to be a faithful wife. I loved my husband; alas! not as I know now, with a wife's love, but I believed it. Yet—let me confess it—at the very bottom of my heart slept my love for you, not dead as I had thought it. I have sinned against you, against him who was my husband, against myself. We must all suffer for my sin. You are strong. I must gather all the strength I can for the duty that my guilt has laid upon me—to bear my fate and to make a ruined life as endurable as unremitting care can make it. My sin was great. Consider my expiation! I must always see before my eyes my handiwork.

"You love me. Do you think that ever a doubt of your love crosses my mind? You will always love me. I know it. But, if you see me no more that love will, in time, become a tender reminiscence—not worth a tear, rather a smile—of pity let it be, for the lives that are wrecked. But from this day forth let your own life present a fair ideal to be realized. One has grown up beside you whose fate is in your hands. The fashioning of her destiny lies with you. To be a happy wife and mother, the lot for which nature intended her, or to live the barren life of a religious devotee; and knowing her as I do, I know that for you, embittered and distrustful by reason of your burden of inordinate wealth, she is supremely fitted to make your life serene and cheerful in return for the felicity you will bring to her.

"Adieu, for the last time. I shall not forget you, but shall love you as long as I live, and as warmly as I love you now. But deliberately, and with unalterable resolve, I have chosen my lot. Nothing, not even the hand of death, can render me fit to be more to you than the memory of one who has lived her life."

He slowly tore the letter into fragments as he had torn the others. Perhaps his mouth twitched as he did so. He looked upon the little heap of paper on his desk. "The Romance of a Rich Young Man," he muttered, and smiled at the conceit. Then he gathered the fragments in his hand and strewed them upon some tinder in the chimney and applied a match. "Gone up in Smoke," he said aloud.

"Did you speak?" asked his mother, who had entered the room.

"I repeated the title of a novel I am going to write," he said. "I wanted to hear how it would sound."

"You must live a romance before you can write one, Mark."

"True," he answered dryly. "I need experience. Where is Paula?"

"Oh, Mark!"

He kissed her. "Yes," he said, "I will do what I can to make you happy, and—gain experience."

Mrs. Joe's eyes beamed through her tears.

"She is in the library."

Leaving the room by the window, which opened upon a veranda, he walked toward the library, the windows of which opened upon the same veranda.

The library windows were divided in the centre, like doors. They were open now, and the thick French plate reflected like a mirror. In the open window pane he saw, as in a mirror, a portion of the interior. Paula was there, and Paula's head nestled against the breast of Father Cameril, and the good Father's arm encircled her while his lips pressed hers.

Mark stole silently away.

He found Mrs. Joe awaiting him in the room he had left. "Be very kind to her, mother," he said. "She will have something to tell you."

"But you have been so quick——"

He smiled. "I shall not be the hero of the tale. Father Cameril is the lucky man. After all, it is better. I could not have made her happy as she deserves to be. I am glad I was prevented from offering her——" He hesitated.

"Your heart," said Mrs. Joe.

"An insult," he answered curtly, as he left the room, strolling toward Eliphalet's tomb.

And at Eliphalet's tomb he recognized that Natalie had been wise. Now that it was lost to him he knew that his last long-neglected chance for happiness was gone. Happiness! Perhaps the word meant too much, but in Paula's companionship he could at least have found, in time, contentment and cheerfulness, and are these not happiness, the highest happiness? What now was left him? Money, heaps of money! It barred the way to honorable ambition; its heavy weight lay on his heart, breeding therein suspicion of the love or friendship of all men and women. For him life must be a solitude. He could never lie beside a wife assured that he had won her for himself. He knew that the deadly poison of distrust must ever and ever more thoroughly taint his being, distorting his vision and rendering the aspect of all things hateful. Yet how many thousand men, whose clothes and dinners were assured them, would be glad to change places with him! "But all I have are clothes and food," he muttered.

"We are all poor critters!" Deacon Bedott had spoken words of wisdom. "But the poorest of all is the Rich Man, Deacon," he said.

And then bethought him that by this time Paula and Father Cameril would have made their great announcement. "Little Paula!" he murmured. "Well, she shall have joyous wedding bells, at least, and smiling faces. For the rest let the fond Father look to it!"

CHAPTER XLIV.

WEDDING BELLS.

The summer sun beat pitilessly upon the burnished cobble stones, driving from the crooked street all except the geese, and even these only languidly stretched their necks, hissing inhospitably at the heels of the dusty wayfarer, the sole object of interest to the landlord of the Red-Ox, who stood in the gateway of his hostelry and blinked in the glare of the sun. "Too old for a student," he muttered, "and no spectacles. Perhaps an artist." As the pedestrian came nearer a puzzled gleam, half of recognition, spread over his features. The dusty traveler stopped. "And so you are here yet!" and he slapped the broad shoulder of the host.

"Here yet, and hope to be for many a year to come," answered the fat host; "and you are here, not for the first time, I dare swear; but who you are, or when you last were here——

"That you can't recall. Why should you?"

"*Ein Amerikaner!* A *studiosus juris*, of the Pestilentia. *Ein alter Bursch* of ten years back! Remember? Surely, all but the name."

"And what's in a name?" shaking the offered hand of the landlord. "Mine is a mouthful for you—Claghorn."

"*Herr Doktor* Clokhorn. That's it. Not so great a mouthful after all." He led the way into the well-remembered garden. "Many a schoppen have you had here," he said; "and many a time sung '*Alter Burschen Herrlichkeit*' at this very table, and many trout——"

"Devoured," interrupted Mark. "That pastime will bear repetition. As for singing, one loses the desire."

"Not so," observed the fat host. "I am sixty, but I lead the Liederkranz to-day. Wine, woman and song—you know what Luther said——"

"I remember. But not even the Great Reformer's poetry is to be taken too literally. We'll discuss the point later on. Now some trout, then a pipe and a gossip."

When the host departed to attend to the order, Mark unstrapped his knapsack and looked about him.

He had come thousands of miles to see this garden! He admitted the foolish fact to himself, though even to his mother he would have denied it. The fat host was right; he had drunk many a flask of wine in this place, roared in many a chorus, had danced many a waltz with village maidens on yonder platform; but of these various scenes of his student days he had not thought until his host recalled them. They were memories, even memories with some of that tender sadness which renders such memories pleasant, but such as they would never have drawn him here.

And now that he was here, so sharp a pain was in his heart that he recognized his folly. The wound was yet too new. He should have waited a decade or more. Then he might have found solace in recalling her to his mind, here where first he had seen her; he, in all the arrogant pride of youth; she, with all the fresh beauty of a school girl. Now no effort was needed to recall her to his memory—she was ever present.

Nevertheless, he enjoyed his fish and his wine. "A superlative vintage," said the host, who had had time to recall his guest more distinctly, and who remembered that in past days *Studiosus Clokhorn* had dispensed money with a liberal hand.

"And so the inn has been enlarged," said Mark, looking about him. "That means prosperity."

"Forellenbach is becoming a resort," replied the host. "We have parties that remain for days. We have strangers here at this moment."

"Ah!" was the sleepy comment.

"Yes; three ladies. Or rather, two ladies and a maid. Mother and daughter—English."

"Ah!" said Mark again.

At this point the host, rather to the relief of his guest, was called away, and Mark adjusted himself upon the bench and dozed. A long tramp, and perhaps the superlative vintage, had made him sleepy.

When he awoke, sunset shadows were about him. He was vexed, having intended to walk on to Heidelberg, which now he must do in part after dark. However, a walk by night might be pleasanter than had been the tramp under the sun. Before leaving he would look about. It was not likely that he would ever again see a place which would dwell always in his memory.

As he neared the cave where the echo dwelt he saw the slender figure of a woman. Her back was toward him, but the garb and mien proclaimed one, not a permanent resident of the village. "One of mine host's guests," he murmured, "a *gnädige Frau* of artistic taste and economical practice." He paused, unwilling to disturb feminine meditation. The stranger stood at the entrance to the cave, on the spot where first he had seen the girl who, later, had become the one woman in the world to him. There was something in her attitude, bent head and arms hanging listless, that interested, even moved him. She, too, looked like some lonely being, saying a last farewell at a shrine where love had been born; and then, as she strolled away, hidden by overhanging boughs of trees and the slowly deepening evening shadows, he smiled at his conceit.

He strolled on to where she had been standing, for, though he smiled cynically at his foolishness, the spot was to him a sacred one. If sentimental folly had brought him a thousand leagues, it might well control a few steps more.

As he reached the place he came face to face with another woman, whose old but sharp eyes recognized him instantly. "Mr. Mark!"

"Tabby!" He was so astonished that he could say no more for a moment. Then he found words: "Was that Natalie?"

Miss Cone, though slightly hysterical from pleasure and surprise, explained that Natalie had just left her. "But what brings you here?" she added.

"Heaven or fate," was the answer. And then he was for following Natalie at once. But Tabitha restrained him. "Let me prepare her," she urged, and to that plea she found him willing to listen.

Then she told him the story of their wanderings. They had brought Leonard to Europe, principally for the voyage, which, however, had been of no benefit. They had remained in Ireland, near Londonderry, where they had first landed. He had never been able to move, but passed his life in a wheeled chair. His mind had been that of an infant, though before he died he seemed to have gleams of intelligence, and had once in an old churchyard expressed a wish to be buried there, or so Natalie had interpreted his babbling. And there he had slept for a year. "And so," sobbed Tabitha, "the poor boy's weary life is over at last. God bless him!"

"Amen to that," said Mark. "Tabitha! It has been a grief to me, God knows. So heavy a sorrow that I have thought I could not bear it; yet, at this moment I can say that I am glad that Natalie forgave him and cherished him till he died."

Tabitha looked up. Her hard, worn old face was softened by her tears. "Those words," she said, "will win her for you; if words can win the heart already yours."

At the appointed hour Tabitha led him to Natalie, who was waiting for him. He could see the swaying of her form as she rose to greet him. He took her in his arms.

"My darling, my darling." He could say nothing else. Her arm had crept upward about his neck; he held her close.

"Why are you here?" he asked, at length, then added: "Bless God that you are here."

"To say good-bye to a place that has often been in my thoughts. And, since heaven has permitted it, to say good-bye to you."

"That you shall never say. I vow before God never to leave you. You and I shall live our lives together, whatever your answer to the petition I now make. Will you be my wife?"

"Mark, I am not——"

"Stop!" he said. "You once declared that as you loved me, so you honored me. I now, with all solemnity, declare that you are honored as you are loved by me. If I do not estimate the fault which you have expiated as you do, I respect and admire the expiation. If you believe me to be a truthful man, learn now that I approve your care of him who was your husband. Let that suffice. And now, once more I swear that I will never leave you. Will you be my wife?"

"Mark, I love you."

"Then the wedding bells shall ring, and Forellenbach shall rejoice." Their lips met, and in the kiss they forgot the years that had passed since last they saw Forellenbach.

THE END.

Milton Keynes UK
Ingram Content Group UK Ltd.
UKHW010718280324
440307UK00004B/253